THE WAVE WALKERS

Pirate Emperor

THE WAVE WALKERS

Pirate Emperor

KAI MEYER

Translated by Elizabeth D. Crawford

Aladdin Paperbacks

New York   London   Toronto   Sydney

❧ ALADDIN PAPERBACKS
An imprint of Simon & Schuster Children's Publishing Division
1230 Avenue of the Americas, New York, NY 10020
English language translation copyright © 2007 by Elizabeth D. Crawford
Die Muschelmagier text copyright © 2003 by Kai Meyer
Original German edition copyright © 2004 Loewe Verlag GmbH, Bindlach
Originally published in German in 2004 as *Die Muschelmagier* by Loewe Verlag
Published by arrangement with Loewe Verlag
All rights reserved, including the right of reproduction in whole or in part in any form.
ALADDIN PAPERBACKS and related logo are registered trademarks of Simon & Schuster, Inc.
Also available in a Margaret K. McElderry hardcover edition.
Designed by Paula Russell Szafranski
The text of this book was set in Centaur MT.
Manufactured in the United States of America
First Aladdin Paperbacks edition January 2008
10 9 8 7 6 5 4 3 2 1
The Library of Congress has cataloged the hardcover edition as follows:
Meyer, Kai.
[Muschelmagier. English]
Pirate emperor / Kai Meyer ; translated by Elizabeth D. Crawford.—1st U.S. ed.
p. cm.—(The wave walkers)
Summary: Jolly and Munk start training with Forefather when they discover that their special abilities as "polliwogs" may be the only way to save the city Aelenium from the Maelstrom.
[1. Pirate—Fiction. 2. Magic—Fiction. 3. Fantasy.] I. Crawford, Elizabeth D. II. Title.
PZ7.M57171113Pk 2007
[Fic]—dc22
2006018132
ISBN-13: 978-1-4169-2474-6 (hc.)
ISBN-10: 1-4169-2474-4 (hc.)
ISBN-13: 978-1-4169-2475-3 (pbk.)
ISBN-10: 1-4169-2475-2 (pbk.)

Contents

The Attack

The scream of the Acherus awakened her. Jolly started up, her head throbbing so badly that she felt as though she'd banged it hard on something. She was lying on a scratchy raffia mat, the twisted roll of a woolen blanket beside her. A narrow stripe of daylight was falling through the cave's crudely carved window, but it couldn't drive away the shadows around the rumpled sleeping place. She must have tipped over the water jug in the night, and its contents had evaporated into the oppressive heat. Even the rock walls surrounding her were sweating in the humid weather.

The scream of the Acherus.

She'd heard it, most certainly.

But now there was stillness—no, not stillness, only the distant murmuring of the Caribbean, the whispering of the wind, and the rushing of the surf. And . . . yes, voices. Very far away.

Pirate Emperor

Where was she? What was she doing here?

Remembering took a moment. But then the images flowed back into her consciousness, most of them no less painful than the throbbing behind her eyes.

They'd gone overboard. In the middle of a raging sea battle, between murderous salvos of cannon and powder smoke, she and Griffin had landed in the water. Jolly recalled how she'd looked for Griffin in the boiling sea, how she'd dragged him onto the rocky shore of an island with the last of her strength. And when the air cleared, their ship was gone.

Their companions had gone with the *Carfax*: Munk, Captain Walker, the pit bull man Buenaventure, the pirate princess Soledad, and the Ghost Trader had vanished into the air with the smoke of the shots.

"Jolly! You're awake!"

Griffin came through the doorway in a crouch. The pirate boy just fit through the narrow opening. Like all the shelters on the island, this one was hardly bigger than a narrow cabin. But after the two of them had been given food and water, the dark rock shelter had seemed like a palace to them.

"I . . . I heard something," Jolly said hoarsely, as Griffin squatted down beside her. "The Acherus, I think."

For a fraction of a second, the boy's face showed concern. But then he grinned and shook his head so vigorously that the blond braids whirling around his head looked like garlands.

"You dreamed it," he said gently. "There's nothing here on the island. At least no Acherus or something else that the Maelstrom could bring down on us."

THE ATTACK

Most probably he was right. Jolly had been dreaming a lot since this whole business had begun.

Again and again she saw images of endless armies of kobalins lurking under the waves as far as the eye could see. She felt the dead fish on her skin as they rained from the heavens and smelled the foul breath of the Acherus. And yet, the evil that had called up these terrible happenings was no more comprehensible because of them. The Maelstrom and the Mare Tenebrosum stayed hidden behind their own creatures—inconceivable, incomprehensible, and thus even more terrifying.

"Agostini said I should call you," said Griffin. "He wants to take us out onto the bridge. You'll come, won't you?"

She nodded vigorously but grimaced at once when the headache made its presence known again. Nevertheless, any distraction was all right with her. She stood up, a little shakily, washed perfunctorily at the spring in the rock cleft, and then hurried outside with Griffin.

The bridge builders' camp was situated in a multitude of tiny caves that ran like air bubbles through the cooled lava on this side of the island. Jolly and Griffin had landed on the north end of the island, where the cliffs of the mountain cones were filled with old, dried-out tree stumps and the ground was colored yellow-brown. But here, in the south, a gray layer of hardened lava several miles wide covered much of the former volcano. It must have belched out of the crater thousands of years ago and gradually cooled on its way to the water. A branching maze of cracks and crevices, cut into the rock by time and weather, protected the inhabitants of this wasteland from the heat and from the much-feared tropical storms.

It had been four days since the two castaways, hungry and thirsty, had stumbled into the camp of Agostini, the bridge builder, and his workmen. The long hours since then had been filled with waiting and doing nothing. Jolly was almost relieved when no trace of the *Carfax* appeared on the horizon on the second and third days. It looked more and more as if their friends had continued on to the city of Aelenium without them. *Let them*, Jolly thought fiercely. Even if she was a polliwog, she most certainly was not keen to confront the Maelstrom. She intended to go aboard the next supply ship and return to her old life as a pirate at last.

"There you are!" cried Agostini, when they left the labyrinth of rock fissures and reached the cliffs.

The master bridge builder came striding toward them, gesticulating fussily with his long arms, giving orders to the workers as he passed, taking a roll of papers handed to him, giving his opinion, handing papers back, spitting chewing tobacco, biting into a banana, and pushing back his broad-brimmed hat—all without slowing down.

Agostini was always doing at least three things at once. And not because he had no time: It was probably part of his nature always to be doing *something*, to be talking, moving, drawing up new plans, or reworking old ones. The man virtually seethed, as if a swarm of ants had taken on human form.

THE ATTACK

Today he was going to take Jolly and Griffin with him onto the unfinished bridge for the first time.

He turned on his heel when he reached the two of them and strode back beside them to the edge of the cliff, across a stretch of ash-gray porous rock covered with tents, workshops, and dark-skinned men. Dozens of islanders were working for him.

Agostini had long, waving hair and wore an outfit that was part torn Spanish uniform, part English captain's attire, and part French farmer's garb, all lumped together. The main thing was, it fulfilled its purpose. His tousled gray hair billowed under his broad-brimmed hat and hardly differed from the faded, drooping feathers stuck under its red hatband.

A crowd of chattering workmen parted as Agostini reached the building site with Jolly and Griffin.

The master builder stopped and, for the first time, stood still for a moment. He breathed deeply. Jolly followed his gaze to the spectacular wooden construction stretching from the edge of the lava rocks into the distance.

When she and Griffin had seen the bridge the first time, they'd scarcely believed their eyes. It spanned an arm of the sea to the next island. It wasn't finished yet, but the sight of the gigantic construction was already enough to take one's breath away.

Agostini's bridge was, in fact, astonishing: two hundred feet long, ten feet wide; curved high over the water like a sickle, but without a single column to support it; completely without ornament, designed only for functionality, and yet, of an elegance that turned the bridge itself into an ornament.

It consisted of a filigreed latticework of planks and timbers that would have to be covered in the next few weeks. Until then, the workers balanced like rope dancers on the wooden crossbeams, only one step removed from the abyss. The bridge ended on cliffs high over the water on both sides. The highest point of its arch was a good twenty fathoms from the surface of the sea.

Clearly the bridge was a delusion of grandeur. What brought a man to erect such a construction in the middle of nowhere? Who was going to use it when it was finished? Why would anyone go to such an expense to create a link between two deserted islands that lay far outside all the trade routes, far from any civilization? Agostini had given them no answers to all these questions.

Jolly suspected that he was simply crazy. However, the master builder had taken her and Griffin in and provided them with every necessity. Until they left the island, they were dependent on his help, as little as it pleased her to be stuck here.

The wind hissed at them as they left the firm ground and walked out onto the timbers of the bridge.

"It was finished this morning," Agostini declared. "The workers closed the last gaps."

Griffin took a slightly worried look at the holes between the planks. Like Jolly, he'd grown up on pirate ships. He moved over the yards of a ship with blind security. But this bridge, for reasons that weren't entirely clear to him, was something else.

They had to take care where they set their feet on the narrow crossbeams—especially Jolly. As a polliwog, she could walk on the water, but to fall and land on the surface of the sea would be fatal—the waves were as hard as stone for her, she'd break all her bones. Even for Griffin, to whom the water was only water, a fall from this height might have serious consequences.

They went along the edge of the bridge, holding on to the railing firmly with one hand. A pair of islanders sprinted nimbly past them—no wonder; most of them had been working on the structure for more than a year.

It took a long time to reach the highest point of the bridge. Jolly was so deeply lost in thought that she hadn't noticed at all that the workers were gradually left behind. Now, when she looked up, she saw that they were alone with Agostini.

Griffin asked a few questions for politeness, but Jolly hardly heard him. It was only when he wanted to know how all that wood could stay in the air without any columns at all and Agostini replied, "By magic," that she became alert.

Magic? But only polliwogs understood the art of mussel magic! Oh, well, not all the polliwogs. Of the two who were left alive, clearly only Munk had this talent. Jolly lacked the patience and also the ability—even if the Ghost Trader maintained otherwise. Munk, however, was far away; probably he'd already arrived in Aelenium with the others.

But what about Agostini? What did he know about magic?

She was about to pry it out of him when the master builder stopped. They were now in the middle of the bridge. Under them gaped a good one hundred and twenty feet of emptiness.

Agostini placed both hands on the railing, closed his eyes, and breathed deeply. His long hair fluttered in the wind like ashes on a breeze.

Griffin and Jolly exchanged a look.

In the distance came the sound of howling. Jolly turned around in fright, but it was only the wind, driving through the narrow gaps between the rock islands. The rushing of the boiling sea was thrown back whispering from the stone walls, the sound of the echo reaching even way up here.

Jolly made a new attempt to get some answers. "Really, what's the purpose of a bridge like this, out here at the end of the world?"

The master builder smiled, looking not at Jolly but over the water to the other islands. The panorama resembled layers of gray and brown shades laid on a blue canvas.

"The purpose of all bridges," he said mysteriously. "It goes from one place to the other." This was the first time he'd spoken so quietly and softly. Jolly had to strain to understand him.

Griffin shifted from foot to foot. His uneasy expression made Jolly fall silent. What did she care? Probably the best thing would be for them to enjoy the breathtaking view for a moment and then return to land.

"That other island over there"—Jolly pointed to the end of

the bridge and the forested knob that rose behind it—"why didn't you set up your camp there? It looks much more comfortable, with all the trees."

Something set off an alarm in the back of her mind, something in her own words, a hidden thought, whose meaning only became clear to her an instant later.

The trees . . . all the trees. Of course: It looked as though not one single tree had been felled over there. They'd all been cut down on the volcanic island, but not . . .

Not over there!

But there could not possibly have been enough trees on the island to create this gigantic bridge. When she thought about it carefully, there could not have been enough trees on the entire island group.

"Jolly?" Griffin had noticed that she was worried about something. "What's wrong?"

She didn't answer but looked silently down at the wood under her feet. It didn't seem unusual. She crouched down and touched it with her fingertips. It felt smooth, although the surface wasn't sanded, and it was fibrous, almost like reeds or bamboo.

"This isn't ordinary wood, is it?" She lifted her head. That same enigmatic smile was still playing around Agostini's lips.

"No," he whispered.

Griffin looked from one to the other, then grabbed Jolly by the arm. "Let's go back."

Jolly stared at the master builder. "Where does this bridge go?"

Griffin's eyes widened. "Where?" he repeated in amazement. "He knows what I mean."

Agostini nodded. "Not to that island over there, anyway."

"But—," Griffin was beginning when Jolly interrupted him: "You didn't think up this bridge on your own, did you? Someone gave you a commission. And a large portion of the wood for it."

Again the master builder nodded. His right hand began to play absently with the brim of his hat. "You came too early," he said. "But now everything will fall into place, little polliwog."

She hadn't told him anything about her abilities.

"Jolly, let's go." Griffin had had enough of the two of them speaking about something he didn't understand. "I'm going alone, if you don't—"

This time it wasn't Jolly who interrupted him but a commotion on the lava cliff. His head whipped around. And Jolly's did the same.

The islanders were running and leaping toward the rocks, where dozens of men had clumped together. Slowly they formed a circle around something that was not discernible at that distance.

"What's going on there?" Jolly asked.

Some of the workers cried out, and in several places the crowd broke apart. Many turned their faces toward heaven, as if they expected to see something out of the ordinary there. But the blue Caribbean sky was as empty and infinite as it was every day. Other islanders fell on their knees and spread out their arms in supplication.

THE ATTACK

Something smacked at Jolly's feet.

"Not again," she muttered between her teeth.

Dead fish plunged down out of nowhere, slapped onto the wooden struts, slid off, and disappeared into the depths. Silvery scaled bodies, octopuses, round spiny fish, crabs with red claws, and swollen bodies without eyes or limbs—they were all raining down now out of a cloudless sky, flowing like a macabre shower of corpses over the bridge, the cliffs, and the surrounding sea.

"Let's get out of here!" bellowed Griffin, about to run.

"Little polliwog," whispered Agostini. And he repeated, still more softly, "From one place to another . . ."

A shimmering body brushed past his shoulder, but the master builder didn't move.

Jolly and Griffin began to run back to land, but after a few steps, they both stopped.

Griffin breathed in sharply. "My god."

Jolly made not a sound. She watched the crowd of men break apart and flee in all directions, a handful even back onto the bridge. It was barely possible to see through the hail of fish bodies, but even that little was enough to explain the workers' panic. Small, dark shadows were appearing among them, figures that uttered gabbling cries as they landed blows with arms that were much too long.

Jolly tore her eyes from the sight, bent over the bridge railing, and looked down at the water. The sea was churning with so many thousands of fish that the waves appeared to boil. And yet it wasn't only the fish corpses that set the sea in motion: Something was also pushing up through the water from underneath, dark forms that floated on the waves like seaweed. Hundreds of them.

"Kobalins!" Griffin started back from the railing as if one of the frightful creatures had popped up right in front of his nose.

Jolly's voice was so hoarse that she could hardly be understood between her gasps. "And something else, too."

Griffin avoided a squid body and was hit on the back of the head by another dead creature instead. He made a face. "Something else?"

She nodded. She'd experienced a fish rain like this twice before. The sign was clear: A creature of the Maelstrom must be nearby. A monster like the Acherus, who had killed Munk's parents.

"But why are the kobalins attacking the workers?" Griffin stared over at the cliffs, where more and more dark forms were now falling on the men, a black, glittering wave of wet bodies, with overlong, much too thin limbs and snapping jaws. "Kobalins don't go on land!" He sounded terribly helpless. "Never!"

"They are now, though." Jolly pushed herself away from the railing and cast an anxious look through the latticework of the bridge down at the water. Between the crests of the waves it was swarming with kobalin heads. "Their leader is driving them onto shore. He must be able to frighten them more than the land and the air do."

Agostini was now on the railing, both arms raised, his head thrown back. "Go, little polliwog . . . ," he whispered.

THE ATTACK

"You are expected." Jolly hadn't seen him climb onto the railing, and she didn't understand how he could stay up there without holding on to anything. But his words froze the blood in her veins. What the devil did he mean?

A deep humming came from Agostini's throat. A gust of wind blew the hat off his head and his gray hair fluttered around his skull like tatters of smoke.

Griffin grabbed Jolly by the arm. "The kobalins are following the workers onto the bridge! Come on, we have to get out of here!" He gestured toward the opposite end of the bridge, where the forested hill of the second island was visible behind the pelting fish bodies.

"No, not that!" Jolly held him back. "Wait!"

Griffin looked back over his shoulder at the volcanic island. Scrabbling, clinging, and leaping kobalins now crowded onto the latticework of the bridge, reaching the fleeing workers and flinging them over the railings into the water below. Once they struck the water, they sank inexorably under the fish cadavers and did not appear again.

"They've seen us!"

"Of course," she said. "After all, they're here because of us." It was a highly probable assumption, but even as Jolly said it, she doubted it again.

"We can't go over there," she cried, trying to raise her voice over the thumping of the dead fish and avoid them at the same time.

"Why not?"

"What exactly did Agostini say before?"

Griffin stared at her desperately, then at the master builder, who was still standing in his posture of submissive worship on the railing. He looked less and less human, his proportions were becoming distorted, as if his reaching arms were growing toward the heavens.

"What did he answer when I asked him where the bridge led?"

"Not to the other island."

"Not to the island," repeated Jolly, and tried to make herself think. *Be calm! Try hard!*

Griffin looked at her, eyes wide. "But then where else would it . . . ? I mean, if not to the island, then . . ." He broke off, shaking his head.

"It's a gate. Or a passageway. Even a . . . a *bridge*," she said helplessly, because nothing better came to her. "Agostini actually did build a bridge, but it doesn't lead to the island over there, even if it looks like it. In reality, over there is something different. Perhaps another world."

"The Mare Tenebrosum?"

"It might be possible, mightn't it?"

Griffin's face hardened, his look became grim. "They're coming. We *have* to get out of here!"

Still Jolly didn't move. She took one step toward Agostini, who kept on humming and whispering into the cadaver rain and not looking at her at all.

The kobalins were coming closer. They weren't as agile as they were in the water, and the height seemed to intimidate them even more than the unaccustomed surface under their feet or the unfamiliar element. And yet their snapping, hissing, squealing mass was threatening enough to prove Griffin right. He and Jolly had to get away.

Jolly ran, but she felt as if someone else were running for her, carrying her forward and making her insensitive to her terror.

Only for a few steps. Then she stopped again. Griffin stumbled and almost slid off, but he caught himself at the last moment with her help.

"There ahead," she said tonelessly.

They had come closer to the other island. And yet it appeared more indistinct than before. Its shape was fuzzy around the edges, like a form of dark smoke. At the same time the air over it was darkened, not by clouds, but as if the light was sucked out of the blue Caribbean sky.

"What is that?" Griffin asked.

The kobalins let out a concert of high, lashing shrieks as they approached from behind. They were now only forty yards away.

"Keep going!" yelled Griffin as he looked over his shoulder.

"We can't—"

"You want to let them tear you apart?" He grabbed her by the arm and pulled her on. "It'll be enough if they throw you off the bridge like the others. The impact will break your neck—or the kobalins in the water will do it."

The darkness had spread over the sky. Not merely over them, it had also grown darker beside and in front of them. The island's hump grew higher and wider and flowed in all directions.

A screech alarmed them and made them both whirl around.

Something sprang toward them with arms outstretched, teeth bared, webbed fingers spread and curled into claws.

"Look out!" Jolly cried.

Griffin ducked. At the same time he drew his dagger from his belt. The blade flashed in the last light of the blue sky that glowed over the bridge behind them like the light at the end of a tunnel. The kobalin avoided Griffin's knife blow, swung his arms wildly, and came to stand astride two wooden crosspieces. His hideous head, with its too many teeth, swung menacingly from right to left, over and over, while behind him the tide of his fellows came nearer.

Jolly drew her own knife from her boot, quickly turned it in her hand, seized it by the point, and in a flowing movement flung it at the creature, just as Captain Bannon had taught her. The blade struck the monster's chest with a dull *fummp*. A last, high scream, then the kobalin lost his balance and plunged between the timbers into the deep.

Jolly whirled around and gratefully took Griffin's outstretched hand. While they rushed forward, the thought flashed through her mind that she was now unarmed.

The kobalins held back, as if the remaining light held them fast.

The island at the end of the bridge was an island no longer but a surging heart of darkness that turned and stretched, pulsing, as if it were alive. The bridge seemed to become longer. They really ought to have reached the other

side by this time. But the structure led ever farther, now curving downward, which made it harder to find enough
footholds to run on the struts and not be swept off their feet
by their own momentum.

"They're . . . they're staying back!" Griffin's voice almost
broke.

I don't know if that's a good sign, Jolly thought, but she didn't
say anything. Her throat felt raw, and there was a horrible
taste in her mouth, somewhere between chewed peppercorns
and spoiled meat.

Suddenly the view cleared and the darkness turned into a
deep, starless night, which extended over a stormy sea like a
dome.

A sea that had not been there. Without islands, without a
trace of land. A sea of black, oily water. The crests of the
waves were crowned by dark foam, which appeared to consist
of millions and millions of tiny creatures; little crabs, perhaps, or water insects.

There was no more light behind them. The part of the
bridge over which they'd come led straight into the endless
night of this place and lost itself in the darkness. The
kobalins had vanished; they could not follow them here. Or
did they not *dare* to?

The end of the bridge ahead of them led in a shallow arc
down into the water. The crests of the waves broke over the
latticework, swirled away over them, and left behind dark,
oily traces.

Mighty bodies moved under the surface, extremely

elongated bodies as wide as Spanish warships. Sometimes something slapped into the waves, after an almost unseen leap in the darkness.

A primal ocean, as it might have been in the beginning of the world, and yet different, stranger, more frightening. A gray shimmer lay over the water. Hazily it outlined the tossing wave crests and house-high waves.

Jolly and Griffin stopped, hand in hand, and stared unmoving out into that sea of timeless blackness and infinite deepness.

Gazed out onto the Mare Tenebrosum.

Bridge of Fire

Jolly felt as if someone had grabbed her by the feet and stood her on her head. She could hardly find any hold on the wooden girders of the bridge. Her body trembled and swayed, and her mind seemed to be lost in a confusing nothingness.

Griffin was holding her hand (or was she holding his?), but his fingers felt cold, as if the emptiness over the endless black ocean sucked all the strength out of them in order to animate them with its own ghastly essence.

In the distance, lightning flickered over the frothing water, across a horizon that in some absurd way appeared to be much farther away than the one in their world. Perhaps the world of the Mare Tenebrosum wasn't curved like their own, or here *everything* was simply more enormous. The distances, the darkness, the mountains of waves.

The living creatures.

Jolly and Griffin just stood there, incapable of moving. And where were they supposed to go, anyway? The bridge continued about thirty yards farther down, then it vanished into the oily waters of the Mare Tenebrosum, washed by black spray and orbited by gigantic shadows that glided in tight circles around the foot of the structure. Sometimes it seemed to Jolly as though she heard an angry howling, prolonged and muffled, as if cries and screams were being uttered under the surface of the water. But the noise of the waves was deafening in itself. And then the wind that swept around the wooden latticework—it sighed and shrieked, and sometimes it also seemed to whisper: words in strange languages, cold and horrible.

It smelled of rotten seaweed and algae, mixed with the stench of dead fish. But there was also another smell, something that Jolly couldn't identify right away.

"Vanilla," said Griffin, as if he'd sensed what was going through her mind. Perhaps she'd spoken her thoughts aloud without noticing it. "It smells like vanilla."

She nodded dumbly, because she was afraid her voice might sound as miserable as his. The sweetness in the midst of all these awful vapors made the scent even more unbearable. It reminded her of the possibility of something more beautiful, better, that was completely unreachable in this place.

"We can't go any farther," Griffin managed to say. Each word was uttered with difficulty, sluggishly, like snails creeping out of his throat.

Behind them there was no sign of the kobalins. The bridge

was empty, an endless arc that melted away somewhere in the blackness. But each time there was a flash of lightning, they saw that in fact the bridge continued into endlessness, thin as a thread, thin as the finest hair, but still visible, as if all the rules of visual range were suspended. The view in this world extended into infinity. Did it also reach out into time, into the past and the future? Was the Mare Tenebrosum in fact a primeval ocean at the beginning of time as well as a state to which all would someday return?

They stood there wondering what they should do, holding tightly to each other's hands, dazed, despairing, overwhelmed by the sheer alienness of this deep black ocean . . . stood there and resigned themselves to their end . . . when in front of them the bridge caught fire.

Flames shot up between the beams. The sudden brightness hurt their eyes. A wave of heat hissed over them.

The bridge was blazing!

The dark froth at the foot of the wooden structure shrank back like a living thing and formed a crater of water. At the same time a shrieking came from the depths of the sea, no longer of the invisible creatures down under there, nor even of the mysterious masters of this world, but of the Mare Tenebrosum itself. Fountains high as towers sprayed into the air, curiously slowly, as if they were frozen in time; they formed marvelous patterns in the blackness and then collapsed heavily. At one moment the spray almost looked like a gigantic mouth, with fangs of water that opened around the bridge and then subsided.

Meanwhile, the flames at the foot of the bridge surged higher and higher and crept along the boards like swarms of glowing ants, rapidly consuming the exotic fibers of the wood—wood that, as Jolly now understood, came from plants from the depths of this ocean, alien shrubs that grew in places that were empty and cold and dark like the gaps between the stars. Agostini must have received his materials from the Masters of the Mare Tenebrosum in order to realize his project, no, *their* project.

A bridge between the worlds, much smaller and less conspicuous than the Maelstrom, who was also going to break through the barriers. The perfect needle eye for any creatures that might want to prepare for the Maelstrom's rule.

Were there other such gates in remote places in the Caribbean? Perhaps even in the whole world?

Jolly had no time left to wonder. She was pulled backward by Griffin. While she'd been staring numbly into the flames, the fire had come closer. Griffin pulled her with him, and they leaped and ran in the direction from which they'd come, toward the invisible transition between this world and their own.

The darkness receded, their surroundings changed, and once more Jolly had the thought that they were perhaps *also* moving in time, that they were returning from the very beginning of the eons into their own, brief, narrowly limited life spans.

The bridge ahead of them shortened, drew itself together into its original proportions. Out of the multitude of images and colors and sounds emerged the bodies of the kobalins, who were frantically darting between the cross timbers of the wooden grid work. But the creatures paid no attention to the pair before them returning out of the mists of time and worlds. Fire was their natural enemy, the enemy of the element into which they were born.

The bridge was also in flames on this side of the crossing. The black smoke of the fire darkened the sky, so that the change between the two worlds was almost unnoticeable. The smoke bit into Jolly's lungs, making her cough. At the same time the heat struck her like a blow, and she had the feeling that the tips of her hair were frizzling and her eyebrows were smoldering.

The flames were everywhere—behind them, in front of them, even on both sides, where they danced on the railings like an army of glowing fire devils.

Agostini was still there too. He stood in the midst of the flames as if they could do nothing to him. His clothing was burning, and the brim of his hat flickered around his head like a grotesque halo.

Yet his face didn't change at all.

Or what remained of his face.

"A shape-shifter," Griffin said matter-of-factly, as if he dealt with such creatures every day. "A wyvern!"

Jolly managed to tear her eyes away for a second from what had once been Agostini to give Griffin an uncomprehending look. "A . . . what?"

"A wyvern. I've heard of them. In the ports they say—"

An outcry interrupted him. Agostini's head rotated on his neck, and the burning hat slid down and disappeared into the wall of flames. The head of the master builder no longer had any human features, or even human size—inflating, it grew to double in girth, a long, extended oval of flickering points that reminded Jolly with a shudder of the living spray foam of the Mare Tenebrosum. In fact, Agostini's body now consisted of tiny crabs, a little smaller than Jolly's smallest fingernail. They billowed all higgledy-piggledy, forming caricatures of human limbs, until they finally slid out of Agostini's burning rags of clothing as a many-armed devilfish.

Jolly first thought that the creature—or the swarm of creatures—would rush at her and Griffin, but the thing's tentacles jerked back and forth in the air. Something seemed to be alarming it, for suddenly it condensed itself and flowed through the openings in the bridge into the deep below.

Jolly had no time to think about what had happened to Agostini. The fire had now almost encircled them. Burning kobalins leaped over the railings in panic, breaking through walls of flame and spraying apart like hot fat, until Jolly and Griffin were alone on the bridge.

"Back to the island!" Jolly cried, without conviction. Anything was better than standing there doing nothing until the fire reached them.

She could see how bad their chances were: The way to land was blocked by a sea of flames, and the other direction, into the Mare Tenebrosum, was also cut off by the hissing conflagration. Nevertheless, she'd rather burn than go back there once more or even take one look into that world of terrors.

They ran, past the burning railings, from which ever new tongues of flame were now spreading to the crisscrossing ground timbers. Not much longer and the bridge would collapse under their feet.

What had at a distance looked like a wall of flame turned out to be a labyrinth of individual nests of flames, between which they might still be able to find a path. If the bridge held. And if the fire didn't keep spreading at such breakneck speed.

"Griffin!" cried Jolly. "You have to jump. The impact on the water won't do anything to you."

"And leave you alone?"

"Stop playing hero and jump, will you?"

He shook his head as he ran. "What good would that do me? The kobalins are waiting down there."

"They're long gone. They're more afraid of the fire than we are." She wasn't certain that was the truth. Whatever had made the kobalins go onto land could make them still hold out in the water, too.

Was the wyvern the commander? Not very likely. After all, the kobalins had attacked the workers before the bridge was finished. The shape-shifter was presumably as surprised by the attack as they were. Someone or something had changed its plans without informing Agostini of it.

But then who had set fire to the bridge?

They'd reached the front third. The wood creaked and cracked under their feet. Their height over the sea here was about fifteen yards, still much too high for Jolly to jump into the water. Through the spaces between the timbers they saw cutouts of the water behind black clouds of smoke. The seething kobalin heads between the waves were gone; but whether they were entirely gone or just submerged was uncertain. Besides, there was still the wyvern, which might be lurking under the surface.

At the last stretch, just before the cliff, there was no longer a way to get through. The beams and crosspieces were all aflame. The heat was almost intolerable, and now it was coming from all sides.

"That's it," Griffin panted.

"Griffin," Jolly said once again, "you *must* jump into the water!"

He was about to contradict her again, but the words remained stuck in his throat. Something dark shot up behind him, over the railing, and to them. Out of the corner of her eye, Jolly thought she saw mighty wings, as dark as the leathery skin of the kobalins. It seemed as if a piece of the Mare Tenebrosum had followed them and now descended on them like a giant bat.

The shadow landed between them on the timbers, the wings—which were not wings—remained open, and a voice shouted, "Here to me! Quickly!"

Darkness fluttered over them and enveloped them. It was material, dark, coarse material, and underneath it smelled musty and warm. But it kept the heat away from them. Underneath the material: a muscular body. Over it: the face of a one-eyed man.

BRIDGE OF FIRE

The Ghost Trader gripped Jolly in his right arm, Griffin in his left, both closely wrapped in the wide cloak.

"Where did you come—"

Jolly never finished her sentence. The ground vanished beneath her. At first she thought the bridge had collapsed and she was falling into emptiness. But then she realized that everything was quite different.

The burning bridge was left behind below them—over them? Beside them? In any case, it was gone, and Jolly, Griffin, and the Ghost Trader floated toward the water, turned into a sea of lava by the glow of the fire.

She'd seen the Ghost Trader make such leaps before, in the harbor of New Providence, when the Spanish fleet was turning the pirate nest into ruins. Now he'd done it again. Not flying. Not even hopping. This was something superhuman, which he accomplished as matter-of-factly as any other man would an ordinary step.

He let Jolly slide out of his embrace. She crashed onto the waves, fought for balance for a moment, and then finally stood upright. The flaming bridge was about twenty yards away, a gigantic glowing sickle in front of an inferno of dark smoke. The heat was definitely palpable down here. Not much longer and the entire lunatic construction would collapse like a house of cards.

They were not alone in the water, even if Jolly was the only one who could stand securely with her feet on the waves. Strange creatures had formed a circle around them, creatures that at first sight looked like horses, except that they were bigger and only rose about halfway out of the waves. The lower part of their bodies were under the surface. Their rough, furrowed skin shimmered with the colors of the rainbow. In place of ears they had stumpy horns, and their eyes were round and fishy. They had no limbs; their entire body was a single, broad fishtail, which was not smooth but horny and graduated in irregular tiers. On their backs they bore odd-looking saddles, which allowed their riders to sit up straight in them. Each of the wonderful animals towered at least six feet out of the water; Jolly guessed that the hidden part was just as long.

The men who maintained their seats on the gigantic sea horses with no apparent effort were wearing simple clothing of leather, which in some places was studded with something that looked like stone. Or coral.

"The riders of Aelenium," the Ghost Trader called down to her from the back of a sea horse. His animal had also been waiting for them in the circle with the others; its sharp head was as white as ivory, the horns the color of amber. The creature's lidless eyes were deceptive; actually, it observed the surroundings with watchful intelligence.

Now Jolly understood why the Trader had set her down on the water: He needed both hands to place Griffin in front of him in the saddle. Only then did he reach a hand down to Jolly.

"Come up!" he commanded urgently. "Hurry!"

She grasped his hand and let herself be drawn up and pushed behind him in the wide, curving saddle. She was held at the back by a network of straps that had tightened around her waist when she sat down.

"Let's go!" cried the Ghost Trader to the circle of sea horsemen. The men were armed with sabers and flintlock pistols. Most carried their loaded guns in their right hand, while their left held the reins of the horse.

Jolly pressed close against the Ghost Trader's back. She didn't yet understand where he'd come from and who these other people were; however, she was infinitely grateful that they'd appeared at the right moment.

"The kobalins," she burst out frantically. "Where are they?"

"They dived."

"But they weren't alone!"

"No." With a powerful jerk, the Trader turned the sea horse around. The other animals followed the motion, maintaining the protective circle formation around them. "The hippocampi sense something." He must have meant the sea horses.

"It must be the wyvern," Griffin called over his shoulder. "A—"

"A shape-shifter," said the Ghost Trader, and he nodded. The sea horses moved forward, away from the bridge, toward a lane between the countless islands. Somewhere in this direction lay the open sea, the endless Atlantic.

"So you know about Agostini?" Jolly hardly had the strength to put this question. To keep from falling, she clung more firmly to the Ghost Trader.

"Agostini? Is that what he calls himself?"

"Not anymore," said Griffin. "Presumably."

"They knew about him in Aelenium. And about this bridge. We came just in time." He looked back over his shoulder at Jolly. "You'll never guess who's come with us."

"Munk?" she asked weakly.

He paused briefly before he answered. "No. Munk is in Aelenium. But Walker is here. And Soledad. The good captain hasn't let the princess out of his sight ever since she smiled at him once too often."

Jolly looked around. Her eyes flitted over the other sea horsemen, but they swam before her like something that wasn't even there. Mere hallucinations. Fantasies.

"Hold on tight!" cried the Ghost Trader as the hippocampus increased its speed. Jolly doubted that there were ships as fast as these creatures.

The formation of sea horses rushed through the island labyrinth. The burning bridge was left far behind them. It had almost vanished behind cliffs and rocks when a horrible grinding and crashing announced its end. Jolly looked back over her shoulder, but her eyes were no longer sharp enough to see anything in detail. All she saw was a glowing stripe in the distance, which abruptly collapsed and immediately vanished into a boiling witch's kettle of black smoke and white steam.

"It's finished," said the Ghost Trader, although she guessed his words more than she really heard them. The waves broke loudly against the horny chest of the sea horse.

White spume sprayed into Jolly's face and deposited a film of salt on her lips.

She couldn't believe that he had really said *finished*. A voice inside her whispered to her that it wasn't the truth. He wanted to reassure her and so he was concealing something from her.

In truth, this was just the beginning.

"Where's the wyvern?" asked Griffin in a voice that sounded just as weak as her own.

"Gone," replied the Trader. "Shape-shifters are cowards, when it comes right down to it."

There was still something else, thought Jolly again, but she was too exhausted to articulate it.

Still something else.

Griffin's voice sounded thin in her ears, carried by the wind, which was beating against them more and more fiercely. "It stopped raining dead fish. Does that mean . . ."

"Yes," said the Trader. "Whatever it was, it's gone. For the moment. We don't know exactly why. When the soldiers of Aelenium appeared and set the fire, the kobalins made no attempt to stop them. On the contrary, right after our attack they withdrew."

Jolly tried to understand the meaning behind his words. "But the kobalins are commanded by the Maelstrom. Why would he permit the destruction of the bridge? After all, he was sent to prepare the way for the Masters of the Mare Tenebrosum."

The Ghost Trader shrugged and sighed. "The power and strength of the Maelstrom grow from day to day. Every move in this war serves a purpose, even if we don't always know what."

Jolly pulled all her reserves together. "War?" she asked in a strangled voice.

Now the surroundings were a blur, so swiftly did the sea horses glide over the boiling sea, toward the northeast, toward their invisible goal in the distance.

The Ghost Trader looked over his shoulder, but Jolly saw only the blind half of his face, the dark band, behind which lay the dead eye.

"The great battle for Aelenium," he said.

The Sea Star City

The hippocampi were tireless. They swept through the deep blue sea like dervishes, seldom needing rest and not sleeping at all—or they recovered themselves without losing any speed, which seemed even more inconceivable and marvelous to Jolly. She herself did sleep some, it was true, but in the confinement of the saddle it was brief and fitful and brought no real relief.

The journey proceeded without incident. They saw no more of the deep-sea tribes. The Maelstrom appeared to have changed his plans. After they'd left the labyrinth of reefs and rocky islands behind them, Griffin was transferred to Walker's sea horse and now was sitting behind the captain in the straps of the strange saddle. Walker was talking with him, but Jolly couldn't understand what he was saying across the distance. Perhaps he was just trying to reassure Griffin, to cheer him up; a strange notion, because it hadn't been so long ago that the pirate captain had wanted to throw the boy over the side of his ship.

Walker had tied his shoulder-length hair into a short ponytail. He still wore the scarlet trousers he'd been wearing when they first met him, and his golden earring. Jolly herself had a half a dozen rings in each ear, besides a pin with a tiny diamond on each end in the skin of her nose just above the bridge. Nevertheless, she thought that the ornament looked silly on Walker.

Soledad, the daughter of the murdered pirate emperor, Scarab, was riding ahead of Walker in the formation of sea horse riders. Like the captain, she was secured to her saddle by additional straps; after all, neither of them had any experience in dealing with those remarkable animals. However, it struck Jolly that Soledad handled herself more skillfully than Walker. In contrast to him, she'd had experience with horses on land. Her long red hair fluttered loose in the wind, and sometimes she sent Jolly encouraging looks or a cheering smile.

During those long hours, Jolly thought often about the destination of their journey: Aelenium. She had no concrete conception of it, but she knew that it involved a sort of floating city, lying at anchor on a long chain somewhere in the Atlantic, northeast of the Virgin Islands. The inhabitants of Aelenium were something like guards, who had watched over the imprisoned Maelstrom for centuries—before he got free and gained new, terrible power.

So far the Maelstrom had kept away from the city. Jolly

had no idea why he was waiting so long to attack; all she knew was that Munk and she were the only ones who could stop him.

The fate of Aelenium hung on their survival and, if she believed the Ghost Trader, ultimately so did the continued existence of the entire world. Only if the Maelstrom were kept from becoming strong enough to tear down the boundaries to the Mare Tenebrosum would they be able to return to their old lives.

She thought about the day when everything had begun. In one stroke she'd lost her foster father, Captain Bannon, and with him the entire crew. Jolly had grown up on Bannon's ship. He'd been father and mother to her and, in addition, the best teacher she could have imagined. But then he'd fallen into a trap. Only Jolly was able to escape. She had no evidence that the Maelstrom was behind it, and she'd always refused to believe that Bannon and the others were dead. But every clue she'd come across so far, every hope, had come to nothing. And although she didn't intend to give up, the experiences of recent days and weeks had pushed her grief over Bannon more and more into the background.

Twice the sun sank into the sea and twice it rose again before a dense field of fog appeared ahead. Jolly tensed when the riders steered their hippocampi straight into the fog. They seemed to float through gray nothingness for a long time before they finally crossed the fog and saw Aelenium before them.

Jolly's heart missed a beat. She'd never seen anything like

it. All the cities she knew were miserable settlements around the harbors of the Caribbean: crooked clusters of badly built huts and ramshackle houses interspersed with dark dives, storage sheds, and the businesses of the fences, rum traders, and tattoo parlors.

Aelenium, on the other hand, seemed to her as though a piece of heaven had taken form, a frosted cake of interconnected coral structures, high as a small mountain rising out of the countless towers and balconies, pointed gabled roofs, crazy bridges and platforms. Everything there seemed to consist of coral, white or beige, sometimes with chocolate brown or amber-colored streaks running through it. The windows and doors were high and narrow, some buildings so finely chiseled that they reminded Jolly of the Chinese porcelain she had seen when Bannon once seized a whole shipload.

But were they buildings? Was there anything there that was really *built*? In fact, it looked rather as if Aelenium had grown naturally, like the miracle of a coral reef. The city rose on a mighty sea star, whose points extended far out into the sea and were used by the inhabitants as natural quays. Most of these points, at least on this side of the city, were covered with low houses; not until the center of the sea star did the houses become bigger; they soared up to dizzying heights around a flattened triangle of a mountain. The mountain itself had steep sides of the same light material as everything else and was traversed by numerous streams of water: some flowing quietly through narrow channels, others plunging over ledges and terraces in waterfalls.

"Impressive, isn't it?" said the Ghost Trader over his shoulder, but Jolly had no answer. "Impressive" seemed the wrong word to use. Aelenium was much more than that, a wonder, a spectacle, something utterly and completely incredible.

And she noticed something else as well: Above the towers of the city, against the cloudless blue of the sky, circled winged creatures—powerful rays, which moved through the air the way the much smaller members of their species moved through the depths of the sea. A rider sat on each of these flying rays, the soldiers of the city.

The sea horses let them dismount at the edge of one of the sea star points. Even the guardsmen were visibly wearied by the long ride. Walker leaped from the saddle, intending to hurry to Soledad—but his knees gave out. He fell flat on the ground. Some of the riders laughed, but Soledad sent him a sympathetic look: She knew that the same thing would happen to her when she tried to stand on her own feet again after days in the saddle.

Someone lifted Jolly down and placed her on a coral block. Griffin was brought to her, his hand felt for hers, but neither one of them said a word.

The *Carfax* lay anchored nearby, badly damaged by the battle. Carpenters and shipbuilders were busy all over the hull and in the rigging, working hand in hand with the sloop's misty ghost crew.

Turning her eyes from the *Carfax*, Jolly looked up at the city in wonder. It seemed to her that a fairy tale had come to life.

Two birds fluttered down out of the sea of Aelenium's roofs and landed on the Ghost Trader's shoulders. He laughingly greeted the two pitch-black parrots. Hugh and Moe usually followed his every step; it was remarkable that they hadn't accompanied him. Hugh had yellow eyes, Moe eyes of fiery red, and anyone who encountered them learned very quickly that both possessed a mysterious intelligence.

New faces swam up around Jolly. Some regarded her curiously, some whispered things like "Is that her?" and "A little slight, isn't she?" Jolly scarcely listened, and when she did, she acted as if she didn't notice how impolitely they were looking her over and speaking about her as if she weren't even there.

Striding out of the crowd, cursing loudly, there emerged a tall, broad-shouldered figure with the head of a dog.

Buenaventure, the pit bull man, flicked his ears, then drew his jowls into a toothy grin. He grabbed Walker, who'd been helped to his feet, embraced him roughly, and thumped him so hard on the back that the captain almost collapsed. Then he discovered Jolly, uttered a relieved yowl, and embraced her, too.

"I'm damn glad you're back with us again, little Jolly! Damn glad!" Smiling his dog smile, he looked over at Griffin, who grinned wearily back. "Glad you made it too, Fresh Brat."

The two shook hands—Griffin's disappearing almost entirely in the grip of the pit bull man—and then Buenaventure turned around theatrically to show them his back. He wore a knapsack, out of which stared the head of a bizarre creature, half caterpillar, half beetle, but as long as a man's arm: the Hexhermetic Shipworm. Below a shield of shell that covered most of his head, a mouth opened.

"My lady Jolly," the creature announced unctuously (he'd never called her that before), "I count myself more than fortunate to see you and your brave companion again."

"Brave?" asked Griffin, looking puzzled. They were certainly used to a different tone from the Hexhermetic Shipworm, the master of ten thousand oaths and even more insults.

"I welcome you to Aelenium," the worm continued undaunted, "and would like to take the opportunity to offer for your benefit a few modest verses which I have created with poetic zeal especially for your arrival."

"Uhh," Jolly began.

"Right now?" Griffin asked.

The shipworm cleared his throat audibly and was just about to begin when Walker's open hand landed on the shell shield.

"Stop!" said the captain, who'd dragged himself over on trembling legs. "Forgotten already? No poems and no verse when I'm in the vicinity."

"Says who?" said the worm excitedly, for a moment losing his dignified formality. "That rule might perhaps have held onboard your filthy, stinking pirate tub, but not here in wonderful Aelenium, where they know how to value high poesie and art."

Buenaventure looked back over his shoulder at Jolly. "The people here honor him. 'Font of beautiful language,' they call him, and 'Maestro Poeticus.'"

"Don't forget 'Wonderworm,'" said the shipworm.

"Six days away," growled Walker, "and already a worm is walking all over me."

"Won-der-worm," the worm repeated in the captain's direction, emphasizing every single syllable. "Mark it well, barbarian! 'Merlin of Marvelous Meters,' someone called me. And 'Diamond of Poetic Art.'"

Walker made a noise that sounded neither marvelous nor poetic.

"Puh!" said the worm, cleared his throat again, and began:

> *The heroes' return in times of gloom,*
> *to storms of joy and women's bliss,*
> *shall lead us all to victory soon,*
> *and thus drive Evil to its own abyss.*

> *My lady Jolly, Chevalier Griffin,*
> *from the enemy's hand made free,*
> *might soon to fame indeed be–*

"Owwww!" screamed the worm. "That hurt!"

"Just like your rhymes," said Walker.

"No one hits a poet!"

"I just did!" The captain came so close to the Hexhermetic Shipworm that his nose almost poked against the shell shield. "I have murdered children, robbed women, and crippled cripples. Who's going to keep me from *roasting* a worm alive and *eating* it, eh?"

"Eating?" asked the worm in a small voice.

"With salt and pepper. And a touch of red wine vinegar."

"Walker!" Soledad gently placed her hand on the captain's shoulder. "He meant well."

"Not with me," said Walker grimly.

Jolly looked at Griffin and sighed. "Welcome home," she whispered.

They reached the interior of a coral palace over steps and bridges. High passages led deeper into the heart of the city. Their way led under slanting, never symmetrical ceilings and past walls from which all kinds of angular structures grew. Seen up close, they no longer resembled anything that an architect could have invented.

Aelenium *was* a coral, the largest anyone had ever heard of: Ancient particles had fastened onto the back of the gigantic sea star and grown with time, layer by layer of fantastic deposits, out of which something had developed that more resembled a termite hill than a city made by human hands.

Paths here seemed always to be longer than necessary, flights of stairs led apparently nowhere, and there were halls and salons in which not even the tiniest corner existed, just round forms, curves, and bulging bays.

"Where's Munk, anyway?" Jolly felt a stab of bad conscience because she hadn't asked after him earlier.

"He's working," said the Ghost Trader shortly.

"Working?"

"On his talents. On the mussel magic."

"Why wasn't he there when we arrived?"

The Trader was silent for a moment, then said without looking at her, "Perhaps no one told him of it."

"But the other people knew all about it!"

Griffin touched her arm. "Maybe he didn't *want* to come."

"But that's—" She broke off, her protest fizzling out unuttered.

"Munk has learned much more in the last few days," said the Ghost Trader, who hadn't failed to notice how disappointed she was. "You have some catching up to do."

She was silent, but she thought that she too would have something to say about what she was going to do with her time. She wasn't a mussel magician like Munk, polliwog or not. And she had no intention of becoming one.

She intended to be a pirate. The most important and most feared woman freebooter in the Caribbean. And she intended to find out what had happened to Captain Bannon and the crew of the *Skinny Maddy*. Let others worry about the Maelstrom and the Masters of the Mare Tenebrosum. Munk, for instance. And the Ghost Trader himself. Jolly was sick and tired of having somebody trying to prescribe for her what she had to do and what she had to allow. And least of all could she tolerate another single one of those forebodings.

"Where are we going?" she asked, and she was already dreading her reception under the coral domes, the sage men and women who would greet her as if the fate of the world actually depended on her.

"I've assumed that you would want to rest for a while,"

said the Ghost Trader. "Therefore, someone will first show you your chambers. Sleep for a few hours. Then we'll see what happens next."

Chambers. Jolly nodded absently. She imagined Munk as she had last seen him: his face reddened with fever, bending over his collection of mussels, which he kept rearranging in new patterns to make magic arise from them.

As if he were possessed, she thought, and she didn't feel very comfortable at the thought.

I am not like him.

I will never be like Munk.

She must have slept for a long time, for when she awakened, her clothing lay washed and dry on a stool beside the bed. Her linen trousers had been replaced with leather ones that were astonishingly light and comfortable to wear. Twilight spread before the high, arching windows, but whether it was morning or evening, she wasn't able to say. No matter—the main thing was that she'd slept enough. The Ghost Trader had given her some nasty herbal brew to drink before she lay down. And whether it was the mysterious drink or the hours of rest she had to thank, she felt fresh and ready for an exploratory expedition. Except that her backside was still hurting from the long ride, and when she looked in a mirror, she discovered she had black-and-blue spots there as big as coconuts.

A little later she left her sleeping place: a chamber much higher than it was wide, with a shimmering, arched ceiling, which had a pinkish glimmer to it that was visible only from certain spots in the room. The door was of wood, as was all the furniture, which made the amazing surroundings seem a little more real. Human beings lived here, not angels or fairies. Human beings from all over the world who'd ended up in Aelenium for the craziest reasons.

Griffin had been put in the chamber next to hers, but when she knocked, there was no answer. He must still be asleep.

So she went on her way alone and followed the Ghost Trader's advice not to climb farther up but always take the downhill direction at crossings and forks—that way you could be almost sure not to get lost in Aelenium, he'd said.

Jolly found the advice odd, of course, but she soon forgot to think about it, for the sight of the city captured her completely. For one thing, she realized that Aelenium wasn't at all the compact mass it had appeared to be from a distance. In fact, most of the houses, even the palace where she'd slept, were rather small and intricately lacy. Behind, between, often under or even on constructed bridges ran a maze of lanes, paths, and streets. And so one walked, even if only for short distances, mostly under the open sky. There were a great number of different smells in the air. Jolly's path took her through markets with fresh fruit, past windows from which delicately perfumed fragrances wafted, or simply onto balconies high over the sea, where she took deep gulps of the salt ocean air, realizing how long it had been since she'd consciously perceived it.

The inhabitants of Aelenium clearly differed from the mobs in the harbor cities. Not that those mobs had ever bothered Jolly—after all, she belonged to them herself. But she couldn't avoid acknowledging that everything here was a little more orderly and pleasant than in the filthy lanes of Port Nassau or the low districts of the Jamaican harbor dives.

For one thing, there were obviously not too many people living in Aelenium, certainly not more than a few thousand. She saw only a few men and gathered that most were preparing for the defense of the city. Women and children were simply but richly dressed. And if there was anything at all that detracted from the impression of a romantic idyll, it was the fact that most people went about their daily business outdoors as quickly as possible and with harried expressions on their faces.

They appeared to know how things stood with the sea star city. The approaching war against the Maelstrom and the powers of the Mare Tenebrosum was obviously no secret in the coral houses and byways. And so this city, in spite of all its beauty and apparent peace, was nevertheless making itself ready for a siege.

Everyone must know what a defeat would mean: the complete destruction of Aelenium and the death of all its inhabitants. Considering that, Jolly found it astonishing that the atmosphere was still one of calm and harmony. But then she remembered Port Nassau and the threat of the Spanish armada: There, too, hardly anyone had worried about the danger, all went busily about their dubious businesses, the pirates, the traders, and the prostitutes. Why should it be any different here? A dweller in Aelenium might be better mannered and a little finer, but possibly all humans were alike when they were looking an unavoidable fate in the eye.

Jolly had a lump in her throat as she wandered over the bridges, steps, and terraces of Aelenium. Gradually she understood why the Ghost Trader staked so much on saving this place. The Trader was old, much older than she could comprehend, and there was an aura of the superhuman about him that sometimes frightened Jolly. Had he found peace in this city—only now to see this peace threatened by the Masters of the Mare Tenebrosum? Was he therefore prepared to offer any imaginable sacrifice for a victory over the Maelstrom?

She shuddered at this thought and clenched her hands a little more tightly around the railing of the balcony from which she was looking down into the lower city. Below her, on the other side of the roofs and towers and minarets, lay four of the mighty sea star points, which stood out in the evening mist like white fingers against the dark ocean surface. Sailboats and hippocampi circled the floating city, and above all, in the air, were the mighty rays with their armed riders, always watchful, always on the lookout for the smallest indication of an attack.

The wind whistled sharply through the narrow coral chasms and sighed like a bizarre organ concert. Jolly pushed back her hair and absently raised her eyes from the waves to the wall of fog that lay around Aelenium in a protective ring.

Veils of fog wobbled and waved, forming fantastic shapes, sometimes also threatening faces, which appeared only to those who looked long enough.

You're brooding, Jolly told herself. And you're driving yourself into defeatism. Aelenium isn't lost yet. There's still a chance to save this city.

It depends on you, whispered the voices inside her. *It all lies in your hands.*

She shook her head as if she could chase away the thoughts like flies, but it didn't help. The Ghost Trader had driven his message into her mind too deeply: Only the two polliwogs could keep Aelenium from destruction. And with the city the entire Caribbean, all that Jolly knew and loved.

"Jolly!" A call made her jump. She was almost grateful for it, even if her heart stopped for a moment.

"Jolly, up here!"

She looked up and saw a mighty shadow over her, triangular like a giant lance point, with wings that rose and fell deliberately, as if they were still swimming in the depths of the sea.

Majestically the ray glided down until both its riders were at the level of the railing, separated from her only by a few feet of utter void.

"Jolly . . . you're all right, thank God!"

One of the riders was d'Artois, the captain of the ray guard and master of the hippocampi. Jolly recognized him. He'd been with the others at the bridge. Yet it wasn't he who had spoken, but the thin blond figure sitting behind him in the saddle.

Jolly sighed, and a smile stole across her lips.

"Munk," she said with relief. "Where the devil have you been?"

Polliwog Magic

"Come on, climb on!"

Munk's face was red, but now excitement seemed to be the reason, not fever and, best of all, not the accursed mussel magic. She stared at him over the void as if she had a ghost before her.

Deep inside she was still angry at him because he hadn't been there to greet her when she arrived. But as he sat there in front of her on the back of this monster, clearly healthier than at their parting a week ago, she was more than willing to forgive him.

Munk had lost both his parents when the Acherus had come to his island. But now he was obviously able to be happy again. The enthusiasm was practically flashing from his eyes, and that was an improvement that Jolly hadn't dared to hope for.

"Climb on?" she asked with a nervous laugh. "Are you crazy?"

D'Artois pulled on the ray's reins and brought him even closer to the railing. Behind Jolly, on a small spot between white coral walls, the wing beats whirled up straw and a few dried flowers.

"I can't climb up there," she said.

"Sure you can," said the captain.

He let out a shrill whistle. Jolly crouched as the ray swept over her and sank onto the ground with a thump. It had no feet or claws, like birds, and Jolly guessed that it usually landed on the water. But here it just lay on its belly, let its wings sink flat on the ground, and waited patiently.

Munk stretched out a hand to her. "Now, come on. We have enough room for three."

Jolly still hesitated. "I don't know."

"The rays can carry up to five of us," d'Artois said with a smile. "And they're gentle animals, much easier to steer than the hippocampi."

"My rear end is still sore."

Munk sighed. "You didn't used to act like this."

Jolly sent him a sharp look, then gave herself a shake, climbed carefully over the pointed tail of the ray, and took a place behind Munk in the saddle. The back of the ray did in fact have places for more riders. There were footholds and handholds for each one, so that they didn't even have to hold onto each other.

Nevertheless, she slid forward close to Munk for a

moment and embraced him from behind. "Great to see you again!"

His face took on the color of a ripe tomato, and his grin reached from one ear to the other. He grasped her hands and pressed them hard. "I missed you."

"Hey, hey," cried d'Artois. "I'm still here!"

Jolly let go of Munk and sat back on the smooth leather saddle. She shoved her hands and feet into the straps, unable to suppress a short groan as the bruises reminded her painfully of the condition of her backside.

"Are you ready?" the captain asked. Jolly nodded. "Good, then let's go. Hold on tight!"

He let out another whistle, and immediately the ray rose a few feet off the ground with graceful wing beats, turned between the houses, and glided out into emptiness. It seemed to Jolly as though she sat in a boat in a calm, so imperceptible were the movements of the powerful body. But in her legs she could feel that under the smooth leathery skin of the animal were tensed muscle fibers as thick as her arm.

The wings kept her from looking down. It was rather as if she were floating on a flying carpet. Only when she looked over her shoulder could she get a glimpse straight down past the ray's tail. However, she immediately became so dizzy that she quickly looked forward again. D'Artois's long hair was blown out almost horizontal in the air, just like her own. The headwind was cooler than she'd expected, but that was because the sun had long vanished behind the fog. Only the upper edges of the bright layers of air glowed delicately like rumpled gold leaf.

The coral roofs of the city were behind them, fifty or sixty yards away. Then the captain of the rays flew a loop, which took them in a spiral around Aelenium. For the first time Jolly got a look at the other side of the sea star city, and so she discovered that there one of the points was missing and two others were broken off at an angle into the sea. The houses on the remnants of these points were destroyed, the debris blackened, as though a great fire had raged there not too long ago.

"What happened down there?" she asked.

"Maelstrom creatures," replied d'Artois shortly. "An attack that we beat back."

"No one here likes to talk about it," said Munk. "It was just a few months ago that—"

"Five," the captain interrupted.

"Five months," said Munk, as if he'd been living in Aelenium at the time. "A troop of kobalins dove under the fog, led by . . . yes, by what, actually?"

D'Artois remained dour; he didn't like this subject. "By something for which there is no name. Larger than the largest ship. And more dangerous than the giant kraken."

Munk looked back at her. "Captain d'Artois and his men beat it back. And the kobalins, too, of course. But there were many dead, and you see what happened to the city."

Jolly nodded somberly.

"Since that attack, rays patrol under the city and protect the anchor chain," d'Artois said. "The deep levels were uninhabited up till now, but now we're not so sure of that. Divers search the halls and grottoes, but it's all much too big and interconnected for us to be certain. If something has settled in down there, it may only be waiting for an opportunity to strike."

"What's that, the deep levels?"

"The city under the city." Munk beat the captain to it. "On the underside of the sea star there's a coral structure similar to the one on the upper side. It's as if Aelenium had a mirror image."

"Innumerable coral caverns and caves," said d'Artois. "In earlier days they were certain there were a few sharks and morays under there, at most. But in times like these? Who knows." He sighed. "Nevertheless—we do our best to secure the undercity."

"How many soldiers are there in Aelenium, actually?" Jolly asked.

"Not enough. A few hundred."

Jolly remembered the host of kobalins they'd seen from the *Carfax* two weeks before. A mighty force of thousands upon thousands, swimming out into the Atlantic. There the Maelstrom was gathering his forces.

Aelenium didn't have the trace of a chance if it came to a battle of men against kobalins.

"I know what you're thinking," said d'Artois, as they flew a second orbit around the city, gradually descending as they flew. "But we will fight, if it comes to that. We have no choice."

"Jolly, look!" Munk's sudden cheeriness sounded a little

too put-on to be real. He wanted to distract her. "That's the traders' quarter down there. See the bazaar?"

"Yes."

"And over there, a little bit higher, is the library. We have to go there early tomorrow." He pointed with outstretched arm to a group of high coral domes, which nestled against the slope of the mountain cone. Several watercourses running down from above ended in basins and canals between the library buildings, creating bubbling waterfalls and pools with exotic plants.

"And there," said Munk a little later, "are the houses of the Council of Aelenium. Right next to them are the Guards' Barracks. And just under is the Poets' Quarter. Well, painters and musicians live there too." He laughed softly. "You should have seen them when the Hexhermetic Shipworm turned up. They sent a delegation to the council to get his own house for him in the Poets' Quarter. And his own ration of wood. He's quite popular here."

"Merlin of Marvelous Meters." She giggled as she repeated the worm's words.

"He is a great poet, your worm," said d'Artois very seriously. "You shouldn't make fun of him just because he's smaller than you."

Munk laughed. "You see? They're like that here. So terribly full of understanding and good will . . . 'just because he's smaller than you,'" he mimicked the captain jokingly. "Probably that's why the Ghost Trader values Aelenium so much, because they're all so terribly nice."

"But mean enough to throw you down from up here if you don't keep your tongue bridled, young friend."

Munk looked at Jolly over his shoulder and made a silent grimace.

"Now we're going down at a steep angle," said the captain. "Hold on tight!"

Jolly slipped forward a little as the ray went into a sort of nosedive. For a moment she felt so sick that she thought she was going to throw up. Only when d'Artois leveled out about three yards over the surface of the water did her stomach recover. The hand grips to which she clung had become damp and slippery.

D'Artois slowed the ray's flight until the animal was gliding forward leisurely over the waves. Down here the darkness was almost complete; only the flickering lights of Aelenium, which were now being lit one by one, broke over the dark surface.

The memory of the Mare Tenebrosum stabbed through Jolly. A deep, black, lightless ocean. Almost like . . . no, not like this one. This was the Caribbean Sea. Waves over which she could walk forward the way others did on firm ground.

Munk pulled his feet out of the foot straps and began to climb up onto the saddle a little shakily.

"Have you gone crazy?" she snapped at him.

"Just watch."

"You don't have to impress me," she retorted snippily. "If you fall onto the water from this height, you break all your bones." Another person would probably not have come to any harm, but Jolly and Munk were polliwogs. And it amazed Jolly that the captain permitted Munk's antics at all—after all, the fate of Aelenium hung on him, much more than it did on her.

"You tell him!" she entreated d'Artois. "This silly fool is going to fall."

"Wait," said the captain. He gave a whistle, and the ray stopped flying, holding its wings completely stiff.

Munk stood up, legs spread, with both feet on the saddle. "Watch!" he said to Jolly. "I want to show you what I've learned in the last few days."

"How to break your neck?"

Munk turned to one side and walked out onto one of the outstretched wings of the ray. It held his weight without the animal's tilting.

"Munk, damn it!" She stretched out a hand to grab him, but he was already out of her reach and was now walking to the farthest edge of the wing as if it were a platform of wood, not the wing of a living creature.

"It's important to dive in with your hands and head first," he said.

Dive in? What was he talking about? Polliwogs couldn't dive. Water was like stone for them. He'd crack his skull if he tried it. "Stop this nonsense right now!"

Munk sent her a smile that was a trace too superior for her taste. Then he turned, flexed his knees a little, bent forward—and pushed off from the ray's wing headfirst.

Jolly let out a scream as he plunged into the depths. Then the ray flew over the spot and Jolly almost dislocated her neck, trying to keep Munk in sight. But the water was too dark to see where he'd landed.

"Fly back!" she urged. "Turn around! Quick!"

"Don't worry," replied d'Artois. "Nothing happened to him."

"Oh no?" She stared as hard as she could at the dark waves, expecting any minute to see Munk's twisted body on the surface. "We're polliwogs! We can die from stunts like that!"

"*You can*—but you don't have to," d'Artois said, and he turned the ray in a wide loop back in the direction from which they'd come.

"Do you mean to say . . ."

"There's a teacher here in Aelenium who knows all about what you can do and what you can't. He isn't a polliwog himself, but he knows about the old records."

"Records?" Her voice sounded scornful. "The first polliwogs were born after the great earthquake at Port Royal. That's just fourteen years ago. So your records can't be so terribly old." She stopped talking, but she could hardly think of anything else except Munk, who was, with the utmost probability, floating dead somewhere down there in the dark.

"False," contradicted the captain. "I certainly don't know everything about polliwogs, but all the same, I know one thing for sure: They did exist earlier, many thousands of years ago—at the time when Aelenium became the guard of the Maelstrom."

"Fine guards you are," she said bitterly. It didn't give her half as much pleasure to wound him as she'd hoped. But at the moment it felt *right* somehow. Even if she only wanted to distract herself from Munk and what d'Artois had just said.

"As guards we have failed, that is correct," the captain confirmed, but his voice had lost some of its objectivity. "Nevertheless, it appears to me that our wise men know you polliwogs better than you do yourselves."

She couldn't think clearly, couldn't listen—not as long as she didn't know what had become of Munk. "Fly lower."

To her surprise, he did as she requested.

"Jolly!" a voice called up to her out of the darkness. "Here I am!"

She slipped into Munk's place in the saddle, the better to be able to see past the captain. "I can't see you!" Her voice sounded raw and husky.

"Don't be afraid for him," said the captain. "He's doing fine."

Her eyes darted nervously over the glinting surface of the sea. And there—yes, there he was.

Munk was *swimming* in the water. Only his head and his arms showed above the waves.

Jolly's heart skipped a beat. "But that can't be—" She broke off, because she couldn't believe her eyes.

Munk could *swim.* He was down there—*in the water!*

But that was impossible. He was a polliwog, just like her. Polliwogs didn't swim in saltwater. Polliwogs walked on top of it. Anything different was like a normal person suddenly sinking between two paving blocks.

The ray swept away over Munk, and again d'Artois made it return in a wide loop.

"You can do it too," said the captain. "Only, it's important that you do it exactly the way he did. With head and hands first."

"That . . . that doesn't make any sense at all."

"It has to do with the speed. Have you ever tried to draw your finger through a candle flame?"

"Every child tries that."

"And? Did you burn yourself?"

"Of course not."

"And why not?"

"Because my finger went through the flame too quickly to . . ."—she hesitated—"to burn."

"Exactly right." D'Artois nodded, but he didn't look at her. "It's just the same with polliwogs and the water. If you whisk through the surface so quickly that it doesn't notice you, nothing happens to you. And once you're in the water, it's just like with any other person. You can swim if you want. Because the surface offers no resistance on the underside, only on top. And, as I said, not even then, if you're quick enough. That's why the header." After a brief pause, he added, "Munk didn't want to believe it any more than you at first. But he learned to accept it."

Jolly tried to sort out her thoughts. "You want me to try it too?"

"Can you swim?"

"Certainly. I've swum in lakes. Polliwogs only walk on saltwater."

"Good. Then try it."

"I'm not sick of life."

"You can do it, believe me. And wait—it gets even better."

"What do you mean?"

"First things first. First the dive. Munk will explain all the rest."

"I don't know."

"Jolly!" Munk called from the water. "It isn't hard. Really, it isn't!"

"Have you ever done a header?" asked d'Artois. "I mean, in a lake?"

"Of course."

"Then you can do it here, too."

She still hesitated, but then she gathered all her courage. With pounding heart she climbed onto the saddle. The ray stretched its wings again so that she could walk out on them. But did she really want to?

"I can't go any lower, or the leap will be too short and so the speed will be less," the captain explained.

"Very reassuring. Many thanks."

He looked back and grinned. Teetering, she balanced her way over the wing of the gliding ray. The animal was again in a straight flight pattern, exactly over the place where Munk was paddling.

"Ready?" d'Artois asked.

"May I please decide that for myself?"

"But of course."

She bounced irresolutely on her knees, at the same time fearing that the headwind would simply blow her off the wing before she had a chance to jump on her own.

One, she counted in her head.

Her neck was stiff. Her back hurt.

Two.

Not to mention her backside.

Three.

Jolly leaped. Not in perfect form, not especially gracefully. But it was a header, all the same.

The surface rushed up to her, met her fingertips—and engulfed her. She dove down. Her breath stopped. A cry escaped her mouth, spraying air bubbles around her face and shooting away to the surface.

Around her was blackness. Emptiness. Cold.

She was drowning.

She could swim, certainly. But not now. Not here. Not in saltwater. That was simply impossible. After all, she was a polliwog!

"Jolly."

Munk's voice. Beside her. In the water.

How could she hear him? Why did she see him so clearly?

Heavens, she must be dreaming all this.

"Everything all right?" he asked her, taking her hand. She was still kicking wildly, but gradually she got hold of herself and nodded.

They were not on the surface but underwater. However, they were moving as if there were no resistance. The two of them sank down, very gradually, as though borne by an invisible hand. But when Jolly moved her arms and legs, she might as well be on land somewhere.

No resistance.

What the devil was going on here?

"I was just as frightened as you the first time," Munk said. He floated downward beside her, ever farther into the depths of the ocean. Jolly followed him and realized in astonishment that she could see Munk more and more clearly. But they must already be too far from the surface for any light to be able to penetrate here. All was blackness around them. It was as if she could suddenly see in complete darkness. Like a cat.

"You get used to it," he said. "No, that's not right. You don't really get used to it. But you cope with it. It's even fun."

"How come I can hear in the water?"

"Because we're both polliwogs."

"And how come we can move as if it were air around us, not water?"

"Because we're polliwogs."

"And why don't we drown?"

He opened his mouth, but she beat him to it.

"Because we're polliwogs," she said. "Obviously."

Munk smiled, strangely pale in the darkness, which for some reason no longer was. In any case, for polliwog eyes.

"Is that the only explanation in those marvelous 'old records' d'Artois spoke of?" She'd intended to sound sarcastic, but it didn't work. There was no point in denying something that she herself was experiencing at this very moment.

Their descent into the depths wasn't diving. And the water wasn't like ordinary air, either, for then they'd have been falling now. But they floated, slowly and calmly, and when

Jolly made a little swimming stroke in the direction of the surface, she moved upward a little. Munk stayed beside her, but he held her back before she could rise any higher.

"I was down underneath," he said.

"On the bottom?"

He nodded. "Not underneath Aelenium, it's too deep here. At least for a start, anyway. But d'Artois took me by sea horse to an area where the water's shallower. Two or three hundred feet."

"You were *two hundred* feet under the surface?" Her eyes widened, and she noticed only then that the saltwater wasn't making them burn.

"Yes. And it was . . . fantastic. Somehow. But also creepy."

"Because of the kobalins?"

"No, not that. I didn't see any at all. D'Artois had probably searched out an area that's relatively safe. And there were divers there. Wait till you see the equipment they dive with. . . . But anyway, I think . . . well, the landscape under there was creepy. The plants only grow quite far up, but farther down it gets so dark that nothing grows there anymore. Everything is gray and bare and somehow . . . sad. There are fish, of course, but otherwise nothing."

"And you could breathe perfectly normally?"

"There was no difference. None at all. We polliwogs can walk on the bottom of the ocean as if we're going for a walk on land. And we can see underwater in the dark. For a few hundred feet; I tried it out. It's as if it were evening and is gradually getting very dark, only the light never changes. For us there's a kind of everlasting twilight down here."

She wasn't sure if she found it so intriguing. On the contrary, it began to make her afraid. She was slowly getting an intimation of what might await her farther down the road—if she decided to take it.

Once again she told herself that she would never, never let herself be ordered by anyone to take up the battle against the Maelstrom. All this—Aelenium, the polliwog magic—this was not her world. It wasn't what she wanted.

Avenge Bannon, be a pirate, become a captain: Those were her goals.

But walking over the dark ocean floor to seal up the source of the Maelstrom . . . it gave her a headache just to think about it. Not to mention that her stomach was already going wild again.

Munk read her expression. "It's scary, isn't it?"

"Yes . . . yes, I'm already scared."

"Me too."

"We don't have to do it. Have you ever thought of that?"

"A hundred times a day," he said, nodding, as they floated deeper. "It's not about what the others say either . . . but Jolly, this place is my new home."

"I thought you wanted to become a pirate with me."

He smiled sadly. "You don't have to *become* one, Jolly, you already are one. You grew up among pirates. But me? I always dreamed of it, sure. But all those days at sea in the last few weeks . . . it was entirely different from what I imagined. That's not for me. Completely the opposite of Aelenium.

The libraries, the people . . . I want to stay here, Jolly. No matter what happens, I belong to them now."

For a moment she wondered if someone had influenced him, whether he was just parroting what had been said to him earlier. But then she saw his expression, the same hardness she'd already seen in him once—when the Acherus had murdered his parents. Munk had made his decision.

"Whether you come with me or not," he said, "I'm going to the Crustal Breach. Even alone, if necessary."

Crustal Breach. That was the place, somewhere in the ocean depths, where the Maelstrom arose from a mighty mussel. A narrow column of water that grew broader and more murderous as he made his long way to the surface. In any case, that's what the Hexhermetic Shipworm claimed. And the teachers of Aelenium must have confirmed it if Munk was speaking of it so matter-of-factly.

Jolly avoided his look. She knew what he was expecting from her. That she would say, *Yes, I'll go with you.*

But she couldn't do that. She simply could not bring herself to. Not that she was afraid—although there was quite a large portion of fear stirring her insides. No, she couldn't because she wasn't sure if she really wanted to. She kept having the feeling that this person here floating in the deep with Munk, who had allied herself with the Ghost Trader and come to Aelenium, was an entirely different person from that Jolly who grew up on the ship with Captain Bannon and had been sure all those years that someday she would be just like him: a famous freebooter on the Caribbean Sea.

Crustal Breach. Maelstrom. Aelenium. Those were words from a fairy tale, a gloomy bedtime story.

"Come on," said Munk, who'd probably realized what was going on in her mind. Was he disappointed? Anyway, he didn't show it. "We have to swim in this direction."

He said "swim," but that wasn't it, really—rather, they were flying through an element that for anyone else would have been water. But for them it possessed no greater density than the sky and the wind.

"You have to make swimming motions, yes, like that. . . . Careful, slower! Keep in mind that there's no real resistance here for us."

Nevertheless Jolly pulled her hands back too quickly, and a single thrust instantly took her a huge distance forward, four or five fathoms.

"Puh," she said as she kicked to reverse and thus made a couple of somersaults by mistake, "that looks easier than it is."

"All a matter of getting used to it."

But did she really want to get used to it? Her life would be simpler if she were still going *over* the water and not flitting around underneath it like a fish.

She needed a few more attempts before she finally succeeded in moving herself forward with some degree of security and calm.

"Where do you want to go?" she asked.

He grinned. "Where do you think?"

She looked ahead again doubtfully. After two more swimming strokes, something appeared out of the darkness far ahead of them, a colossal, colorless wall of branching coral structures. The bizarre slopes fanned apart over them and ended at the underside of the sea star. Only now did Jolly grasp that for a long time she and Munk had been below its enormous point. When she looked toward the bottom of the coral wall, she realized that the mighty thing tapered to a point in the depths like a gigantic icicle.

So this was the underside of Aelenium. The deep levels of which d'Artois had spoken.

"You want to go in there?" she asked Munk without looking at him.

"Wouldn't you like to know what you're supposed to fight for?"

She couldn't take her eyes off the fantastic forms that now appeared more and more clearly out of the darkness. Munk had said that the underside was a sort of mirror image of the above-ground Aelenium. But that wasn't quite the way it really was.

The underside was very much rougher and more rugged. Jolly had assumed that the city on the upper surface had grown, not been built, but now she realized that the truth lay somewhere in between. The inhabitants of Aelenium had probably worked the coral mountain in order to form houses and little streets and squares. Here, on the other hand, was the rough, uncut condition in which the upper side of Aelenium had probably been at one time too, a proliferating, many-armed, dangerous-looking thing of points, teeth, and knife-sharp edges. The largest coral in the world.

Pirate Emperor

D'Artois had spoken of sharks who lived here. Of morays. And of something else.

Something had possibly settled in there, he'd said. Something that was only waiting to strike.

The water suddenly became very much colder.

Underwater

The closer they came to the deep levels, the better Jolly learned to manage the underwater world. It was a different kind of seeing. The rough, crannied outer surface of the corals appeared to her in a light gray, sometimes shot through with a tinge of color like the coral up on the surface. But unlike the surface corals, the shadows between the projections were such a deep black that each crevice, each crack, and each cavity became a threatening maw. In every hole a monster could be lurking, behind every projection a kobalin. So while her new darkness vision lent a welcome security in these unknown regions of the sea, it also increased her fear of whatever might be waiting for them down here.

She felt as if she were being observed from every single one of the branched shadow shapes, and she asked Munk if he was feeling the same thing.

"It's worse in the beginning," he answered, "and probably the fear never disappears entirely."

"And yet you want to go into the deep levels, of all places?"

"I was here before, along with some divers."

Munk floated through an irregular opening in a coral wall. "Think about moving slowly. If you go too fast in the tunnels and caves, you can get caught in a crevice."

Or on a coral thorn. "That's comforting."

Munk looked over his shoulder and smiled encouragingly. "I'm here with you, after all."

"Then I feel much safer already."

Me and my big mouth, she thought.

She followed him—very carefully, almost warily—into a tunnel into the interior of the coral mountain. For reasons she didn't understand, her vision decreased markedly. The end of the irregular tunnel lay in complete darkness. Cracks and crevices branched off on both sides, and sometimes, too, openings that were as big as archways.

Jolly lost any sense of how long they wandered through the labyrinth of the deep levels. Munk led her as surely as if he'd often been down here already. Mostly they floated between floor and ceiling, moving forward with swimming strokes, but sometimes they also sank down to the coral floor and walked. Munk was right: They could move along the firm bottom as well as they did on the surface—they could walk and jump, even run. The only difference was that Jolly had the feeling she was out of breath sooner down here. She didn't want to think that that might be because she was sucking saltwater into her lungs instead of air.

And yes, the salt . . . they weren't immune to it entirely. She'd developed a strong, salty taste in her mouth, which not only made her thirsty but gradually hit her in the stomach as well. It would probably have been too wild for the whole business not to have any side effects at all.

"You get used to that, too," Munk said when she complained about it. "But there are a couple of other things that are uncomfortable. The water pressure, for instance. Of course we don't really feel it, but sometimes you can get a backache, as if you'd been carrying heavy sacks around with you for hours. And sometimes, after you surface you can get headaches. Forefather says the brain doesn't understand why it isn't being squeezed from all sides anymore, or something like that."

"Who's Forefather?"

"Our teacher. You'll meet him tomorrow."

"Did *he* teach you all this?"

"Yes. But Forefather can only tell about it. He isn't a polliwog himself, but he knows all about us, just the same. Well, almost all. I think he knows every book and every scroll in Aelenium's library by heart."

Jolly was going to ask another question, but Munk stopped at a fork. Confused, he looked around. "Hm," he said. "I think we've gotten lost."

Marvelous! "Lost?" she asked.

He raised an eyebrow. "Off the path. Taken the wrong way. Climbed through the wrong hole."

"I *know* what lost means!"

"Why'd you ask, then?" He grinned again, pale and wan in her underwater vision. "Besides, I was just pretending. I know exactly where we are."

"Oh, very funny."

He scratched the back of his head guiltily. "I'm sorry."

"Can we go up again now? I just can't wait any longer for the headache and backache."

He sighed—something else that appeared supremely strange underwater—then nodded and went on ahead. After two dozen bends, coral halls, and shadowy holes, they came to a wide shaft, which led straight up.

"Up here," he said shortly.

They pushed off and rose effortlessly upward, now clearly faster than before. Maybe Munk wasn't as sure of himself as he pretended to be. The walls of the coral shaft were irregular, and so they kept having to avoid sharp-edged outgrowths and projections. Once Jolly pulled Munk to one side just before a sharp coral blade could slice his back.

"Thanks," he muttered, and she wasn't sure if he was really frightened or was secretly angry because she'd protected him and not the other way around. He enjoyed the role of leader, that was impossible to miss. The fact that he knew more than she did made him arrogant. And careless.

The shaft was endless. Jolly hadn't been aware that they'd gone that far down. The crevices and gulfs in the walls formed intricate patterns of shadows and flashes of light. Some were big enough to offer shelter for animals. And all the time, Jolly kept expecting that a head would shoot out of the darkness, open-jawed, with teeth as long as she was.

But perhaps d'Artois's men had done a thorough job when they searched the deep levels for intruders.

At some point, a fissured ceiling appeared over them, the shaft made a bend to the side and now ran horizontally. Jolly and Munk halted for a moment.

"I thought this shaft led up into the city," said Jolly anxiously. She no longer made any attempt to conceal how very much she feared all the empty caverns and tunnels.

Munk frowned. "Actually, I thought so too."

"Are you trying to say that now you *really* don't know where we are?"

"It can't be that bad. Anyhow, we've already come a long way up."

She made a wry face.

"We simply follow the shaft farther; it certainly has to lead to the upper side sometime." He took her hand to give her courage. "If necessary, we'll go back the same way we came."

"Down there again?" She looked into the abyss, which narrowed to a dark, shadowy point far below them. "Most certainly not."

Was the darkness stretching at the foot of the shaft? Her heart stopped for a moment and then pounded like a fist against her chest.

Was something coming up toward them from down there?

"I want to get out of here," she said.

He followed her eyes down to the depths. Did he see it too? Did he *feel* it coming closer?

"Right," he said, and he pulled her behind him into the horizontal shaft. "We can hurry if you want."

The abyss was behind them, but at the moment that was no great reassurance. Jolly kept looking around, back to the bend and the darkness, which lurked there like an oily black puddle.

They quickened their swimming strokes and now drove forward with considerable speed. It was reckless, certainly, and if they weren't careful, their unease would turn to utter panic. But Jolly couldn't help it, and, looking at Munk, she saw that he felt the same way.

A sound rang in their ears, a rasping and splintering, as if something were shoving itself through the shaft behind them, something too wide for it that was breaking off coral combs and outgrowths with its body. But when they looked around again, the tunnel was empty and nothing showed in the distant bend.

Imagination, she said to herself. *You're just making yourself crazy.*

"Do you hear that too?" Munk asked.

"Yes."

They increased their tempo, without wasting another word. Fear made them careless, and they constantly bumped against coral arms and edges.

"There's an exit up ahead!" Jolly cried.

"Not much farther," Munk said between clenched teeth.

Several hundred feet in front of them the walls of the

shaft ended in a gray oval. What lay behind it wasn't discernible—it was too dark there. If they were lucky, it was the open sea. But it might only be another cavern in the coral labyrinth of the undercity.

Again Jolly looked over her shoulder. The water behind them appeared to flutter, like the air over a burning ship, but she still saw nothing that should have made her really worry. If something had followed them out of the deep, it had perhaps given up the chase.

"It *is* an exit!" cried Munk triumphantly.

They rushed up to the oval opening, and now Jolly realized that he was right. Like two cannonballs they shot away over the edge and found themselves in the middle of the ocean again, under them an entirely different sort of abyss, bottomless and yet only half as scary as the creepy shaft.

But couldn't the thing that had followed them also have been seeking a way to the outside?

They were rising toward the surface, arrow-swift, like hornets on the attack, when Munk suddenly said, "Look over there."

She froze inside as her eyes followed his outstretched arm. But her fear was groundless.

To their left, the anchor chain of Aelenium extended diagonally across their entire field of vision, a slanting rope. It originated in a tangle of steel and coral on the underside of a sea star point and stretched stiffly taut down below, where it lost itself in the dark gray of the sea after some hundred feet. The chain itself must have been about thirty feet wide, each link as big as a house. Algae and other water plants waved, buffeted by invisible currents. The metal of the chain was covered with dark brown rust where it showed between the strands of plants.

"How long is it?" Jolly wanted to know.

"From here to the sea bottom is three thousand feet."

"That far?"

"The Crustal Breach is almost ten times as deep."

For seconds she forgot to breathe. *"Thirty thousand feet?"*

Munk nodded while they swam toward the edge of a star point. "Anyway, that's what Forefather says."

Jolly said nothing as they continued their ascent. She tried to imagine a depth of thirty thousand feet. That was almost—

Six miles!

People were expecting them to dive down six miles to the bottom of the ocean in order to close the source of the Maelstrom there?

She could not conceive of the depth, the darkness, and the loneliness that must reign there. And yet an aura of it brushed over her and made her shiver inwardly.

They broke through the water surface at one of the sea star points and climbed onto dry land. Meanwhile deep night had descended. The city's coral cliffs were sprinkled with hundreds of lights, and the wall of fog had sunk into complete darkness.

Six miles.

Through the icy cold, through darkness. Through a

landscape that was not comparable to anything that she knew from the surface.

For the first time tears came to Jolly at the thought of her future. She didn't want to cry, not in front of Munk, not in front of anyone at all. But she did it anyway, sobbing softly to herself and not allowing him to comfort her.

Soaked to the skin and wordless, they trotted up into the city, through empty streets, across deserted squares. In some places it was as dark as if Aelenium itself had already sunk into the deep.

Jolly's tears overcame her when she saw the coral palace in front of her again. Somewhere inside was Griffin. She had to talk with someone about all of this, with a person who wasn't a polliwog himself. Someone who bore no responsibility in this horrible war.

Someone who wasn't Munk.

The Plan

In her room again, Jolly took off her wet things, dried herself off, and slipped into the clothes someone had laid out for her—again tight leather trousers, this time black, and with them a sand-colored shirt with a wide belt and high, laced sandals. In addition, she found a silver-embroidered vest, which she put on over the shirt.

At least no one had gotten the idea of laying out a skirt or a dress for her. No one here seemed to see her as a mere girl.

Although at the moment, even that would have been all right with her: She could have acted naive and helpless and no one would have expected her to be a match for the Maelstrom. But everyone in Aelenium appeared to conclude quite as a matter of course that she would take up the challenge.

Munk was right about the backache, but anyway, her head didn't ache. However, the thoughts were whirling in her head, impressions and images, so fast that everything was becoming a flickering, whirring confusion. She didn't know what she should think. She didn't know which way to turn.

She didn't have a chance to look for Griffin, for there was a knock at her door, just as soon as she'd finished changing. A servant stood outside in the hall and asked her to follow her to the council assembly room.

"At this hour?" asked Jolly, but she earned only a shrug of the shoulders, and so she followed the young woman downstairs and over bridges to a high portal. It must have been going on midnight when they arrived, and two guards with expressionless faces and muskets on their shoulders let them in.

Behind the portal, in a broad hall with an arching coral ceiling, Jolly was awaited by her comrades—and by other men and women she did not know. Most were sitting a very long table, and some were standing in groups, conversing.

Princess Soledad was leaning against a white coral column, one knee bent, and deep in conversation with Walker. The pit bull man stood beside them, looking bored and rolling his eyes silently when the captain said something to Soledad. When Buenaventure saw Jolly, he detached himself from the two of them with a relieved sigh and hurried over to her with thumping steps, his boots hammering on the coral floor as if he wanted to break out pieces of the surface with their heels.

"Thank God, Jolly . . . the flirting of those two drives me crazy."

She returned his smile and noticed that he wasn't wearing the knapsack with the Hexhermetic Shipworm. Obviously

Aelenium's new prince of poetry had not been invited to the assembly.

Instead she caught sight of Griffin, who looked up at the same moment. Bored, he'd been sitting at the table with his feet on the edge of it. Now he leaped up with a joyful grin and quickly came over to her.

Griffin and Buenaventure, she thought, and felt an unexpected warmth rise in her. If there were two people to whom she'd entrust her life unconditionally, it was these two.

Possibly Soledad, too, but the princess's goals still appeared a little too opaque to her: Soledad wanted to topple the pirate emperor Kendrick and enter into the rightful inheritance of her father, Scarab. But what price was she willing to pay for it? Would she ever value anything more highly than the throne of the Caribbean pirates?

Then there was Walker, himself a pirate, who knew how to sail a ship as scarcely any other man did. Walker was here for one reason primarily: He was speculating on the gold that the Ghost Trader and Jolly had promised him.

The scalding thought came to her that Walker must still believe the half-finished tattoo on her back was part of a treasure map. Jolly had told him that tall tale to get him to carry her and Munk to Tortuga without charging them for passage.

Walker also had a second motive, however: He was hoping to win the princess's affections, and she obviously didn't intend to reject him outright—whether out of honest feelings for the captain or to secure his support was still a mystery to Jolly.

THE PLAN

And finally there was the Ghost Trader, who was now standing at the head of the table beside a man who wore the clothing of a European nobleman, not sumptuous but of fine materials. His cloak was embroidered in a manner similar to Jolly's new vest, and she wondered if this correlation perhaps had a deeper meaning.

Was she so highly prized as a polliwog that she might wear symbols similar to the rulers of this city? She felt flattered, even though she knew how irrational that was.

The Ghost Trader was certainly the least transparent person of all those present. He was a living mystery, a man who could be friendly at times, almost fatherly, then cold and calculating, if it suited his secret purposes. He was the only one of the friends who had not put on new clothes: As usual, he was wearing his dark, floor-length robe, but his hood was thrown back and his haggard face was displayed openly. The narrow-lipped mouth and the piercing, dark blue eye did their part to make him seem more sinister, which perhaps in fact he was. On his shoulders sat the black parrots Hugh and Moe, imitating his every head movement in an irritating way.

Jolly turned to Griffin and Buenaventure, who were now standing beside her, as they waited for instructions or advice. Both obviously felt just as uncomfortable and out of place in this remarkable gathering as she did herself.

They'd hardly exchanged a few words when the doors at her back opened again and Munk came in.

He wore a long-sleeved dark jacket with silver embroidery, which matched that on Jolly's vest and on the clothing of the nobleman at the head of the table. Munk was supporting a gray old man in a long robe, who needed the additional help of a staff to walk. That must be Forefather, the teacher of the polliwogs.

Munk gave Jolly a smile, but before she could return it, a gong struck somewhere in the depths of the hall. All conversation died.

"Please, my friends, sit down," said the nobleman at the head of the table to those who were still standing. "We are present in full number, now that our two polliwogs have arrived."

All eyes turned to Jolly and Munk. Forefather uttered a soft, satisfied mutter. Some of the men and women murmured stealthily to each other. Jolly's doubts returned: They'd never be able to live up to these people's expectations.

Those who hadn't been sitting now streamed to the table. Munk steered toward a place beside Jolly, but because he was leading Forefather on his arm, Griffin got there before him. Buenaventure let himself down on her left side.

Ill-humoredly, Munk placed the old man on the opposite side of the table and sat down beside him. Jolly met Forefather's eyes and smiled nervously when he nodded to her. His wrinkled features appeared serene and relaxed; he radiated a tranquility that did her good.

Walker took the chair next to Buenaventure, then looked in Soledad's direction and pointed inquiringly at the empty place next to him. The princess winked at him, but she sat down between two women, who regarded her with frowns.

THE PLAN

Among the aristocracy of Aelenium, people were obviously not in the habit of associating with pirates.

The nobleman at the head of the table waited until everyone had sat down, then he began to speak again. "I am Count Aristotle Constanopoulos. My grandfather came to Aelenium many years ago with a fleet of ships from Greece. He was allowed to remain and in time was initiated into the secrets of this city. The council chose him to be ruler, and after him this honor was bestowed on my father. I myself have served Aelenium for four and twenty years now." For an instant his gaze wavered, but then he resumed. "Under my guardianship the Maelstrom has burst his chains and has succeeded in gaining new power. I bear the responsibility for this catastrophe, and I will—"

"Excuse me, Count," the Ghost Trader interrupted, without rising from his seat, as would have been usual practice. "But you don't bear the blame for this misfortune. No one could have held the Maelstrom."

Count Aristotle smiled sadly. "It is kind of you to seek to defend me, but I cannot agree with you. Since ancient times it has been Aelenium's task to hold the Maelstrom imprisoned in the Crustal Breach, and for whatever reasons he has regained strength—it happened under my aegis."

The Ghost Trader was about to contradict him again, but the count cut him off with a wave of the hand.

"It is a fact, my friend," he said. "But today we will not speak further about that. There's something more important that must be decided in this meeting."

Jolly was amazed at how much the Ghost Trader subordinated himself to the count. His nodding in agreement and becoming silent now did not appear to fit with his usual behavior. But perhaps that was a part of his wisdom: to recognize the moment when it was better to respect another's opinion.

"Some of us already know what stands before us and in what way we must fight against it," said the count. "I think, however, that we owe it to the two polliwogs to call the thing by name just this once." Then he turned his eyes to Jolly and Munk and was silent for a remarkably long time while he regarded them. It seemed to Jolly as if his eyes pierced her eyes and behind, in the far distance, discovered something quite astonishing.

A pirate girl and a farm boy. Possibly he was just realizing how hopeless the situation was.

"Everything began with the magic," the count explained, and the Ghost Trader at his side nodded slowly. "Magic is only another word for the power that streams through our world and thus flows through veins under the surface like blood through the body of a human being. It is this power that keeps us all alive, even if only a few learn its secret and hardly anyone understands it. It is this power, this magic, that comes to the world's aid when it is threatened, as now. Just exactly as it did once before, many thousands of years ago."

Jolly felt that Forefather was still observing her. Munk was also looking in her direction. She returned his look briefly and noticed in surprise that he first blushed, then smiled.

THE PLAN

"At that time, the Maelstrom threatened for the first time to tear down the boundary of the Mare Tenebrosum and open a pathway into our world. Then, it was inhabitants of this island who succeeded in turning aside the danger and imprisoning the Maelstrom in a mighty mussel on the bottom of the sea. Today we call the place where the mussel lies the Crustal Breach. For a long time the Maelstrom was safely confined there, for the magic veins bunch together in the Crustal Breach. They keep the Maelstrom enclosed.

"Nevertheless, some creatures of the Mare Tenebrosum succeeded at that time in getting into our world through the Maelstrom, before it could be sealed in. In this way the ancestors of the kobalins crossed over, it is said, and there were men who mated with them. Thus the kobalins received the form they have today."

Walker, obviously uncomfortable in this meeting, raised his voice. "Does that mean the kobalins are half human?"

Some of the gentry sent the captain reproving looks, but Count Aristotle nodded patiently. "Human blood flows in them too, certainly. How much, no one is able to say. Are they more of this world or are their roots in the Mare Tenebrosum? I do not know, and I doubt that any other here knows the answer to that." He turned to the Ghost Trader, but the Trader shook his head silently.

"But it is not the kobalins who concern us at the moment," said the count after a short pause. "I have only mentioned them to illustrate what might await us if the Maelstrom opens completely."

He took up the earthenware goblet that stood before him and drank a sip. "The kobalins came to us because the border between the worlds was down for only a moment, perhaps a few seconds, perhaps a heartbeat. No one can imagine what would come over if the Maelstrom opened it for an hour or a day."

"Or forever," added the Ghost Trader, and his parrots nodded wisely.

"Or forever," the count repeated. "There were polliwogs then too, in the first war against the Maelstrom. Only they were probably called something else at that time. The world opened the veins of its magic and let a little of it escape, and where it ran among men, polliwogs were born soon afterward. Exactly as it happened fourteen years ago."

"The earthquake," Jolly murmured softly, but in the stillness that followed the count's words, everyone in the room heard her.

Aristotle nodded. "The great earthquake of Port Royal. It did not cause havoc there alone, but also deep on the ocean floor. Down in the Crustal Breach. The mussel opened and the Maelstrom was able to escape. The magic veins that crossed there were disrupted, and some were obliterated, and the power of the mussel diminished. That is the calamitous result of the earthquake, but there was also a good one, for the world keeps a balance in all things. Around Port Royal, there where the temblor broke to the surface, magic escaped from the burst veins and created new polliwogs. It is predestined for them to repair the devastation in the Crustal

Breach." He snorted scornfully. "No one could guess that once again men would have nothing better in their minds than to misuse the magic of the polliwogs for their own purposes. You all know what happened. The polliwogs and their families were hunted, and so today there are only two of them sitting here among us, the last survivors of the massacre."

Jolly knew the story. Munk's father had told it to her. But to hear it again from the count's mouth sent chills down her back. Against her will came renewed doubts as to whether Bannon had told the truth when he claimed he'd bought her as a little child in the slave market on Tortuga. What if he'd been one of those who'd hunted the polliwogs, murdered their parents, and abducted the children? Anyway, he'd profited all those years from her being able to walk on the water.

No, impossible. Not Bannon.

She was glad when Count Aristotle resumed his speech and turned her to other thoughts.

"It is predestined that the polliwogs take up the battle against the Maelstrom. With the help of the mussel magic they must"—he looked piercingly at Jolly and Munk—"*you* must close the Maelstrom into his mussel in the Crustal Breach again and thus seal the gateway to the Mare Tenebrosum."

Soledad raised her narrow hand. "May I ask a question?"

"But certainly, Princess," said the count.

Soledad registered the title with satisfaction. Not everyone saw a princess in the daughter of a pirate emperor; probably far less polite words would have come to mind for many of them. "I'm wondering why Aelenium isn't anchored directly over the Crustal Breach, but here, many miles away."

Count Aristotle nodded as if he'd already heard this question frequently. "Aelenium is a floating city, which is held in its position only by an anchor chain. But the length of such a chain, however strong it may be, is limited—the currents would tear it apart otherwise. Therefore, the depth of the sea under the city may be no greater than it is at the place where Aelenium lies now. One hundred feet more, and the danger of breaking the chain arises. But the Crustal Breach lies very much deeper. Here was the nearest possible place to anchor Aelenium, even though we are almost two hundred miles from the Crustal Breach." The count looked at Soledad. "Does that answer your question, Princess?"

"There's something else that worries me. If the chain is as breakable as you say, then it will certainly be the first point of attack."

"We are aware of this danger, and we are doing our best to protect the chain. Divers patrol along the links, at least as far as it is possible for them. We do not know exactly how it looks on the ocean floor. The divers cannot go to such depths."

"But we can," said Munk.

The count frowned.

Munk didn't give him time to argue. "Jolly and I need practice. Before we go down to the Crustal Breach"—he looked quickly over at Jolly, uncertain, but also with a flash of triumph—"we could see if the anchor is all right down on the bottom."

"Too dangerous," said the Ghost Trader, shaking his head so vehemently that Hugh, on his right shoulder, took a stalking bird step to one side. "We cannot risk your lives unnecessarily."

"Quite right," agreed Count Aristotle, and a murmur of agreement arose among the others. Jolly was glad about it, but she also saw Munk's face harden.

She was becoming increasingly aware of how much he enjoyed the power of the polliwog magic; he was positively basking in the recognition the others showed him. It angered him to have his suggestion rejected.

Griffin had noticed too. "Our good Munk is sulking," he whispered to her.

She nodded but said nothing. Munk might seem sulky to Griffin, perhaps offended. But she was afraid that the unexpected rejection had hit him much harder. She didn't like the way the magic had changed Munk. She didn't like it at all.

And she herself? Was she immune to it? What would become of her if Forefather took her under his wing and initiated her into the mysteries of her origin?

"The plan looks as follows," continued the count. "Our soldiers have been bumping into spies for some days now. It appears there's only a little time left before the kobalin armies will begin the attack on Aelenium. The preparations for the battle and defending the city are moving forward. Building of the barricades has long since begun. But the polliwogs' training has priority—Forefather, that is your task."

The old man nodded his head but still said nothing.

"In twenty days, at the latest, perhaps even sooner, the sea horses will take Jolly and Munk as close as possible to the Crustal Breach. From there on, you two are on your own. None of us can accompany you down to where you must go. The Maelstrom will direct his gaze to the battle for Aelenium. He will not expect his opponent to approach over the floor of the ocean. And that is our chance. *Your* chance."

There was unconcealed sadness in his eyes now, and his voice sounded depressed. "I know what I am asking of you. You will be alone down there in the dark. You will be able to rely only on each other. No one can prepare you for the dangers—for no one knows them. If all goes well, there is only a strenuous hike ahead of you before you reach the Crustal Breach. If not . . . well, we are not capable of foreseeing."

Jolly blinked. All at once she was dizzy. It was as if she'd walked into a dream from one moment to the next. The boundary between reality and madness was suddenly fluid.

She felt Buenaventure shove his huge hand over her small one.

"They're children," he said to the gathering in a thundering voice. "Just children."

Count Aristotle dropped his eyes, took a deep breath, and then looked up. "We all know that. But when the fate of the world rests on children's shoulders, then they must bear this burden. This was not our choice."

The pit bull man growled something that was lost in the storm of other voices. Suddenly everyone was talking at once. Soledad was arguing with the Ghost Trader. The aristocrats buzzed with excitement. Forefather spoke with Munk, and Walker was talking animatedly about God knows what. Even the parrots were squawking.

Only Jolly said nothing. Before her inner eye spread a dark, dead landscape, an underwater mountainous region, full of deep crevices, like gaping mouths in the crust of the world. No green, no plants, only gray and deep shadows. She was afraid as she had never been in her life before. Not even the Acherus had filled her with such fear.

Griffin bent toward her, but she took in what he had said only when he was looking at her expectantly.

"Let's vanish," he'd whispered in her ear. "First thing tomorrow. We'll go away and everything will be fine."

But perhaps that was only a part of this waking dream, this jumble of truth and miracles and out-and-out terror.

For nothing would be fine, she knew that for certain.

Nothing would ever again be the way it had been before.

Visit by Night

Forefather's voice was dry and cracked.

"Just try it," he said. "You can do it. You need only to want to."

Jolly stared at the three mussels lying on the floor in front of her. The opened mussel mouths looked as if they were grinning sneeringly.

"There's no point in it. I can't do it, and I don't ever want to either."

"That's the excuse of someone afraid of herself."

"Nonsense." But she didn't look at the old man as she said the word. For deep inside her the truth dawned. Forefather was right. She was in fact afraid of herself, what she might learn about herself if she delved deeper into the unknown regions of her innermost feelings. She felt as if she'd ventured into a strange area of the sea without charts and compass, that under the waves lurked murderous reefs and currents.

"Try it," the old man commanded again.

They were in Forefather's book room, a part of the library that he had all to himself. It was a very large room with irregular walls, like almost all the rooms in Aelenium. Therefore it was next to impossible to install regular bookshelves. There were thousands upon thousands of volumes piled on the floor, some in hills like funeral pyres, others in exquisitely precise interlocking towers and book fortresses, circular or horseshoe-shaped, layered over one another like walls of roof tiles. If you wanted to withdraw one of the books underneath, you had to be nimble: You grabbed the book with your left hand, holding a second one in your right, ready to shove it into the resulting gap before the entire book structure could collapse.

Jolly hadn't credited the fragile Forefather with so much agility, but he surprised her the first time he displayed the trick. His bony fingers were as artful as a pickpocket's. Neither Munk nor she could exchange the books as swiftly as he could. "This way," he'd explained to her, "there's never disorder. All the books are lying there where they should be, and no new piles develop to need putting back in their places every few weeks. For every book the library gives, it demands another. A proper exchange."

Forefather insisted that all these mountains of books were arranged in a precise order, and he knew the exact place where every single volume was located.

"Jolly."

His voice snatched her from her thoughts.

"You will do it. Trust me."

She blinked from her three mussels to him. His face was as brown and fissured as a ship's keel. It seemed to her that he nodded; although he was looking at her without moving at all. It was his eyes that spoke to her. Like no other person she knew, Forefather understood how to impart something just with looks. Sometimes she wasn't even sure if the words she thought she heard from his mouth had really been spoken aloud.

He stood beside her, his back bent, leaning on his whale rib stick, his brow knitted into a perennial frown.

"You did it before," he said deliberately. "Now work at it. Work on yourself."

Jolly sighed, closed her eyes, and tried again to concentrate on the three mussels. In the darkness behind her eyes they seemed like the fireballs one sees after looking at the sun for too long.

"You must feel them," whispered Forefather.

She imagined how her fingers groped over and reached into the open mussel mouths, which were much bigger in her mind than in reality. She slipped her hand inside—not the real hand, only the imagined one—felt the magic under her fingertips, and pulled it out like a long piece of thread, like undoing a seam. She brought one thread after another together into the center of the mussel group until she felt that the connection was established.

"Very good," said Forefather.

She opened her eyes and yes, there it was: A glowing pearl

floated among the mussels, just there where she'd connected the magic threads in her mind.

"Now try to control them." The aged man's voice was gentle and demanding at the same time. "You've created the tool, now use it."

Jolly didn't take her eyes off the glowing pearl. She'd awakened the magic of the mussels and formed the pearl—the first step of any mussel magic. Now she must direct the magic to a particular purpose, an object, an action.

"What shall I do?" She tasted salty sweat on her lips.

"You decide. It is in your power."

A book, whispered her inner voice. *Pick out a book, pull it out, and replace it with another, before the pile can fall down.*

Her mental fingers groped toward a heavy folio with a broken leather binding, a good ten steps away from her. *That one*, she thought. *That's the one.*

The pearl glowed brighter, blinded her.

The book moved, the man-high pile shook. Then the volume slowly slid itself out of the carefully built structure of book spines. With a rustling sound it kept sliding forward.

Now another, she thought. *Any one.*

She grasped a second book at the top of the pile that had the same mass as the first. Slowly it floated off, carried only by her mind.

Do it! Now!

The folio slid out of the gap, slid across the floor, and opened as if by a ghostly hand. The pages fluttered as if in a storm wind.

The pile teetered.

The second book pushed into the empty space.

Yes! Jolly thought. *Done!*

But the pile was still shaking. She'd rammed the book into the gap too hard and now it had caused the artfully arranged tower of books to begin swaying.

The pages of the first book rustled even more strongly, as if they'd been awakened to life by Jolly's magic.

The upper books on the pile slid, fell forward.

Jolly swore.

"The pearl!" cried Forefather. "Don't give up now!"

She looked at the glowing pearl, which still floated among the mussels. Jolly concentrated again, but doubt had spread in her mind. She couldn't manage it. It was too late.

The pile of books tipped. Hundreds of books started teetering, then sliding. Finally they fell.

And stopped in midair.

Did I do that? Jolly asked herself. Her eyes sought Forefather, but he gently shook his head.

The books hovered in the air like a swarm of wasps that couldn't decide whether to attack. They trembled, barely noticeably. Then they slid, one after the other, back into their original positions. The pile built itself up again, one book after the other, and a few moments later the tower of books stood there completely undamaged.

The fluttering pages of the first book came to a standstill; it lay there open.

Jolly looked over her shoulder and saw Munk sitting at

some distance, in front of him a dozen mussels arranged in a circle. A trace of a smile played around the corners of his mouth. It was he who'd held the book tower. His magic had repaired what she'd spoiled. Her failure was his triumph. Not for the first time.

"The pearl," Forefather reminded her again.

With a furious snort she turned to her three mussels, seized the glowing pearl with her mental fingers, and flung it into one of the open mussels much more vigorously than necessary. The mussel seemed to utter an angry sound as it snapped shut and swallowed the magic pearl. The two others also closed up.

Forefather nodded thoughtfully, but now even his eyes were silent. Jolly clenched her fists and heaved an exhausted sigh.

It was the third day of her training.

Her twenty-second failure. She'd been counting.

The easiest thing for Jolly now was the dive into the sea and movement under the water. She'd begun to enjoy the hours in the ocean, not only because her initial insecurity diminished but also because it was a welcome change from the hours of instruction in Forefather's library room. She was expected to arrive there right after she got up, have her breakfast with Munk and the old man, and begin the daily practices. Without any interruptions worth mentioning, it went on that way until evening—with the exception of one or two hours in the water. Usually it was d'Artois who called for them, or sometimes one of the other ray riders.

Gradually it turned out that underwater Jolly was the more skillful of the two polliwogs. She flew—for her it was much more flying than diving—fast loops and spirals, completed turns a lot faster than Munk, and learned to let herself sink half a mile down in a few moments without becoming sick or dizzy.

Munk didn't betray any sign that he begrudged her the progress. On the contrary, he encouraged her to dare wilder maneuvers and to keep on hoping that things would soon be going better with the mussel magic, too.

She'd had her first real success with the magic exercises on the fourth day, right after the noonday meal. With the help of a magic pearl, she'd succeeded in making Forefather's whale-rib staff rise to the cathedral-high dome of the library room, where it twirled around very fast while balancing three books on its end and not losing any of them.

Forefather had rewarded her with euphoric applause, and Munk grinned as proudly as if he'd performed this feat himself. She was gradually feeling closer to him again. Perhaps it had something to do with their having passed so many hours together, but possibly it was also because she hardly saw Griffin at all these days.

Once, when they'd briefly met in the evening, he reported to her that d'Artois had assigned him to one of the stable masters as a pupil. The man was teaching Griffin how to control the sea horses and to ride them. Twice already, he told Jolly excitedly, he'd crossed the fog with a troop of d'Artois's men and chased across the open sea on the other side. By the third day he was going out with patrols regularly, especially since he'd shown the soldiers that he knew how to handle blades and pistols as well as they.

For the present, Griffin had given up any thought of leaving Aelenium. He and Jolly wasted no more words on it. She felt that he was more comfortable here than he admitted. Perhaps it was the same with her. So in their own ways, the two of them weren't unhappy with the course of things, aside from the fact that there was so little time they could spend together—which wasn't all right with anyone except Munk.

Jolly knew all that. She could foresee the distance that was gradually building between her and Griffin, the lack of understanding over why they really were staying in Aelenium. And she also felt Munk's relief that she and Griffin hardly saw each other.

What is going on here? she thought once, at an inopportune moment when she was just diving from a ray into the depths. *What's happening with us?*

But she repressed the answers to such questions. The more she pushed the uncomfortable truths away from her, the more accomplished she became in handling the mussel magic.

On the fifth day, through the power of her thoughts, she interchanged books at three different places in the library, all in the same breath, and made the three volumes flutter through the coral dome like the gulls that gathered around the towers and gables of Aelenium.

She didn't think of the Crustal Breach, nor of the gray lava mountain range of the sea bottom. She didn't think of the Ghost Trader and only seldom of Griffin.

She was becoming an apt polliwog student, and Forefather praised her as only he could.

But in spite of everything, Munk remained the more skillful magician. She made three books fly, he did the same thing with six. She let a storm wind sweep through the canyons of books, he created a bolt of lightning that turned a whole pile of folios to ashes. She made the ghosts on the *Carfax* dance, he created from smoke the image of a kobalin with teeth bared.

It was a competition, certainly, and on the outside it looked like a contest of strength between friends. But in fact, envy slipped into what they were doing—envy of Munk's greater powers, envy of Jolly's skill underwater, envy of every praise from Forefather, and envy of the approving calls that came from the windows of Aelenium when they walked through the streets.

On the fifth evening, she wanted to visit Griffin in his room, but he wasn't there, and someone told her that he was now a member of the ray guard and on a nightly ride over the ocean. Then Jolly was even envious of him, of his freedom and the work with the sea horses. She'd always liked animals and would rather have spent her days in the stables than in Forefather's dusty library room.

On the sixth day, at sundown, there was a knock on her door. "Your tattoo," said Griffin, who was standing there in the torchlight on the other side of it. "It isn't finished."

"I know," she said.

"If you want . . . I mean, I can do that, if it's all right with you."

She smiled and had stripped her shirt over her head before he was through the door. "I thought you'd never ask."

He'd brought along what was necessary. Black ink. A long needle, not too sharp. A cloth. Even a basin with warm water, which he'd gotten from one of the kitchens.

With her upper body uncovered, Jolly went to the bed that stood near the arched windows. She wasn't ashamed in front of Griffin. The old trust between them was established instantly again, as if there'd never been any doubt. She shoved the covers and pillow aside and lay on her stomach with her hands under her chin. From here she could see out to the red-golden sky and observe the ray riders in their rounds over the city.

Griffin sat down beside her, placed the basin of water on the bed, and dampened the cloth. Then he gently rubbed over Jolly's back, following the outline of the half-finished tattoo with the warm cloth and then patting the skin dry.

"If you know it's supposed to be a coral, you can really see it quite well," he said.

"Trevino did it, the cook on the *Skinny Maddy*." She hesitated briefly, then added sadly, "That was just before the *Maddy* went down. I saw Trevino get bitten by the spiders and collapse."

"Did he do tattoos for the crew often?"

"Sometimes. He said tattooing someone was like telling his fortune. You have to find a motif that means something to the person, something that could be important for him."

"I never thought about that before."

Jolly looked thoughtfully into the evening twilight. "The coral . . . it just came to me a few days ago. But it's really quite obvious."

"Do you think Trevino foresaw that you would come here? Into a city of coral?"

"Perhaps it's just coincidence."

"Anyway, it's pretty strange." Griffin dipped the needle in the black ink and made the first prick to get the color under her skin. "Does that hurt?"

"I've survived worse."

He smiled. "I know."

They were silent for a time, while he filled in the irregular outline Trevino had made with shapes and shadows. He kept patting the color and the sweat from her skin, now and again uttering an affirmative sound, as if he were satisfied with his work.

"This is going to take a few days," he said.

"If it gives us the chance to see each other more often—then take your time." She felt his eyes on the back of her head. Perhaps he was hoping she'd turn around to him so he could see if she meant it seriously. But she kept looking out into the glow of the evening. The fiery light bathed the light coral walls of the room in yellow and red. The bedclothes glowed as if they were in flames.

"I'd love to ride on sea horses too," she said as the sky over the wall of fog gradually darkened. "That must be great."

"Do you still have black-and-blue marks?"

She giggled. "*Those* I am certainly not going to show you!"

"Anyhow, mine are twice as big now and almost black," he said, laughing.

"Interesting idea."

"D'Artois and his men must have calluses as thick as tortoiseshells on their rear ends."

She liked that he could make her laugh. She'd had much too little fun in recent days. Forefather was always terribly serious and, God, so *wise*. And Munk doggedly pursued his wish to improve his capabilities, in spite of all the nearness to her.

Griffin, on the other hand . . . well, he was just Griffin. A pirate and a trickster and a loudmouth. Sometimes, anyway. And from time to time he was also the way he was today. Himself, and yet somehow very different. As if all that she'd secretly liked about him earlier had suddenly become much more obvious. Had he changed? Or was she only seeing him differently?

"The whole city is talking about you two," he began again after a pause. "About the two rescuers and saviors and—"

"Please, Griffin, stop."

"The needle?"

"The talk of rescuers and saviors. That we most certainly are not."

"Munk, anyway, gives the impression that he isn't altogether averse to that idea."

"He likes his role. And he enjoys the attention. But you have to understand that for fourteen years he met absolutely no one except his parents and a few traveling traders. And now the entire world appears to be revolving around him."

"Then he should watch out that he himself doesn't some-day . . . oh, well . . ."

"What?"

"If everything is revolving around him . . . if he stands in the middle and enjoys that, then he's something like a mael-strom himself, isn't he?"

She pictured what Griffin had just said and unwillingly had to agree that he was right.

Wasn't that the greatest danger that threatened them: that they themselves would become what they wanted to defeat?

"I've spoken with Forefather about that," she said.

"About Munk?"

She shook her head. "About what's happening to us. How we're changing. That it's only about conforming to the expec-tations of the others—and it really isn't important anymore what we expect of ourselves."

The needle pricks in her back stopped for a moment.

"What is it?" she asked, and tried to look up over her shoulder at him. He was now working by the light of several candles. Night had arrived outside the window.

"But it's true," he said softly. "You really are something special."

"Only because I'm a polliwog? Because my parents were in the right place when they conceived me? That doesn't make me anything special." She was talking more and more excit-edly, even though she knew she was not being honest with herself. She'd thought a great deal about these things recently. "Other people can just ride very well. Or draw. Or learn foreign languages. I can walk on water. To be precise, that's no great difference, and not at all a question of talent. I simply *can*, you understand? I never have to do anything for it. I don't have to exert myself."

The needle was still at rest.

"That's not what I meant at all," he said quietly. "I said that *you* are something special. Not your abilities. Only you, Jolly."

She felt warmth spreading through her. She tried to turn around to him, but he held her back with one hand.

"No, don't. You'll smear all the ink."

She remained lying on her stomach, but she almost put her neck out of joint to look around at him. "You've spoken quite nicely."

He smiled, and for the first time she saw him almost abashed. "The advanced pirate school of conversation," he said. "Some people just have it in their blood."

"Sure," she said, grinning. "Come here a minute."

"I'm already——"

"Closer, I mean."

He bent forward and closed his eyes. She lifted her torso to kiss him. When she touched his lips, it was as if needles were sticking into every pore in her body. But it didn't hurt, it only tickled. She was hot and cold at the same time, and that was something new, something altogether confusing.

He opened his eyes and looked at her as they kissed. She couldn't remember ever having been so close to any person.

"Jolly——," he was beginning, but he was interrupted by a

sound. Hastily he turned around. They both looked toward the other end of the room.

"I . . . knocked," stammered Munk, who stood in the open doorway, pale as a ghost. "But no one said anything . . . and so I . . . I mean . . ."

He fell silent and stared at them: Jolly on the bed with her torso naked, Griffin very close to her, one hand on her waist.

Then he turned on his heel, left the door standing open, and ran away.

"Munk, wait!" Jolly called after him.

Griffin sighed deeply, took the cloth out of the now cold water, and patted her back clean with it. She fidgeted uncomfortably and rubbed a hand over her face, but then let herself sink down onto her stomach and remained lying there.

Griffin looked at her in surprise. "Don't you want to go after him?"

Jolly rolled onto her back. "Would that change anything?"

Forefather

Forefather was sitting in his wing chair and explaining the world. Jolly was alone with him in the high cathedral of books.

No one knew where Munk was. She'd knocked on his door in the morning, but he hadn't opened it. None of the servants had seen him. Forefather was as surprised as she was that Munk hadn't shown up for class.

Soledad had warned her. Jolly ought to have known this would happen sooner or later. But why should she deny her own feelings just to keep Munk from being angry at her? That would only have made *her* angry at *him*. All in all, a heap of trouble, for which, sighing, she took the responsibility herself.

"The world," said Forefather, in his sonorous, impressive voice, "is really not *one* world but consists of many. Some say these multiple worlds lie beside one another, and they touch from time to time. But I think they are arranged over one another, like round slices. Imagine a pile of plates. That is the universe."

She had other things on her mind than imagining worlds as dishes. And yet something of what he said got through to her.

"Then one of the plates would be our world," she said, "and another the Mare Tenebrosum. Do you think there are many others?"

"Innumerable ones."

"But our world is already so big . . . and so hard to understand." It must have sounded to him as though she were thinking about the blank places on the maps, of the unknown continents and faraway countries. But in truth she meant something entirely different.

"Just because you cannot count all the stars in the sky, they don't become fewer, do they? No one is interested in what humans can grasp and what they cannot. Every world has its own conflicts to settle, every one has its own concerns."

At the moment she didn't care. She had a world to save— and a friendship. And did not the one possibly depend on the other? How was she going to explain *that* to anyone?

Forefather went on, without noticing the haze of tears in her eyes. "Most people think of the past and the future of our world as a line that begins somewhere and will end at a distant point somewhere. Or one not so distant, depending on whom you ask." His smile was impish, like that of a child, and at the same time a little sad. "But in reality, time moves in a circle. There is no beginning and no end. Time is only the edge of the plate, it always leads back to itself again. The world is made of repeats."

"I don't understand."

"Your battle against the Maelstrom, for example. Others have done the same thing thousands of years ago. The same opponent—a similar battle. And if you look back into history and tradition, there have always been individual human beings whose task it was to save the world from the worst. And has one of them ever refused?"

"Perhaps I'm the first." She ran her fingers nervously through her hair. "That makes me feel much better right off."

He shook his head. "Listen to me, Jolly. Things repeat themselves. *All* things! Only we don't necessarily recognize it. Time is a circle, it rushes around the plate at a furious speed, over and over again."

"And what good does it do for me to know that?"

"You say that you are only a girl. But that isn't right. Anyway, not anymore." He raised a hand. "No, wait, listen! The worlds never overlap of their own accord. Some people maintain the opposite, even your one-eyed friend. But the truth is that there is no overlapping. Only beings who live in the worlds can create a connection."

"And?" She was gradually becoming impatient. Where was he leading?

"Most people never get to look into other worlds. They don't grasp the connections, they never even try to. They live in the moment and, quite literally, never look over the edge of the plate. But there are exceptions, those who risk a look and sometimes very much more. Those are the painters, the poets, the artists, and the shamans—they look over and describe what they have discovered to all the others. But not even they are capable of going over there. They can see events and images, they can tell of them, but they can't really visit those other worlds. That is reserved for a very few only. The elect. People like you, Jolly."

Again he made a gesture to stifle her objection. "And it is this that makes you something unique, whether you want to be or not. You have the power to leap from the speeding gallop of time, from one plate edge to the next. You and Munk—and the Maelstrom. For he also is a living being, and he also is elect."

"Are you saying that we polliwogs and the Maelstrom . . . we are alike?"

"Like siblings."

Griffin's words rose from her memory. Munk would himself become a maelstrom, he'd said. She shuddered.

"That is not all," said Forefather. "Even if it's hard for you, you must try to understand these things. Every discovery of the other worlds, every conscious venture there involves dangers as well. Sometimes they could mean ruin, as perhaps for Aelenium. But sometimes they help us to something higher. You, Jolly, will grow into one, already *are* growing into one, who can take up the battle against the Maelstrom."

She stood up. "I don't know if I've understood any of all that," she said. "But it frightens me."

"It need not. It shouldn't disconcert you just because it's something new. You probably need to think for a while." He pointed to the door of the room. "Feel free to go, if you wish. Go somewhere where you can be alone. Think about what I've said. The lesson is ended for today."

She didn't argue with him, merely nodded to him and left the library. Forefather's eyes followed her until she'd closed the door behind her.

"Jolly!"

She whirled around and saw Soledad, who was hurrying toward her across a coral platform on the west side of Aelenium, not far from where the steep mountain cone in the center of the city merged into the tangle of houses and little streets.

Hundreds of gulls circled around the towers, but their screeching was drowned out by the rushing of the waterfalls that poured from the coral mountain down into the canals of the city.

During her rambles, Jolly had discovered that the story-tellers of Aelenium met here. They sat cross-legged on blankets or skins, some even on raised podiums, and gathered small groups of listeners around them, usually children, because the grown-ups were busy with the defense prepa-rations.

Jolly had wandered from one storyteller to another and picked up little snippets here and there, fairy tales and fables, but also episodes from the history of the city, of the Caribbean, and of the beginnings of colonization.

"I was looking for you." Soledad smiled. "The old man said you'd surely be up here somewhere."

Jolly hadn't spoken with the princess at all for days, or with most of her friends from the *Carfax*, actually.

For the first time she felt guilty on that account.

"I had to think about something," she said.

"Oh?" Soledad tilted her head and raised her eyebrows.

"Oh, don't make such a face." Jolly forced herself to give a halfhearted laugh.

"Is it on account of Griffin and Munk?"

"You never let up, do you?"

Soledad studied her, hesitating, then she shrugged. "That's your business, I'm not going to get into it. I wanted to talk with you for another reason." She walked closer to Jolly and took her hands. "I want to say farewell."

"You're going away?"

"Only for a few days, if all goes well."

"What are you going to do?" Jolly had thought she'd be the one who had to do the leave-taking when the time came for departure. The thought had been following her all day long like a spook.

Soledad released her hands. "I'm going to end what I began in New Providence. I will avenge my father. Finally Kendrick's going to bleed for having grabbed the pirate throne so treacherously."

Jolly stared at the princess. She'd known that sooner or later Soledad would go looking for the pirate emperor again. But recently she'd simply forgotten it. Or repressed it. Like so much, she thought. Like her own feelings and her search for Captain Bannon.

"Where do you intend to find Kendrick?" she asked.

"A rumor's been going around for months that there's going to be a big gathering of all the important pirate captains of the Lesser Antilles," said the princess. "Kendrick's going to meet with them. The pirates in that area have never accepted the pirate emperor. My father and his predecessors tried to force them, but it didn't work. They have their own organization, and the decisions of their council are the only ones that apply in that region."

"Then why a meeting with Kendrick?"

Soledad brushed back a strand of hair. "It's said he wants to make them an offer they can't refuse. No idea what he has in mind. My father ran into a brick wall with their stubbornness, and I doubt it will turn out any differently for that bastard."

Jolly frowned. "Do you know where they're meeting, then?"

Soledad grinned. "To be honest, it would probably be easier to get into the Spanish viceroy's treasury than to get any information about the meeting place. But I have a plan." She gave Jolly a piercing look. "An opportunity like this doesn't come along often." Jolly was just about to respond to that when Soledad went on. "Someone else is also going to take part in the meeting. Tyrone."

"Tyrone!"

"Amazing, isn't it? Looks as if he's going to leave his hidey-hole in the Orinoco delta for it."

"But Tyrone . . . he doesn't belong to them anymore. He quit the others." This news had actually been a small sensation. Tyrone was a legend, a pirate whom even the other captains of the Caribbean feared. When, years before, he'd been driven into a tight spot by a Spanish armada, he'd fled onto the mainland and traveled up the Orinoco River on a raft with the rest of his crew. It was said that all the pirates in his crew had been killed and eaten by cannibals—with the exception of Tyrone, who in some mysterious way had managed to make the natives believe he was one of their gods. Since that time, rumors kept circulating that he'd risen to be ruler of the Orinoco cannibals, recruited new crews, and was making plans to fall on the islands of the Caribbean with a powerful fleet of pirates and man-eaters.

Most people brushed these off as just wild stories. Even Bannon had believed that Tyrone had probably been wiped out by the cannibals along with his crew.

And now Tyrone was supposed to appear to meet with the Antilles captains? That was almost as incredible as if the Devil himself had said he was coming.

Jolly took a deep breath. Soledad was planning nothing less than poking a damned wasps' nest. "We need you here," she said, holding her ground against the gaze of Soledad's dark eyes.

"No," the princess contradicted her. "Only you are important. And Munk. We others aren't important at all. In comparison to you, even the Ghost Trader's unimportant."

"But—"

"He's going with me. Really, it was his idea how we could find the meeting place."

Jolly stared at her. "The Ghost Trader? But . . . he can't just leave us in the lurch!"

"No one's leaving you in the lurch, Jolly. With some luck, we'll all be back here again before you leave."

"We'll all? Does that mean—"

"Walker's going too. And, no, before you ask: Buenaventure and the *Carfax* are staying here. Walker, the Trader, and I are taking hippocampi."

The fact that Buenaventure and Walker would separate— even if it was only for a few days—was unusual. But at the moment Jolly wasted no thought on it. "How come the Ghost Trader's going too? It must be all the same to him whether Kendrick remains pirate emperor or not."

Soledad agreed. "In any other situation it wouldn't matter to him. But if the captains listen to me, then perhaps I can make them understand the danger we're all in—even they and their crews. If they believe me, I'll turn back with an entire fleet that can support us in the war against the Maelstrom."

Jolly made a face and didn't try very hard to conceal her lack of understanding. "You're going to inform all the pirates of the Caribbean that Aelenium exists? And where it's anchored? What do you really think they'll do first of all?"

"I know the risk. That's why it's so important to have the Ghost Trader there. He can assess whether we have a chance or whether the entire plan is madness."

"But they'll turn up here with their ships, and then

Aelenium will have *two* fronts it has to fight on. The pirates will plunder the city and leave the ruins for the Maelstrom."

Soledad stroked Jolly's hair. It was the first time that she'd permitted herself such a familiar gesture. "You're smart, Jolly. But don't underestimate me. I've learned a lot from my father. I know how you talk to those fellows. And what you have to promise them to have them eating out of your hand. It's about their survival too—they just don't know it."

"All the same, it's madness. What does Count Aristotle say about it? And the council?"

"They've agreed that it's a chance. Perhaps the last one. You both need time to get to the Crustal Breach. And even if you and Munk are successful in sealing in the Maelstrom, it's still more than likely that Aelenium will be attacked first. In that case, we need all the support we can get."

Jolly saw that she couldn't convince the princess. The plan had been under way for a long time without anyone letting her and Munk in on it.

"When are you leaving?"

"Right now. That's why I was looking for you. I wanted you to learn it from one of us, not from the old man or one of those big shots in the council."

"And Munk?'

"You tell him."

"What about Griffin?" Jolly felt her heart beating suddenly harder.

Soledad pricked up her ears and smiled in amusement. "Griffin?"

"Is he going with you too?"

"No, Griffin's staying here. Don't worry."

Jolly blushed. She felt discovered.

"Take care of yourself." Soledad pulled Jolly to her and hugged her hard. "Remember what I told you. You and Munk will be dependent on each other down there."

"Munk is furious with me."

"He'll calm down again. He's probably sitting somewhere and sulking. Men are like that, believe me."

They looked each other in the eyes. Jolly blinked away her tears before they could roll down her cheeks.

"We're coming back, no matter how it turns out," Soledad said.

"Yes," Jolly answered weakly, "sure." She took a deep breath, as if the burdens on her shoulders had become doubly heavy at one stroke. "I'm afraid."

"We all are."

Jolly shook her head. "Not of the Maelstrom or the kobalins. I'm afraid of being down there alone with Munk. He . . . he's my friend, but . . . oh, I don't understand myself what's the matter."

"Don't you trust him?"

"I don't know!"

"And that's the worst, isn't it? The not knowing."

Jolly embraced her again. "Oh, Soledad, I'd much rather go down there with any other person. With any one of you."

The princess pressed Jolly's head against her shoulder and said nothing.

The Truth About Spiders

The Ghost Trader's plan was as crazy as it was obvious. It was based on a story that was being told all over the Caribbean.

A few months before, one of the most powerful Antilles captains, a certain Santiago, had been marooned on a desert island by his men. The crew had mutinied because they felt the captain had cheated them in dividing their loot (and anyone who knew Santiago knew that their feeling was sure to be right). The men headed for an island, hardly more than a solitary sandbank, and set their swindling leader on land there. At his own request they'd given him only a large barrel of rum for nourishment—this, too, was just what you'd expect of Santiago.

No one wept a tear for him when the story made the rounds of the dives in the harbor cities. A drunk, tyrant, and swindler, the captain had had very few friends among the leaders of the Caribbean pirates.

The whole thing would soon have sunk into oblivion, but not long afterward, another crew, sailing within sight of the island, started the stories all over again. From the railing, the men had clearly made out the gigantic rum barrel on the shore—and the two legs sticking up out of it. Obviously Santiago had become a victim to his boozing, fallen headfirst into the cask, and drowned miserably in rum.

Since then, it was said, the cask with the corpse stood on the bank of the island like a memorial. Even the most hard-boiled pirates shuddered when the story of Santiago's end was recounted for the benefit of people in the taverns. Yes, people laughed about that greedy gut, but secretly the vision of the lonely rum cask with the pirate's boots sticking out gave chills to many. Of course Santiago wasn't the first to become a victim of his own insatiable thirst, but the way he did it was unprecedented. Soon the talk was of a curse the captain was supposed to have uttered in a gurgle and celebrated with his last swallow of rum.

All the same, however many stories made the rounds, it was a fact that Santiago had doubtless been one of those who'd have known of the secret meeting of the Antilles captains with Pirate Emperor Kendrick. The Ghost Trader's plan was thus as follows: He and Soledad and Walker would ride on sea horses to the island, where he would call up Santiago's ghost and get him to reveal the meeting place of Kendrick and the pirates; the living might well fear the consequences of a betrayal and keep silent, but Kendrick's threats could mean nothing to a dead man. The Ghost Trader was confident his plan would succeed.

The three riders intended to then proceed from Santiago's island to the captains' meeting place, for d'Artois's spies were reporting that the meeting with Tyrone and Kendrick was going to occur soon. Haste was thus in order, not just because of concern for the attack by the Maelstrom, but also because the meeting might be over before the comrades even got there.

Soledad told Jolly all this while they descended through Aelenium's narrow little streets together, passing under the shading awnings the inhabitants had stretched from house to house. It took them almost half an hour to reach the stables of the hippocampi down along the water. There Walker and the Ghost Trader were already waiting.

The sea horses' stables were located in an extensive complex on the shore of a sea star point. Grooms hurried around, some carrying two or three large baskets filled to the rims with tiny fish that were freshly caught. Others rolled hip-high balls of dried algae and trailing plants, which were harvested from the plantation-like fields on the walls of the undercity. Both were used as fodder for the sea horses, which were, despite all their stamina, still vulnerable to nutritional deficiencies and, as Jolly had learned from d'Artois, to catching cold in cooler waters. This was one of the reasons why the sea horses never moved outside the boundaries of the Caribbean Sea.

THE TRUTH ABOUT SPIDERS

The interior of the stables consisted of a center walk, several hundred feet long, with water-filled pools sunk into the floor on both sides of it. The sea horses romped around within the pools, frequently underwater, sometimes also lined up beside one another. With their great round eyes, they curiously observed the men and women who were busy keeping the pools clean, adding new streams of water, or scrubbing and feeding their charges. It smelled of algae, saltwater, and the soaking-wet clothing of the workers in the stables. The fishy smell you might obviously have expected there was missing almost entirely, for the sea horses had an earthy smell, a little like shore mud and damp stone.

Walker and the Ghost Trader were waiting for Jolly and the princess at one of the pools. Three saddled sea horses rocked quietly beside them in the water. Stable hands held the bridles, scratched the animals' bony plates, and whispered soothing words to them.

Walker grinned at Jolly, while the Trader nodded thoughtfully and uttered only a growling "hmm, hmm." Perhaps he'd been afraid Jolly would disapprove of her friends' departure and refuse to accompany Soledad to the stables. His two parrots were nowhere to be seen; they were to remain in Aelenium so that in case of an attack, they could quickly fly over the sea and warn their master.

Walker hugged Jolly. She flinched slightly, his grip was so strong. "Don't let any of these fatheads get you down, little one! Just remember: In better times we'll rob the whole store, drive these powder puffs into the sea, and sink the city."

Jolly assumed her darkest pirate mien and nodded.

"And one other thing," said Walker, before he released her. "If any one of them wrinkles his nose at you, break it for him. Punch it right in the middle! Is that clear?"

"That is clear!"

Soledad, too, hugged her again. "We've come quite a long way together, haven't we? From Kendrick's hole in New Providence to here?"

Jolly grinned. "Right."

The princess punched her lightly on the shoulder. "Damn, who would have thought it?" She took a deep breath, looked for a long moment as though she was going to add something, then shook her head and stepped back to make room for the Ghost Trader.

"Take care of yourself," he said as he went into a crouch in front of Jolly in order to bring his eye on a level with her face. "You're a brave girl. And no matter what Munk can achieve with the mussels—he needs someone like you to go along with him."

"And I'll need *him* down there at the Crustal Breach."

"If everything works out, we'll be back before you leave," he said. "If not . . . well, you two are the only ones who can do it."

He patted her on the shoulder and stepped back without embracing her. The three climbed onto their sea horses, waved once more, then turned the animals toward an opening in the coral wall. No one else had come to see them off. Jolly guessed that the official leave-taking had taken place already, in the council room of the count, probably, or in another hall in the great coral palace. But why hadn't Buenaventure shown up? And Griffin?

She gave herself a shake and ran along the central walk to the exit from the stables. Under the archway she stopped, shaded her eyes with her hand, and looked out across the water. In the distance she saw the three riders on their sea horses growing ever smaller, until they disappeared into the billowing fog wall. A last streak marked the place at which they'd gone into the fog, but only for a moment, then everything settled back to a uniform gray.

Jolly stood there for a long time, paying no attention to the growling of the grooms, in whose way she was standing. Sorrow filled her, as if she'd seen her friends for the last time. The whispering of the waves sounded like an invitation to run out onto the sea after them, away from Aelenium and the people who lived here; away from the Maelstrom and the Mare Tenebrosum; away from a responsibility she didn't want to bear.

What would Griffin think of her if she simply stole away? Would he consider her a coward? Perhaps.

But what if she had a good reason, one that weighed more heavily than her fear? If she, like Soledad, remembered her own goal again?

Would he understand her?

Yes, she thought, *Griffin understands me. For sure.*

Suddenly she had an idea, and she was amazed that the thought hadn't come to her much earlier. She cast a last look at the fog wall, then raced up the steps and little streets to the palace. She stormed excitedly into her room and searched through her things for the little box with the dead spider, the only proof she had that she hadn't imagined the attack of the poison spiders on the *Skinny Maddy*. Not that she mistrusted her own memories. However, it was a reassuring feeling to hold a witness to this catastrophe in her hand—even if it had eight legs and hideous bristles.

With box and spider she hurried to the great library again, not to Forefather's book room but into the main buildings. There she began her search.

The spider had a Latin name, which Jolly had to divide into syllables in order to read it. When she said it out loud to herself, it still sounded as though she were spelling it, instead of saying it in one word.

It had been late afternoon when she finally worked her way into that part of the library. Armed with a ladder and a telescope she'd searched room by room, from the lowest piles of books to the highest. When she was just about to give up, she chanced to go through a small door and discovered behind it the Division of Jungle Organisms and Intestinal Diseases in Tropical Climates—obviously not an often requested subject among the sages of Aelenium.

After the long search, it felt almost as if the finger of Fate pointed to the book with the information she sought lying right on top of a pile that rose just next to the dusty reading desk. It had been written about three decades before by a monk who—as Jolly learned in a little note appended—had lost his life in a shipwreck after the completion of the book.

On page 426, she found the first clue that might possibly give her information about Bannon's fate. Again and again she compared the striking markings of the spider body in the open box with the illustration in the folio.

According to that, the species of spider to which the dead one in the box belonged came from a region on the coast of South America. Not just any coast, not just any region—but from exactly that region that Jolly had already encountered once today in her conversation with Soledad.

The Orinoco delta.

That part of the jungle into which the legendary Captain Tyrone had fled and where he was said still to rule today as a cruel despot over a population of cannibals and pirates.

A coincidence? Possibly, but very improbably.

The spiders in the reefed sails of the galleon that had been waiting for the boarding pirates from the *Skinny Maddy*; the spiders that Jolly had barely managed to escape and to which all the other members of the crew had fallen victim—they came from the cannibal kingdom of Captain Tyrone.

Jolly gasped with fright, inhaled a load of dust, and coughed for half a minute before she was quiet again. Then she compared the light brown pattern on the spider's body with the illustration once more. There was no doubt. She also studied the text again, but it gave no indication that this species of spider appeared in any other regions.

It all fit together. The ambush, the spiders, and Tyrone's

sudden readiness to work with the pirates again after such a long time.

But why? Why should a man like Tyrone set such a trap for Bannon? What interest did he have in the crew, the ship—or in Jolly?

Supposing Tyrone had in fact been after the polliwog from Bannon's ship—did this mean there was a connection between him and the Maelstrom? Or was there something she'd overlooked?

One thing was established, anyway: She now had a clue. For the first time since the fearsome attack by the poison spiders, Jolly felt real hope spring up in her. If Tyrone had set the trap for them, then there was a possibility that he'd supplied Bannon and his men with the antidote in time. Always provided he had an interest in getting his hands on Bannon alive.

Jolly slapped the book closed. Clouds of dust arose and veiled her sight. When it had settled again, the library room lay as still and extinct as it had all the years before.

At night the sea around Aelenium was as black as a bottomless pit. The fog ring swallowed up a major part of the starlight. Therefore Captain d'Artois had given the order to kindle giant fires on floats. Their light was supposed to illumine the night and warn the defenders before kobalin attacks. Blazing, the platforms floated on the dark water, but their circles of light were nowhere large enough to illuminate the entire upper surface. It was as if someone tried to become lord of the darkness with a handful of fireflies.

Jolly took cover behind a pile of logs. The repair work on the *Carfax* was finished, but the rest of the materials and the tools still lay near the quay. The sloop rocked gently at the edge of a sea star point beside a dozen fishing boats, whose low masts were dwarfed by the *Carfax*.

While she strained to look over to the quay from her hiding place, it seemed to Jolly for the first time that the ship had something majestic about her. And the thought of her plan gave her conscience a painful stab: Walker had inherited the sloop from his mother, a much-feared freebooter, whose urn he kept in the captain's cabin as a reliquary. It was wrong to steal that ship. But damn it, Jolly was a pirate. Walker would understand. At least for a second—before he beat her brains out.

Jolly knew that soldiers were hidden everywhere in the darkness. In the late afternoon d'Artois's men had run into a troop of kobalins in the fog; they had been observing the city out of the mists. Since then they'd known that the Maelstrom's soldiers were moving inexorably closer. The watches had been doubled along the shores of the city and in the watchtowers.

Jolly's plan was crazy, and she knew it. Escaping from Aelenium unnoticed was impossible. She could only hope that no one would presume her to be aboard the *Carfax*. She had possibly a one- or two-day lead before anyone drew the right conclusions. Even then, the sea horses were still fast enough to catch up with her. But perhaps they'd understand that Jolly was not suited for what they asked of her. After all,

Munk was still there. He was the braver polliwog and the more powerful mussel magician, better prepared for the battle against the Maelstrom.

She felt a sharp pang at this thought and was forced to recall the Ghost Trader's words at their parting. She could turn it and twist it however she wanted: In the end it came down to the fact that she was leaving Munk in the lurch. He'd have to go into the deep alone, have to walk to the Crustal Breach alone.

Stop that! Don't make it harder for yourself than it is already!

She tried to breathe quietly and regularly. When she had herself somewhat under control, she looked around for a last time, then scampered, stooping, across the open harbor landing to the quayside. The gangplank to the *Carfax* vibrated as she went on board. Her steps sounded hollow on the deck.

She took cover behind the railing and looked back. Not a human soul far and wide. Soldiers were in the vicinity, but possibly they had their eyes only on the water, not on the quayside. Probably no one figured that someone would steal a ship.

But the cone of the mountain, with its hundreds upon hundreds of spires, towers, and bridges, appeared to lean over her if she raised her eyes to it for long enough. Then it was as if it were tipping forward infinitely slowly, and she had to fight the urge to whirl around and run away. Even in the dark she couldn't get entirely free of this feeling. Perhaps it was just the worry that somewhere up there someone was looking down at her.

She crouched again and crossed the deck. It smelled of

fresh sawdust, of tar and carpenter's glue. The workers of Aelenium and the ghosts on the *Carfax* had done good work, as far as it was possible to tell in the dark. Although Jolly had never encountered ghosts in the city anywhere, dealing with the misty beings seemed to be nothing new for the people of Aelenium.

Jolly had tried before to command the faceless beings, without success. But after her lessons with Forefather, she knew what she needed to do to control the ghosts. She'd proven it in a competition with Munk only two days before.

Now she ran up to the bridge, loosened the safety rope on the wheel, placed her hands on the grips, and concentrated. Her lips formed silent words that only she herself knew and that had meaning exclusively for her; for magic, she'd learned, was something entirely personal. There was no fixed spell that anyone could use, no written-down charm formulas. Books of magic and magic scrolls? All nonsense. One formed one's own devices to work the magic. The words and syllables for it were found deep in one's innermost thoughts. The mussel magic also worked on a similar principle, only it was far more powerful and its effects much more dangerous.

Jolly's call to the ghosts sent a gust of wind over the boards of the *Carfax*. It nestled gently around the masts and crept up into the ropes and sails. Like an invisible power, it danced over the rigging and forced under Jolly's command the lost souls of all those who'd died aboard this ship.

It took only a few moments for the foggy outlines and silhouettes to rise from the wood, with fuzzy borders and blurry faces, making it impossible to differentiate one from another. Soon they were all on the main deck and gathered on the bridge around Jolly and the wheel. A ghost as shifting as a shred of fog even wafted up into the crow's nest on the new topmast. Jolly let her eyes travel over the deserted pier of Aelenium once more. She'd never sailed alone in a ship before, not to mention commanded an entire crew. But she couldn't allow herself any doubts now. Bannon had taught her all he knew about seafaring. She lacked only experience.

The ghosts manned all the important positions on deck and in the rigging. Only the rustling of the unrolling sails, the groaning of tautened ropes, and the creaking of the anchor winch were to be heard. In a few minutes the *Carfax* would be ready to run out.

"Haven't you forgotten someone?"

Jolly whirled around. Behind her, in the shadows of the railing, a thin figure was seated cross-legged. On the dark deck shimmered a circle of small, bright dots.

"Munk!"

He sighed softly. "Yes, just me. Too bad, huh?"

"What do you mean?"

He looked up at her. "You'd rather it was someone else."

She glared at him angrily. "Stop that foolishness. This isn't the time for—"

"Why don't you take Griffin with you? Now that you understand each other so well."

"This is my affair alone. Not Griffin's. And not yours either."

"Hmm," he said, tilting his head as if he had to think about that. "Haven't you overlooked something?"

She considered whether she should order the ghosts to throw him over the railing on the spot.

She had neither the time nor the patience for arguments of this sort. And especially not with someone who was acting like an offended little boy.

"The Crustal Breach," he said, thus unerringly hitting her sore spot. "So you mean for me to get the job done alone."

"I have to find Bannon. I intended to do that from the beginning, and you know it."

"And Aelenium? The people here and in the entire Caribbean? I and—devil take it—oh, all right, Griffin, too? Don't we matter to you?"

"I must do what I must do."

"Good Lord, Jolly! Can't you think of anything more original?" He stood up, walked carefully around the mussel circle on the deck, and stopped close in front of her. "Admit it. You've got the jitters. Bannon is only an excuse to run away."

"I'm no coward."

"Ah, no? And how do you think it's going to look when you do what you're doing?"

She placed a finger against his chest like the barrel of a pistol. "You're jealous—that's all! I am afraid, that's true, but so are you. And my fear isn't the reason why I'm leaving Aelenium."

"You want to find that Bannon—that *pirate*," he said disparagingly. "How noble!"

She stared at him and found simply no entry to his thoughts. "It isn't so long ago that you wanted to become a pirate yourself."

"That was before. And I was a different person."

Jolly looked at him. Yes, he was right. He was a different person. "And do you like yourself this way?" she asked softly.

His eyes became narrow slits, and suddenly she was glad that in the dark she couldn't see every nuance of his expression. His voice sounded cold and filled with seething fury. "It's not about that, Jolly. It's a vocation. *Our* vocation!"

Jolly got gooseflesh. Several days ago she'd still thought his transformation might go back to the death of his parents. But she'd been mistaken. It was this city and the people's expectations that had changed him. *Savior*, she though coldly. *Vocation*.

"Do what you want," she said. "Save the world if you think you can. I wish you luck with it."

He seized her wrist. "We have to carry out this job *together*. Just us two."

"I'm not the heroine that all these people see in me." She tried to free her hand from his, but his grip was too strong. Jolly lowered her voice to a whisper. "Let—me—go!"

She feared that he wouldn't give in. That he'd actually try to force her to stay in Aelenium. She readied herself to hit him in the face as hard as she could.

But then he loosened his fingers and she could move her arm freely again.

"Don't you ever do that again," she hissed.

"I don't want to quarrel with you, Jolly."

"You already have."

"Come back on land, please." But it sounded like an order the way he said it.

"No. *You* get off this ship. And right now."

Munk's hand felt behind him, as if he were going to pull something from behind his back. But instead he fanned his outspread fingers in the direction of the mussels. Instantly a light blazed up.

He must not have to look at it anymore to create a pearl! flashed through Jolly's head. *He's so much more powerful than I am.*

Munk's expression did not change.

The glowing pearl rose slowly out of the circle, floating higher and higher.

Had he merely been playing with her for all the past days? Letting her believe she had a chance to beat him in their absurd competitions? So that she at least *tried* to impress him?

"Stop that," she said, forcing herself to be calm.

The pearl was now almost at eye level.

"Munk, quit that!"

The glow radiated more brightly, pulsating slowly. Now the pearl bathed the entire deck of the *Carfax* in light so that the goings-on aboard were visible far away. Probably the first watch would be alerted at once.

Jolly closed her eyes. In thought she stretched invisible hands toward the floating pearl, willed them to surround it, pluck it out of the air, and . . .

"Ow, damn it!"

She snapped her eyes open when her real hands suddenly

felt as if they'd gotten too close to an open fire.

"That hurts, Munk!" One last time she controlled herself. "Is that what you want? To hurt me?"

"I want you to see reason."

"*Your* kind of reason."

He shook his head silently. The pearl rose higher and higher, now hung over them like a full moon.

Jolly gave one of the ghosts a wave. The phantom shot forward, not at Munk but toward the circle of mussels behind his back. The being's foot gained mass. Then the mussel shells burst under his soles.

A high whistle sounded and the pearl turned blood red. Munk's eyes widened in fright as he abruptly lost control over the magic. The pearl began to wobble, caught itself again, flew a loop, and rushed like a shot back toward Munk. He cried out in pain, was flung at Jolly, who tried to catch him. But the power of the blow threw them both back. Jolly groaned as she was pinned between Munk and the wheel for a moment. The wood pressed painfully into her spine.

Munk slid past her to the floor and crashed onto his knees. The pearl had gone out without causing any greater harm. But in Munk's features there now shone such a fury that Jolly retreated in fear and again banged against the wheel.

"My mussels," he whispered, looking up at her. His eyes were deep, dark lakes, like shadow holes in his face.

"You wouldn't have it any other way," she retorted. "And now, get down off this ship!"

He sprang up faster than she'd thought possible. The flat

of his hand shot forward and struck hard against her breast bone. He pressed her against the wheel with all his strength.

"If Griffin hadn't turned up," he panted, "then everything would be the way it used to be. You'd never have attacked me . . . it's all his fault."

"You attacked *me*."

"It's because he's so like you . . . that's why you like him more than me."

"That's silly, Munk."

"I thought so from the beginning. Ever since we saw him the first time, in New Providence."

"That's enough, Munk. Once and for all!"

She gave the ghosts the order merely with her eyes. Half a dozen of them started moving.

Munk was seized by several shadowy hands. Although he struck out around him and cursed, the ghosts bore him off the ship, back down the gangplank, and onto the pier.

"Jolly. Don't go!"

She shook her head and saw him thrown to the ground. The landing hurt her almost as much as him, but he'd left her no other choice. Why did he have to change so?

"Don't go!" he bellowed once again.

The anchor banged against the stern as it was pulled out of the water. Ropes were made fast. The *Carfax* began to shake like an animal waking from sleep.

The ghosts held Munk firmly on the ground until all was ready. Then they drifted foggily across the quay and on board and pulled up the gangplank behind them.

Munk scrambled up, but he didn't try to follow the misty figures. His eyes were fixedly looking toward Jolly. She bent, shoved the remains of the mussels into their leather sack, which lay beside the destroyed circle on the deck, and flung them over the railing. Munk caught the bag easily, almost without looking at it.

High above the mast something fluttered. Two dark shadows let themselves down onto the yards on both sides of the topmast. Red and yellow eyes looked down toward the deck.

Jolly sensed the parrots more than she saw them. Her hands grasped the wheel, then the *Carfax* left the sea star point and glided out onto the sea.

"Let her go!"

The old man's voice rang out from the pile of crates on the pier behind Munk.

"Forefather?" He turned around, but he could see no one.

"She has made her decision."

"The wrong decision."

"She must find that out for herself."

"But we need her here!" Munk gave up searching the darkness for the old man's stooping figure. He looked back at the *Carfax*, which had left the crowd of fishing boats behind her and was now gliding without any lights over the open water toward the black fog wall.

"The watches will not stop her," said Forefather. "I've seen to that."

"But she—she doesn't know what she's doing," Munk stammered despairingly.

"Oh, yes, she does, exactly. Only she cannot foresee the consequences."

Munk had to force himself to tear his eyes from the ship. He took a step toward the shadows, half expecting to find no one there. But Forefather was indeed standing between the crates. In the dark he looked even smaller and more fragile than usual.

"I can't go to the Crustal Breach alone," Munk said.

Forefather's face remained expressionless. "You used the magic against her. But far worse is that you forced her to oppose you. She did not want that. But you left her no other way out."

"But only to . . . to . . ." Munk fell silent and dropped his eyes.

"There is also some good in it," said Forefather.

Munk snorted scornfully. "Oh, yes?"

"She is not ready yet. She's different from you, Munk. There is a lesson that neither I nor anyone else can teach her. A lesson that you have already learned and that has given you your strength."

Forefather raised his stick and thumped it softly on the ground at Munk's feet. "Let her go and gain her own experiences."

Munk could hardly breathe, the lump in his throat was so large. "What lesson do you mean?"

"Loss," said Forefather thoughtfully. "The experience of losing something that she loves more than herself."

Swallowed

"She's gone."

Griffin started up and turned around when he heard d'Artois's voice behind him. He'd been leaning on the parapet of the watchtower and polishing his saber, which had been issued to him with his new soldier's uniform. He didn't feel comfortable in this clothing. But if he intended to make himself useful—and furthermore, to learn how to handle the sea horses and the flying rays—it wouldn't work without the uniform. The leather was soft, and yet it pinched him under the arms. And no one could tell him the purpose of the corals decorating it.

"She's *what?*" He set the saber on the parapet of the tower with a *clink*. A good three hundred feet below him shimmered the surface of the sea.

"Jolly is gone." D'Artois examined him closely.

Griffin grew dizzy. "That can't be."

"I'm afraid it is, though."

Griffin whirled around and stared down the furrowed slopes of the sea star city and out onto the water. From up here, it looked like a pitch-black surface sparsely sprinkled with individual fire floats. D'Artois had commanded their number to be tripled in the coming nights.

"She took the *Carfax*," the captain said.

Griffin still didn't understand. "Why so early? They say her training—"

"She isn't on her way to the Crustal Breach."

"Where, then?"

"I don't know. I wanted to stop her, but Forefather ordered us to let her go." D'Artois came closer to Griffin at the ledge of the tower. "I very much hope that he knows what he's doing."

Griffin battled his impatience. Everything in him screamed to simply turn his back on the captain and run down to Jolly's room to see for himself that it was all just a misunderstanding. But he controlled himself.

"Someone must know what she has in mind."

"I thought perhaps you could give me an answer about that."

Griffin shook his head. "She didn't say anything to me."

The captain placed a hand on Griffin's shoulder and turned him halfway around toward him. "Is that true?"

"I swear it." Griffin shifted restively from one foot to the other. Jolly was leaving the city and he was standing around and talking.

D'Artois sighed, and now he, too, looked out into the darkness. From up here the fire floats looked scarcely bigger than the individual stars in the sky.

"Have you any idea how hard it is for me to obey Forefather in this matter?" D'Artois put the question without waiting for an answer. "Especially since he has no authority to command. But I respect him and his decisions. He is . . ."

"Wise?" suggested Griffin.

"More than that. He's the soul of Aelenium. There's no one here who is more important for the city and its task."

Griffin pricked up his ears. "In the council he didn't seem to be especially . . . important. No one paid very much attention to him."

D'Artois smiled, but he gave no explanation. Instead he bent over the ledge and stared down into the darkness.

"You know, for years they've told us the polliwogs would save Aelenium if the Maelstrom ever attacked. When it got serious, we all waited for them to finally turn up. There were some who even prayed to them, can you imagine that? And then, out of nowhere, appeared these two children—no offense, Griffin—and we're supposed to believe that they're our saviors. That's certainly hard enough. And when we've finally accepted it and said to ourselves, good, they *are* the ones, they'll save us, then one of them suddenly runs away. Just like that." D'Artois's eyebrows came together, his face darkened. "And I could stop her. But now I'm supposed to let her go . . . and thus perhaps seal the fate of this city."

"There's still Munk," said Griffin, while an icy hand clutched at his heart. "Or did he go with her?"

"No," said d'Artois, and for that Griffin could have hugged him. "Munk is in the city. Forefather is looking after him."

"Perhaps it will be enough if Munk goes to the Crustal Breach alone. He's the more powerful of the two of them. Jolly has said that more than once."

"Maybe." The captain's hands curled around the edge of the parapet as if they wanted to break a piece out of it. "But according to my sense of it, we need *both* of them down there. Munk may possibly have more power—whatever that means. I understand too little of magic and all those things. But in his eyes I see things that I . . . I don't know . . . that I can't reconcile. Wanting to be admired, and arrogance—and yes, of course, power also, in a certain way. In the eyes of your friend, however, there is much more: humanity and warmth and enough courage to win this whole damned war with. I described her before as a child, but that was wrong. She may look like one, but inside . . . there's much more concealed in her. Things that I don't see in Munk." He heaved another sigh. "And therefore, Griffin, it's of no importance to me what the others say about his capabilities. All hollow magic, I say. What matters is what's in here." He pointed to his heart. "That's the power we need. And of that, Jolly has more than he does."

"I know what you mean." Griffin missed her more with each of the captain's sentences. The idea that she was gone almost strangled him. Why hadn't she taken him with her? Why had she left without even saying good-bye?

"I cannot call her back," said the captain, and this time there was an odd tone in his words. "I've promised to obey Forefather, and I will do that. Perhaps another, someone who might possibly disobey my order, would . . . but not I myself."

Again their eyes met. Griffin's heart was racing.

"How would it be if I took over your watch up here?" asked the captain.

"You want—you mean—"

Another look, then d'Artois again turned to the panorama of the night. "I need quiet to think. This is a good place for it. I come up here often, especially at night. You are free to go to bed, if you want."

Griffin seized his saber, shoved it into his belt, and rushed over to the steps. A thousand thoughts were shooting through his head at the same time. *To go to bed* . . . he understood only too well what d'Artois meant.

At the steps he stopped again for a moment, stammered a half-swallowed "Yes, sir!" and then jumped down the stairs. He had the feeling that d'Artois was looking after him out of the corner of his eye. And smiling.

The number of steps seemed to him to be increasing by themselves—there'd never been so many before. Griffin kept taking three at once, finally even four.

When he got down, he ran through the deserted streets down the mountain. No candles burned behind most windows; it was shortly before midnight and the people had gone to bed. For most of them the next day would again be filled with a thousand tasks that the approaching siege brought with it: filling and piling up sandbags in the most important defense positions; building protective walls; storing emergency rations in the houses but also in the shelters deep under the city; sharpening all kinds of blades; cleaning gun and pistol barrels.

Griffin looked neither to the right nor left. His thoughts were centered on Jolly, on her smile, on how her skin had felt under the tattoo, on her voice and the sparkle in her eyes when she teased him. And on what lay ahead of her: her path in the darkness at Munk's side.

It was this last thought that made him hesitate in front of the entrance to the stables. He stopped, tried to catch his breath, and leaned on one hand on the doorpost. Did he *want* to bring Jolly back to Aelenium at all? Did he really want her to go down to the Crustal Breach on a mission that might cost her her life?

Maybe she'd done the right thing when she turned her back on the city. This way she'd soon be out of danger. And that was what mattered, after all. What mattered to *him*.

But then a conviction slipped into his thoughts, sobering him in an instant. Jolly was no coward. She wouldn't run away, not even from the Maelstrom and the Crustal Breach. If she'd left Aelenium, there was something else behind it. Something that had nothing to do with fear and most certainly was no less dangerous.

He entered the stables and ran down the middle walkway.

Despite the night hours, the grooms were at work. Some of them had to be on duty at all times because of the patrols. They looked at Griffin in amazement as he ran as if the Devil were after him to the pool where his own sea horse was sleeping with eyes open.

He clumsily set about saddling him until one of the more experienced grooms came to help. The man asked no questions, it wasn't his place; but his frown made it clear that the boy's late departure made him mistrustful.

A few minutes later Griffin was under way. He turned his sea horse beneath one of the arches to the sea and splashed out over the dark water, past the flaming fire floats bobbing like buoyant pyres on the waves.

The night was warm and moist in the Caribbean at this time of the year. Yet the humidity of the day had subsided. Griffin noticed how very much easier it was to breathe freely at this hour. In spite of his task, in spite of the worry about Jolly, an irrepressible feeling of freedom came over him. He was riding out entirely alone for the first time, and the power of the wonderful creature under him seemed to carry over to him. He felt as if he were reborn.

Before he reached the fog and everything grew dark around him, he looked back over his shoulder to the city and tried to locate the tower where he'd stood with d'Artois a little while before. But he didn't find it quickly enough. Already the first patches covered his vision, and then suddenly it became so dark that for a long moment he was overwhelmed with panic.

The fog surrounded him, not with mist and gray gloom,

but with absolute blackness. No light from the city penetrated; even the light of the nearby fire floats glowed behind him like the points of dying candlewicks. The blackness gave him a foretaste of what lay ahead of Jolly if he brought her back to Aelenium. She might be able to see under there with her polliwog eyes, but it didn't change the fact that she would find herself in the most complete darkness that could be found anywhere in the world.

Fear entered through his clothing with the blackness and wrapped itself around his body like a shell of ice. It wasn't even one day ago that the soldiers had come upon the troops of kobalins in the fog. Now, in this darkness, there might be hundreds of them swimming around without anyone discovering them. Surely they could sense the presence of the sea horse, perhaps follow the powerful tail fin from the depths with their small, malicious kobalin eyes.

"Fast, Matador, faster!" he urged the animal forward. One of Aelenium's master breeders had given him the name. Griffin guessed that the man had Spanish forebears, and in fact, most inhabitants of the city seemed to have ancestors in the Old World. That too was one of the countless paradoxes of this place: If Aelenium had actually been in existence for centuries, even millennia, then how come its guardians came from Europe and not from the surrounding islands?

The fog had no end. Blindly Griffin clenched Matador's reins, and his thighs gripped the saddle firmly as if his life depended on it. If necessary, he would still be held by the belt, which was indispensable for riding on the hippocampi.

But it was hard for him to have confidence in *anything*. He even distrusted his own perceptions. Wasn't there a soft chattering piercing the fog—whistling, high sounds? Wasn't the splashing and rushing of the waves around him louder and more frantic? And wasn't something gigantic, formless, moving through the darkness in front of him?

The last impression, at least, must have been wrong: He could see nothing, not even a hand before his face, never mind gigantic bodies in the distance. The darkness had certainly been playing tricks on him.

He only now became aware of what trust d'Artois had placed in him, to send him on such a mission alone and in the face of the ever-nearing enemy. But at the same time Griffin began to doubt. Had the captain really *sent* him? In any case, he hadn't verbally given an order, and it could all turn out to be a horrible, lethal misunderstanding. Perhaps he really had only intended to relieve Griffin so that he could think. Maybe he even believed that Griffin had been in bed long since, just as he'd advised him.

The sea horse uttered a whistle, the alarm signal when it scented something unknown.

Griffin scratched the creature's neck with trembling fingers. "What's the—?"

He didn't have a chance to finish his question. Something struck against the horse from underneath, raised him out of the water with tremendous force, and flung him out of its path. The animal's whistling grew louder and broke off for a moment, as he plunged sideways into the waves. The belt cut into Griffin's flesh. A fearsome jolt went through his neck and down through his spinal column. Saltwater streamed into his open mouth, and his hoarse shout went unheard in the waves.

The sea horse was back upright again so quickly that Griffin was hardly aware of the motion. He flew over the waves in a panic, while Griffin tried desperately to figure out what was happening in the darkness. At least his head was no longer underwater, he could breathe freely, and had swallowed hardly any water. The horse had taken control and was carrying him forward as fast as he could go. Griffin had no idea whether he was racing out over the open sea or turning back to Aelenium to the security of his stable. He almost didn't care. The main thing was to get away from here. Out of the fog, somewhere where there was light and he could see what had attacked them.

Something had rammed the sea horse from underneath. Something that was massive enough to have flung the twelve-foot-tall animal through the air like a toy.

Griffin closed his eyes. It made no difference in the dark, but he had the feeling it would help him guide his churning thoughts into orderly pathways. The sea horse was going on his own, anyway.

When he opened his eyes again, they'd almost left the fog behind them. The last arms of mist still held him in their grip, and stars were invisible, as always. But then he saw the open sea lying ahead of him, a network of sparkling wave crowns and vague reflections. Matador had not chosen the way back but had swum to the other side of the fog wall.

Pirate Emperor

The sea horse and his rider escaped the last clouds of fog and emerged into the glittering glory of the Caribbean firmament. They rode over waves in which the stars and the crescent moon shimmered, and through a cool breeze that carried Griffin's fears away with it.

Not that he assumed for a moment that the danger was over. Whatever had attacked them could have followed them. It might still be lurking somewhere, concealed under the waves. But the familiar sight of the night sky and the breadth of the sea reassured him so much that he could think clearly again. It was almost as if he were aboard a ship, on one of those quiet night watches that he used to enjoy so much.

His eyes swept over the ocean and along the dark horizon. There was bound to be only one direction for Jolly and the *Carfax*: southwest, the course that would take her back to the islands or to the mainland.

Matador knew the direction. The sea horses were trained to discern the scents of the larger land masses, even over hundreds of miles. That was one of the countless wonders of Aelenium, its inhabitants, and even its animals. There, the magic that was concentrated in the polliwogs touched every being, just as if the magic veins Count Aristotle had spoken of ran through the middle of the city.

Griffin's eyes had to get used to the light at first. Then he saw the outlines of the sails in the distance, many miles away, gray rectangles that were carrying the *Carfax* forward on a strong breeze.

With a loud cry he urged the sea horse on and steered him

onto the ship's course. Matador was a great many times faster than the sloop, and with some luck he'd have caught up with her in less than half an hour.

Foam sprayed into Griffin's face as the sea horse dashed through the waves. His heart raced. Again and again he looked back over his shoulder. He could hardly make out the fog. Behind them was only a dark stripe that extinguished the sparkle of the water surface and the starry sky, as if someone had wiped away part of the horizon with a cloth. The black wall was several miles high and concealed the towers of Aelenium and the coral cone in its center.

Griffin didn't get far.

The sea in front of him curved up into a mountain, at first almost imperceptibly, like the gentle incline of a hill, then more and more steeply. At the sides of the mound the waters poured down like a waterfall.

Griffin was about to turn the sea horse around, but the animal reacted even faster. Matador swerved to avoid the giant that was breaking through the surface in front of him. But it was too late. The waves seized sea horse and rider, and this time the saddle straps did not hold. Masses of water whirled over Griffin, a wall of salty foam. Then invisible hands pressed him under the surface. Suddenly he was alone, without the sea horse that might have carried him to safety.

Jolly! flashed through his mind in the darkness, and he realized that he was going to die, that if he didn't drown, he was going to be swallowed by this thing, this living mountain of darkness.

The same forces that had pressed him beneath the water now seemed to drag him up. His face broke through the surface of the sea and he gasped for air, but he sucked in water again and now threatened to choke, despite the clear night air. His wet uniform pulled him down, but he kicked his legs so hard that he was able to keep himself afloat. Coughing, he snapped his eyes open, saw no horizon anymore, no sky, again only blackness, but this time as massive as an island that had unexpectedly risen up in front of him.

Yet it was no island. And most certainly the gigantic silhouette in front of the stars betokened no rescue.

A new current seized him, a powerful vortex that pulled him forward with masses of water as if a hole had opened and was swallowing him and the whole Caribbean.

The Maelstrom! he thought.

But no, it was not the Maelstrom.

It was a throat as large as a church door, a stinking, glistening inferno of flesh and heat and rows of bright teeth. Griffin felt the sharp points tearing his uniform as he was whirled across them on his back. Then he was thrown against a soft, warm wall, in new darkness, slid farther, got no more air, and whizzed down through a tunnel, sideways.

It swallowed me! he was just able to think before the certainty of his fate extinguished any further thoughts.

Behind him the gigantic jaws closed, the suction eased. The beast that had swallowed Griffin dove down into the depths of the ocean.

The Ghost in the Barrel

Some legends tell invented stories that are nevertheless true. Others are only lies if those who hear them close their ears to the truth. And some stories—however improbable they appear, however crazy and far-fetched—paint a picture that the reality vastly surpasses in poignancy and truth.

The story of Santiago and his death in the barrel was not freely invented. But within a few months it had grown far beyond a simple rumor, repeated hundreds of times, exaggerated and embellished.

And yet in this case, the reality exceeded all the stories: It was the craziest, most macabre, and out-and-out wildest picture that Soledad had encountered in all her years as the daughter of a pirate emperor.

On the face of it, there was only a wide sandy beach with a large barrel and a pair of boots sticking out of it. But *seen* and *felt*, it was a sight that burned into Soledad's mind so deeply that she'd never forget it.

It wasn't only the image itself that impressed her so deeply. There was more. In the desolation of the island, among the sand dunes, Santiago's ghost was as perceptible as an ocean breeze that comes up and dies down again.

"You feel him too, don't you?" The Ghost Trader's voice broke through the silence that had settled over them since their arrival at the island.

Soledad and Walker nodded at the same time.

"No other human being has ever died on this island before," said the Trader, frowning. "The loneliness must be a thousand times harder for a ghost to bear than for a living person."

Soledad nodded again as if she knew exactly what the Trader was talking about. She could almost taste on her lips the feelings of loneliness and confusion that surrounded the entire island.

The sea horses were moving through the shallow waters at almost a walking pace. They were being extremely careful not to touch the ground with their sensitive tail fins. Finally they stopped, and the three riders had to cover the rest of the distance on foot.

The air over the sand appeared to blur when Soledad reached the beach and turned toward the barrel. Only ten yards separated her from her goal. The Ghost Trader had chosen to remain some distance behind. He sensed that the island was completely under the dead man's control.

Vague forms peeled out of the shimmering air before

Soledad's eyes, images of ships, of battles, and of drinking bouts. But also distorted impressions of ragged children on the beach, of men in uniform, prison cells, laughing and screaming women, fire and gold and blood seeping into the sand. None of it was real, and by the time the Ghost Trader called over to her that these images must be the life experiences of Captain Santiago, Soledad had already come to that idea on her own.

These pictures did not appear in any organized sequence; they overlapped and mixed with each other. Grown-ups suddenly had the faces of children, and the other way around. Clothes changed in the wink of an eye. Ships turned into fortresses into forests into swamps into harbors. All had the feeling of wild dreams in which things seen and imagined were bound into a whole that had strayed far from the path of reason.

And there was death. Over and over again, death.

Flickering figures collapsed lifeless, dying under saber blows, strung up from the yards, in burning shipwrecks, and in hails of bullets. Soledad had seen many men die in her life, in battle, from age, and under the knives of cowardly murderers. But these images surpassed her experience by a great deal. Whether they were deaths Santiago himself had witnessed or the fate that he'd imagined for the mutineers was uncertain. An unsavory mixture of both, probably.

Walker came closer to Soledad and took her right hand. She flinched slightly, but she didn't withdraw her fingers.

"I recognize a few of them," he said, while the visions

around them became more horrific and bloodthirsty with every moment.

"They all look like ghosts themselves," said Soledad, spellbound.

Now the Ghost Trader also came closer. "That's deceptive," he explained, the only one who remained unruffled. "They're only dreams and wishes and recollections from Santiago's confused mind. No reason for you to be afraid of them—as long as they're not following you, at least."

Walker's expression wavered nervously. He grasped Soledad's hand a little more tightly. "Follow? What exactly do you mean by that?"

"If you expose yourself to the images for too long, they might settle into you. Then you take them away from here with you and they follow you for the rest of your life."

Soledad and Walker exchanged a meaningful look. "And how long is *too long*?" asked the princess.

"You only know that when it's too late."

Walker bent toward Soledad's ear. "I knew he was going to say something like that."

She nodded worriedly.

The Trader reached under his robe and pulled forth the silver ring that gave him power over the ghost world. The simply wrought ornament had the diameter of a plate and looked something like what jugglers ordinarily use to perform cheap tricks.

The Trader held the ring horizontal and let the fingertips of his right hand circle over it. As he did so, he closed his eyes, murmured something to himself, and was silent again. His eyes remained closed; he did not move.

"What's he doing?" whispered Walker.

Soledad shrugged her shoulders. "Something terribly powerful."

"Wrong," replied the Trader. "I'm concentrating on the mosquito bite on my left heel, so it will stop itching."

"Oh," said Walker, nodding seriously.

"Mosquito bite?" Soledad repeated.

"I can't catch any ghosts if my foot is itching. I beg you for a little more understanding."

"But of course," said Walker spitefully.

Soledad shook her head, speechless.

"So now," announced the Trader, taking a deep breath, "I shall begin."

"Good idea," the captain muttered.

Again the Trader stroked his fingers over the silver ring. The images from Santiago's crazed mind drew nearer to them and pulled themselves into a cocoon of past and potential future around them. Soledad fought against the impulse to avoid the slashes and blows of the flickering figures, but she was unsuccessful. She closed her eyes and hoped that way to be able to shut out the horrendous images. She focused her mind wholly on the touch of Walker's hand, although she was troubled by conflicting feelings as she did so. Anger at herself, but also reassurance. Shame, because she was so inconsistent, but also . . . affection?

Gracious!

Very shortly she felt that the visions were nevertheless seeping into her. They streamed into her thoughts like water into a leaking hull.

Soledad opened her eyes and realized to her horror that it was no longer Walker holding her hand but a fat fellow. A striped shirt stretched over his potbelly, exposing his navel. He had hair on only one side of his chubby head; the other side was covered by a network of old burn scars like a leather cap. Over his shirt he wore a threadbare coat, with its right arm hanging in tatters. A knife wound in his forehead had stopped bleeding a long time ago, but it was still gaping wide open.

"Santiago," Soledad whispered dazedly.

The fat pirate turned his face toward her and opened his mouth. An indescribable stench of rum and dead fish met her, as if he'd bared the teeth of a wild animal. She tried to pull her hand free and at the same time draw one of her throwing knives with her left hand. But her movements were too slow and strangely irresolute, as if she were sharing the power of her body with someone who kept wanting to do exactly the opposite.

"Soledad . . . little Soledad," said Santiago, tilting his head. Only now did it hit her that he was even more grossly bloated than he had been at their last meeting some years ago. At that time he had, of course, been alive and not stuck headfirst in a rum barrel.

She hoped very much that the yellow-brown fluid dripping over his bulging lips was in fact nothing else but rum.

"You've come to see me," he said. "That's nice of you." At every third or fourth word little bubbles formed at his mouth, then popped a little later. "Do you know what those fellows did to me?"

"They marooned you."

"They mutinied. They deserve to be strung up for that. Drawn and quartered."

"People say you tried to cheat them out of their share."

"Pah! A little mistake in arithmetic, nothing else."

"Sure."

"Drawn and . . ." He stopped, as if he'd forgotten what he was going to say.

"Quartered?" she suggested.

"Quartered," he confirmed with a ghastly grin. "What do you want of me?"

Soledad looked around the island's shore but discovered neither Walker nor the Ghost Trader. The visions had also dissolved into the air. Only the rum barrel was still standing in the same place. But no boots were sticking out of it anymore. Instead, damp footprints led to the living corpse at her side, which continued to clutch her hand. His fingers felt soapy.

She pulled all her courage together. "Do you remember my father?"

"Old Scarab? But of course. A son of a bitch, but one who stood by his word."

"You know what happened to him?" Her voice sounded thick at the memory of her father, especially here, in this strange in-between world.

"Kendrick slit his throat."

"Yes . . . he did that."

"And now you're out to get Kendrick, right? You were already a Satan's brat as a child. Once I tried to buy you from your old man, but he didn't want to give you up, not even for ten barrels of rum."

Silently she sent a prayer of thanks to pirate heaven. "You know something that could help me."

"What have you got in mind?"

"I have to find Kendrick. And I want to get the Antilles captains on my side."

Santiago shook with laughter. "What, you think they give a damn about you? Or about what you have in mind?" With a shake of his head, he let go of Soledad's hand and trotted toward the barrel again. Soledad followed him with heavy, sluggish steps.

"Wait!"

He didn't even turn around. "Why should I?"

"Because . . . because we called you up and you must obey me."

"You?" He laughed again. "Maybe your one-eyed friend . . . yeah, probably him. But you? Dream on about the pirate throne, little Soledad, but leave me my peace."

He was faster than she, in spite of his substantial weight and his sodden limbs. It infuriated her to have to stare at his broad back but not be able to summon him back.

"Peace?" she asked. "You call this peace? Beset by your own memories and nightmares?"

"What do you know, anyway?" he said with a shrug and stomped on.

THE GHOST IN THE BARREL

"Santiago!"

"What?"

"I won't try to fool you. I can't help you. But I need *your* help!"

"Doesn't sound like a good deal." He reached the barrel. The metal-banded edge hit him at his belly. Instead of climbing in, he simply leaned against it with a groan and let himself fall over forward. He sank headfirst into the barrel until only his sun-bleached boots showed.

Soledad felt that the situation was getting away from her. She couldn't just give up.

She placed both hands on the edge of the barrel and looked in. There wasn't much to see: Santiago's broad behind blocked her view.

"Scurvy fellow!" she cursed him.

"Leave me in peace," he grumbled. Coming from the barrel, his voice sounded hollow and subdued. So there couldn't be any rum left in it. Even while dying the old souse had drunk it empty.

Helpless, she looked up from the barrel and the fat man and scanned the beach. The entire island consisted of an extended sandbank with a few palms and bushes growing on it. It might be the unreal atmosphere of this place, but she didn't wonder that Walker and the Ghost Trader hadn't accompanied her into the between-world. Anyhow, this had been *her* idea and it was her mission alone.

"Are you finally gone?" came from the barrel.

"I have no intention of being gone."

"You're a damned plague, little Soledad. You hear me? A plague!"

"Damn it, Santiago, you drank up a whole barrel."

"You think I didn't notice that?"

"A *whole* barrel, for God's sake!"

"Bring me another and maybe I'll help you." Now he sounded sulky, like a little boy who wanted a second piece of birthday cake.

She kicked the barrel angrily. "That'll be the day!"

"Ow!" he wailed. "That was loud!"

"Oh, really?" She kicked it again. And a third time.

"Ow-ow-ow," whimpered the ghost.

"Come out of there again, right now!"

"Ow-ow-ow."

Still another kick. And another. Now an especially hard one.

The captain's wailing from inside the barrel sounded spooky. Soledad was gradually realizing that there were far more reasons to pity ghosts than to fear them.

"All riiiight," he howled, "I'll be right there."

Somehow he succeeded, with much kicking and cursing, in crawling backward out of the barrel, which was by no means a pretty sight. His shirt rode up, then also his sash, and finally Soledad tactfully turned her eyes away until he stood panting beside her and had put his clothing to rights.

"Humiliating," he grumbled. "And that in front of a lady."

"Nice of you to call me that," she said, giving him a captivating smile.

"Oh, no," he cried hastily, raising both hands defensively.

"No, no, no . . . that's not going to work. That's nothing for me anymore. I mean, just look at me."

Soledad abandoned her seductive arts and placed her hands on her hips resolutely. "I want nothing but information from you, Santiago."

He scratched his chin. Beard stubble and tiny shreds of skin sprinkled down onto the sand. "Well, then," he said grumpily, "if you'll disappear again, for good."

"That's a deal!" she cried with delight.

He began to clean the fingernails of his right hand with those of his left. One broke off. "So?"

"The secret meeting of the Antilles captains. Where is it taking place?"

"That's all?" He raised a doubting eyebrow.

"That's all," she confirmed.

"After that you'll finally get out of here?"

"For sure."

"And promise never to kick my barrel again?"

"Agreed," she said, raising one hand to swear it.

"Good, good." He cleared his throat and coughed up a little gush of rum. "Saint Celestine," he said. "That's where they're meeting."

Her tension vanished in an instant. "Saint Celestine! That isn't far from here!"

"But you understand that Tyrone is going to turn up there? The cannibal king?"

"Do you know him?"

He nodded. "Be careful of him."

"Yes. I will."

He expelled a gurgling sigh. "They should all just leave me in peace out here."

"Don't worry. None of them dares to come to your island. There are rumors, you know. About a curse."

He perked up. "A curse?"

"An especially nasty, gruesome one."

"*My* curse, by any chance?"

"But of course."

He gurgled again, and for the first time he looked happy. "They're saying that about me? That I cursed the whole filthy lot?"

"That's what I'm telling you!"

"By Henry's red beard, damme!"

"You're famous, Santiago. And feared."

"You don't say!"

"Nice that it pleases you."

He grinned with self-satisfaction for a moment and then turned to his barrel again. "Good luck, little Soledad."

"You too, Santiago."

He let himself thump into the barrel again and waved farewell to her with his left foot.

She closed her eyes, thought about Walker, and at the same moment felt his hand on hers.

I know it, she thought proudly and repeated it once more aloud: "I know it."

"Yes," said the Ghost Trader, when she opened her eyes again. "You reek quite horribly of rum."

Alone at Sea

Jolly wiped the sweat out of her eyes. She was dog tired. Even the excitement at having fled Aelenium wouldn't keep her on her feet much longer. She could hardly feel her hands on the grips of the wheel, and her knees felt as flabby as octopus arms.

She'd now been standing at the wheel of the *Carfax* for one day and two nights. Occasionally she'd tied it with a rope and slept for an hour, eaten and drunk something now and then. But that didn't change the fact that she was completely exhausted, and her stomach was growling so loudly that it was audible even over the breaking of the waves against the bow.

On a calm sea she could have left the wheel unsupervised. But not on this one. A sharp wind was blowing across the Atlantic from the east, the waves formed valleys and hills six feet high. Spume dashed against the hull and sprayed over the deck. It wasn't a real storm, nothing that should cause concern in an experienced steersman. And Jolly understood navigation and cartography, too; she knew how to steer a ship and what dangers wind speeds like this brought with them. But what she lacked was pure physical strength. The wheel was as high as she was, and she had to keep her arms outspread to hold it. Each time the *Carfax* plunged into a wave trough, or an especially furious breaker crashed against the prow, it felt as if her arms were dislocated. A grown man might not make much of the strain. But Jolly was too small and, as she had to acknowledge to herself as she ground her teeth, not strong enough for this task. Let alone for a day and a half.

She'd tried to give the unmanageable wheel to one of the ghosts. But the vaporous beings weren't suitable for this duty: Countless sailors had lost their lives aboard the *Carfax*, certainly, but not a single one of them had been a steersman. The ghosts stood there helplessly, without any of the sensitivity that was necessary to sail a sloop. A steersman must assess each vibration of the hull, each thrust against the bow, and be able to respond to it. With the ghosts, on the other hand, it was as if you tried to get a wooden doll to ride a stallion: You might tie the doll into the saddle ever so firmly, yet somehow the horse would shake it off or smash it against a post.

If the weather didn't change soon, Jolly's situation was hopeless. She would hold out a while longer, three hours, maybe four. But then she'd finally have to admit she was beaten. The wooden colossus under her was stronger than she was, and she had vastly overestimated herself when she'd assumed she could sail it, all alone, with only the help of the ghosts, to the mouth of the Orinoco.

The sun had come up some time ago, but that didn't make Jolly's situation any more hopeful.

During the night hours Jolly had asked herself the same tormenting questions over and over: Why the devil had she gone off alone? Why hadn't she taken Griffin with her? She hadn't seen him again since that evening two days before. But all the more painfully, she was becoming aware of how very much he meant to her. And now she'd left him behind in Aelenium without a word. Without saying good-bye, without explanation. Had she actually believed she had to carry out her search for Bannon alone? Or had she simply been too proud?

She missed Griffin more than she could have thought possible. Missed his gibes, in which there was usually some truth, his laugh, and the concern he felt for her. She thought of the tattooing on her skin and of what he'd said before Munk appeared in the doorway. If she closed her eyes, she could feel how his fingers had moved over the image on her back, as if his touch was caught within the pattern and was wandering gently between the lines of the coral.

Jolly pulled herself together and forced herself to concentrate on the *Carfax* and the sea in front of her. Gray clouds covered the sky, though occasionally sunbeams broke through the mist and shone over the sea like glowing pillars. The Atlantic was boiling all the way to the horizon in shades of treacherous beauty: color blocks of gray, silver, and ice blue lay sharply delineated next to each other and augured uncertain wind conditions and changeable seas.

Jolly and the wheel seemed to have become fused in all the hours together as they held each other mutually upright. More and more often she felt her vision darken and her thoughts stray in a way she knew only from the minutes shortly before falling asleep: moments in which reality and imagination mixed with each other and both became plausible at once. She thought she was watching as the sea around her turned black, with foam crowns of tiny creatures. But her mind was no longer alert enough to realize that she had seen this image once before, at the end of a bridge, in the gulf between the worlds.

The sun must really have risen higher, but for some unexplained reason it was darker. The glowing pillars of light that had been supporting the clouded sky a while back grew thinner and finally disappeared altogether. All at once darkness came down on the *Carfax*. In the bright light of morning it became night again.

The wind was no stronger, but now the hull creaked, as if there were something in the pitch-black, foaming water that was compressing it on all sides. Jolly's head sagged forward, but her fingers were so firmly curled around the grips of the wheel that she remained standing upright. Her black hair fell over her forehead and tickled the tip of her nose. She started up, was suddenly wide awake, but the darkness remained, and the waves were no longer water but something that possessed a life of its own. The foam that sprayed over the railing on both sides of the ship did not seep into the boards but formed on deck into hordes of iridescent crabs, as small as water fleas, but there were thousands and more thousands and they kept forming ever new designs: stars, swelling spots, and netlike, pulsing patterns.

The Mare Tenebrosum has come to me, she thought with surprising matter-of-factness, and she repeated the thought to herself until it sounded quite logical, quite self-evident: *It has come to me.*

The same thing had happened before, and each time, the Mare Tenebrosum had swallowed the ships that had met it. But Jolly wasn't fazed. Not anymore. The Mare Tenebrosum had come because it wanted something from her. She doubted that it had the power to kill her at this moment. Others who were not familiar with the sight of the Mare might fall into panic in this alien, hard-to-comprehend unreality and cause their ships to sink. But Jolly was not seeing this night sea for the first time, and though it terrified her to the marrow of her bones, it did not completely rattle her either.

And again there was the same phenomenon as on Agostini's bridge: The water's surface appeared to extend to infinity, without losing any sharpness. It wasn't the horizon that formed the edge of it, only Jolly's sight. At last she had to turn her eyes away in order not to lose herself completely in this endlessness.

"What do you want from me?" she cried out into the tumultuous sea.

No one gave her an answer. What had she even expected?

A bodiless voice that spoke to her? A sea monster that raised its hideous head and talked with her?

Only blackness. Only the endless ocean.

"Say what you want or leave me in peace!" she cried, holding the wheel as tightly as if it were her last hold on reality.

To the larboard there was something going on in the distance. She couldn't say how far away the place was, for all estimates were invalid in the superclarity of her surroundings. It might be ten miles or it might be a hundred.

The oily waters of the Mare Tenebrosum then erupted into frantic motion, as if the millions upon millions of black foam crabs on the wave crests were creating a particular form. The seething and boiling turned into something that resembled human features, several miles long and just as wide, spread out across the ocean.

It was her own face.

She wasn't certain how she recognized it, for she was looking from a strange angle over chin and lips, the towering mountain of the tip of the nose, along the cheekbones to the eyebrows and the forehead. The features could have been those of any human. But Jolly was sure: The Mare Tenebrosum was confronting her with her own image, formed from the waters of the primeval ocean.

The hills of lips moved, as if they wanted to speak, but there was only the rushing of the sea and the flapping of the sails to be heard. Single flashes flared through the darkness, blue-white tongues of fire flickered in the rigging.

"What do you want?" screamed Jolly into the distance again.

The gigantic mouth opened and closed faster and faster before it exploded in an eruption of black water. A house-high tidal wave rolled toward the *Carfax*, but it subsided before it reached the ship. The distance must be much greater than Jolly had assumed—and the face inconceivably bigger. Where it had just been, a whirlpool was forming, first slowly, almost lazily, then faster and faster, until it became a rotating chasm that quickly spread in all directions.

The gigantic vortex soon had a diameter of many miles. Now it even seemed to suck the lightning from heaven, for more and more branching arms of light flashed down into the boiling abyss.

The *Carfax*, however, lay untouched in the water, shaking, creaking, and groaning, to be sure, but without being drawn into the devilish suction. That was the last sign. Now Jolly was certain that the only danger here threatened her understanding, not her body—and that she could put an end to all this with her own power. She must only want to, she must believe in it.

"That's enough," she whispered and then cried resolutely into the darkness: *"That's enough!"*

The vision faded, drew into a dark nucleus in the middle of the abyss for a moment, and then tore into thousands of shreds, which vanished like fog patches in the sunshine. Light flowed at Jolly from all directions, striking her like a barrage of fire. She cried out, in fear but also in relief, and then she slowly slid to the deck.

The last thing she was aware of was a dog nose bent over her, the face of a pit bull. Then a voice.

"Oh my God," wailed the Hexhermetic Shipworm, but if he invented some ghastly rhyme about it, she wasn't hearing him anymore.

"If Walker were here, he'd wring your neck," said Buenaventure as he looked around at her.

Jolly crouched in front of the railing on the bridge, only three feet from the wheel that the pit bull man was holding effortlessly on course with his hairy hands. The Hexhermetic Shipworm was peeking out of Buenaventure's knapsack, which leaned beside her against the balustrade. He was surprisingly quiet. Since she'd opened her eyes again, he'd said hardly two sentences, and those were neither rhymed nor overwhelmingly caustic.

"You were aboard the whole time?" she asked in bewilderment.

"No," Buenaventure teased, pulling his jowls into a grin. "I'm good at backstroke, you know?"

"I can't believe it." She shook her head. "You were below deck the entire time while I was up here. . . ." Again a shake of her head.

"Well, we had a few problems down there, too. The shipworm ate one of the Spanish throne chairs. And the three-eyed Madonna. Walker won't be exactly thrilled, but I couldn't see the little fellow starve."

"And what about me?"

"You've learned your lesson, I hope."

"I almost died out here."

"I doubt that. We kept an eye on you all the time. Actually, you didn't do your job badly. Until yesterday, that is."

Jolly hadn't told the two of them anything about her visitation by the Mare Tenebrosum, less from fear of calling up the vision again than from inability to describe the images.

"Until yesterday? How long have I been asleep, then?"

"A day and a night."

She looked up at the sun in disbelief.

"Did you find the food beside your cabin?"

"If I hadn't, I'd probably have eaten the worm already." She sent the little fellow a crooked smile, but he repaid it with only a cool snort. Only a few days before, a remark like that would have goaded him into a minutes-long tirade of scolding. But now he was quiet.

"What's wrong with you?" she asked him.

"Humpf," said the worm.

She raised an eyebrow. "Humpf?"

"He's sworn to silence," said Buenaventure. "He swore it when I got him out of a . . . well, an uncomfortable situation. Right, worm?" He laughed softly.

"Humpf."

"What kind of an uncomfortable situation?" Jolly asked.

Buenaventure laughed even louder and shook his head.

"The thanks for my poetic art," said the worm morosely, but he didn't give any further explanation.

"You know," said Buenaventure, "that the good burghers of Aelenium were crazy about our friend here."

Jolly nodded. "The Merlin of Marvelous Meters," she reminded him, grinning.

"Wonderworm," growled the worm. "Puh!"

"So," she said, "what happened?"

"They gave him a house in the Poets' Quarter. And then they—"

"What's a worm supposed to do with a house?" the worm interrupted him. "If it had at least been made out of wood. But no—coral. Everything out of coral. Yeech!"

"They brought him wood. To eat."

"Sawdust," corrected the worm. "Lumpy, damp sawdust!"

"For that he was supposed to give a taste of his . . . hm, lyrical talents every day at sunup and sundown."

"So?" Jolly asked. "On Tortuga you used to give a public poem every day. One more or less shouldn't be a problem for the Maestro Poeticus, should it?"

The worm sank a handsbreadth deeper into the knapsack. "You're just making fun of me!"

"The problem," said Buenaventure, "was not the insufficient wealth of invention of our highly prized bard, but his ravenous appetite."

"Sawdust!" cried the worm once again, scornfully. "*Damp* sawdust!"

"He used the time between his poetic presentations to eat up half a dozen street barricades that the inhabitants of Aelenium had erected against the enemy. He ate two weeks of work, mind you. You can imagine that he can't let himself be seen in Aelenium for the time being."

"That means we aren't sailing back?" Jolly asked hopefully.

"Yes," replied Buenaventure. "I can understand why you

couldn't take the city anymore. It hit me the same way—and after all, they don't want to send me down to the Crustal Breach."

"I didn't take off because I was afraid," she said. "I mean, I *am* afraid, of course. But I also swore to find Bannon."

Buenaventure nodded without looking around. "It's your decision."

"Does that mean you'll help me?"

"I have nothing better to do right now, the way it looks. Besides, I promised Walker to keep an eye on you." He laughed his odd dog's laugh. "Oh, well, would have done it anyway. Without the promise, I mean."

She leaped up, although it made her so dizzy that she almost fell over again, and embraced the pit bull man from behind. It felt as though she'd put her arms around the trunk of a jungle tree, he was so massive.

"Thanks," she whispered.

By afternoon Jolly was already feeling so well that she could climb up to the crow's nest. She sent the ghost who had been doing lookout there back to the deck. He whisked down as shreds of fog and took on the vague form of a human only when he got to the deck.

Jolly let the wind blow around her nose. Her black hair danced on the powerful breeze like the pirate flag for which she was named. From up here the waves looked small and harmless, and although the ship was rocking considerably, the sea had become quieter. Looking like a scratched mirror, it stretched endlessly in all directions, glinting in the sunlight. There was no land in sight anywhere. The *Carfax* would probably be under way for three or four more days before the forested jungles of the Orinoco delta appeared on the horizon.

Jolly held on to the tip of the mast with one hand. Over her the English flag waved in the wind—the usual deception ploy. The skull and crossbones, the symbol of the freebooters, would be raised only for attacks or pirates' meetings.

She kept her knees loose, in order to match the rocking of the ship. That wasn't hard for her, since her legs still felt a little wobbly. The meeting with the Mare Tenebrosum had taken more out of her than she wanted to admit to herself. It annoyed her that she was so vulnerable, susceptible to the visitations of her enemies. On the other hand, at this moment, not even that could ruin her mood. She was finally on the way to Bannon. She had never thought about whether he'd actually been a sort of father to her—she didn't even know how it felt to have a father. He was just Bannon, the captain of her crew and one of the smartest buccaneers on the Caribbean Sea. He'd taught her everything she knew— about the sea, about people and the art of privateering. She loved him as much as other children loved their parents, that was certain.

And she missed him.

Carefully she pulled the little box with the body of the dead spider out of her pocket, gazed at it one last time, and let the cover snap shut. The hideous cadaver had accompanied her for a long time, from the sinking of the *Skinny*

Maddy, through the flaming hell in the harbor of New Providence, through Tortuga to Aelenium, and now even out of it again.

The hairy body had fulfilled its purpose: It had brought her on the trail to Orinoco. And she'd climbed up to the crow's nest to fling the box into the sea from here—a kind of burial, and at the same time a further turning point in her life. Until a few days ago, her fate had unfolded entirely according to the plan of the Ghost Trader. Now, however, she'd taken it into her own hands, and it was time to separate herself from this remnant of her past as well.

She stretched out her arm to throw, when she felt something settle itself on her left shoulder. Claws poked into her skin. There was suddenly a mighty fluttering beside her ear.

Startled, she whirled around, letting the box drop. It landed at her feet in the crow's nest. She struck out with a cry. She just managed to hold back the blow when she recognized what had clawed at her arm.

"Moe!" she exclaimed in surprise.

The Ghost Trader's black parrot ran along her arm with stiltlike bird steps until he was in an upright position again. His blood red eyes sought her gaze as if he were trying to deliver a piece of news with his look.

"Is Hugh here too?" She searched around and located the second bird on the foremast. He was also staring at her, motionless.

She remembered having seen the two of them on the pier at Aelenium. They'd flown over the ship during her quarrel with Munk and sat on one of the yards. After that, however, she'd completely forgotten the parrots. Had they been aboard for the whole voyage? Then she really would have to have noticed them. On the other hand, she'd been so busy piloting the ship, maybe she'd overlooked the birds.

With a flap of his wings, Moe moved onto her shoulder. It irritated her that she couldn't look at him directly anymore, and she half expected him to whisper something in her ear. But the parrot was silent and sat there for a moment. Then he took off, fluttered toward the starboard, flew a few dozen yards out over the sea, and began to circle there.

Jolly followed his flight, frowning, before she grasped what he was trying to tell her. She looked at the water's surface beneath Moe.

There was something in the waves, a dark outline. An icy shudder ran down her back. Everyone knew that the sea around the coral city must be crawling with kobalins and other creatures of the Maelstrom. They might not show themselves, but they were there: scouts and observers, a vanguard of the fighting power that the Maelstrom would very soon send into the field against Aelenium.

No wonder that one of those creatures had followed the *Carfax*. But why hadn't it attacked them yet?

She still couldn't recognize any clear outline. It could be a whole swarm of kobalins or a single mighty creature. But one thing amazed her: Whatever it was, it didn't come any nearer. Instead it remained on a course parallel to the *Carfax*, as if it wanted to observe it, investigate it, but not attack. Or was it waiting for a suitable moment? Hardly likely, for there'd been more than enough of those.

Moe flew a last loop, then returned to the ship and landed next to Hugh on the foremast. The two mysterious birds looked over at her with red and yellow eyes.

Jolly picked up the little box from the floor, stuck it back into her vest pocket, and speedily climbed down the shrouds to the deck. Moments later she was standing beside Buenaventure and telling him of the parrots' discovery.

The pit bull man asked her to take over the wheel for a moment, hurried to the railing, and stared grimly in the direction Jolly had told him. But from down here the outline wasn't discernible—the light reflections on the waves and the flat angle of sight made it invisible.

"There's something there," Jolly asserted.

Buenaventure nodded. His dog face did not betray how concerned he really was, but the wrinkles in his forehead meant nothing good.

"We can place it under fire," suggested the Hexhermetic Shipworm. "A few shots in the ribs, and *voom!* we're rid of the thing. Very simple."

"Very simple?" repeated Buenaventure. "Perhaps in the eyes of a half-blind worm."

"What, pray, is *that* supposed to mean?"

Jolly leaped in before the pit bull man. "That we can't afford to fight something that so far hasn't acted hostile toward us."

Buenaventure gave her an approving nod. "Even if it was

a swarm of kobalins, which, to be honest, I don't believe it is, we should beware of attacking. As long as he doesn't come any closer, he's of no further concern to us."

"A mob of kobalins doesn't concern you?" The worm's voice was shrill. "By my mother's chisel tooth and the six hundred legs of her tattered tribe, you aren't really serious!"

The pit bull man looked out at the place in the sea once more, then silently took over the wheel again.

Jolly climbed back up to the crow's nest and was glad to be able to leave the shipworm's ranting behind her. Buenaventure was right. It was senseless to risk a battle now.

The peculiar silhouette was still beside the *Carfax*, not a hundred paces away. She blinked in an effort to see the thing more clearly, but even that didn't help.

Hugh and Moe fluttered over to her and landed on the yards to the right and left of the lookout. Almost imperceptibly they followed Jolly's eyes. Only now did she realize that Buenaventure wasn't the only one who'd been assigned to her.

The parrots were also here to look after her—or to keep an eye on her.

The Man in the Whale

Griffin spewed out a high arc of seawater, which tasted like cod-liver oil with a note of rotting fish and a good pinch of salt. He gagged and spit until his throat and stomach hurt, and even then he still wished he could exchange his tongue for a new one, so horrible was the taste that had settled on it.

He was crouching, bent forward, in the midst of a confusion of split and shattered planks, black nets of seaweed, and a great deal of indescribable stuff that might be the wreckage of ships but also the remains of living creatures. A trace of light lay around a tunnel of semicircular arcs quite near him—either the ribs of an enormous fish or the boards of a destroyed ship's hull. He felt no great need to find out which of the two possibilities was correct.

On the other hand, what *was* of burning interest to him was the answer to the question of why he was still alive. And where the beam of light in the stomach of a sea monster was coming from.

Unhappily, he wouldn't stay alive long enough to solve this riddle. The stinking broth that was lapping at his legs was presumably a mixture of his vomit and the stomach juices of this monster. The thought made him retch again, but there was nothing left for him to bring up.

He pulled himself up and tried to wipe the slime and muck from his uniform, but when he noticed that his hands were only patting around helplessly on his clothing, he let it stay.

Now, for the first time, despair overwhelmed him. It hit him late and therefore that much harder, and it pressed him to his knees. He buried his face in his hands and closed his eyes for a while in hopes of mastering this nightmare.

A jolt made the surroundings tremble—an undulating tremor that began on one side of the cavelike space, rolled toward Griffin, almost swept him off his feet, and then continued on away from him, flinging up bones, ribs, and scraps of wood, and finally subsiding again. When the ground under him had steadied, Griffin listened tensely in the silence. There was a steady rushing, like the roaring of a waterfall behind three-foot-thick walls. And something else, a rhythmic thumping, deep and far away: the beat of a gigantic heart.

Griffin supported himself on one of the tall arcs and took a deep breath. It stank horribly, as if someone in a fishing harbor had laid out the guts of a whole week's catch to dry. The air was humid and so close that it settled itself on his larynx like an oily film. He cleared his throat, coughed, and spit, but nothing helped.

The giant heart kept on beating in the distance.

Griffin's hand felt along the rounded arc. Too smooth for the plank of a ship. It was actually a bone, the arching rib of some gigantic animal that had been stranded down here some unknowable time ago.

He moved forward slowly. In the vague half light that filled the cavity, he had trouble seeing where to put his feet. He saw outlines, black silhouettes of parts of wrecks, and mountains of ribs. Now and then he stumbled on human skeletons. Nothing about them betrayed how these poor devils had lost their lives. Had they drowned? Or had someone down here slain them?

He picked up a metal rod that was sticking out of a knot of half-rotted wood, weighed it in his hand, and decided that it would make a passable weapon if necessary. His saber had vanished; maybe he'd lost it in the fall into the mouth. He also discovered no trace of Matador and earnestly hoped that he'd escaped the suction of the gigantic mouth. The sea horse would find his way back to Aelenium without his rider.

How long had he been unconscious? A few hours? Even days? Since his stomach was growling, his arrival down here had presumably been quite a while ago. Besides, his skin was all soft and wrinkled in the places that had been lying in the water and digestive juices. He found it quite disgusting and hoped it would soon get back to normal.

Pirate Emperor

Not that it mattered, if he was going to be digested in a short time anyway.

And he simply could not imagine what kind of a gigantic creature might have swallowed him.

The pictures of the Mare Tenebrosum assembled themselves before his eyes, movements in oily water, the murmurings of huge bodies under the surface. Was this thing here one of those creatures? Good heavens! Was he even in his own world still?

Despair overwhelmed him again, but this time he was armed against it. He clamped his teeth together and clenched the fingers of his left hand into a fist so hard that it hurt. That distracted him for a short time, and when the pain died away, panic and resignation went with it. A trick he'd learned from an old seadog in Haiti.

The iron bar in his hand felt slippery and pretty well rusted, but its weight provided him with a touch of confidence. If there were something here that could be dangerous to him, he'd defend himself.

But what could he do against the digestive juices? When it began raining acid and a wave of poison whirled him deeper into some sort of intestine?

"Good day," said someone beside him suddenly.

Griffin jumped back, stood astride a spot between debris and fish cadavers, and swung the bar in a semicircle before him like a sword.

"Uh," said the voice, and there was a clatter as its owner stumbled backward to the ground. Then the light went out. Darkness clutched at Griffin from all sides.

THE MAN IN THE WHALE

"That was . . . not nice," said the voice, with a groan. Griffin heard the man patting his hands around in the wetness.

"Who are you?"

"Ebenezer Arkwright. At your service."

"My . . . service?"

"That's what people say in my calling, young man. And a little more courtesy would likewise do you very well." To judge from the sounds, the man had picked himself up and was brushing off his clothes.

"What is your . . . calling, then?" Griffin asked.

The man cleared his throat. "The hospitality trade," he declared formally, taking a tentative step forward.

"Don't come any closer to me!"

"Do I perhaps look as if I wanted to do anything to you?"

"It's dark, I can't see anything at all."

"Ah, the dark . . . how careless of me. When one has been here long enough, one's eyes get used to it and one sees almost as well as in brightest daylight." There was a rustle as he pulled something out from under his coat. "Wait . . . now." The sound of steel on flint, then a flame. "So. Is it better now?"

The flame leaped from tinder to a candlewick. The yellowish glow drove most of the shadows from the man's face, but deepened some others. He had full, round features and big, chubby cheeks. His eyes were very bright, either blue or of a catlike green, and stood in remarkable contrast to his plump appearance. His lips were narrow and scarcely distinguishable from the folds of his multiple double chins.

Whatever Ebenezer Arkwright was doing down here, at least he didn't suffer from hunger.

Griffin's stomach growled again, but he tried to ignore it.

"A meal would certainly do you good, boy," said the man, who hadn't missed the sound. "I have a few new recipes to choose from in there."

Griffin recoiled. He could already see himself landing in the cooking pot of some kind of madman—before it became clear to him that Ebenezer meant it completely seriously. He was in fact inviting him to a meal.

"Fish recipes, I'm afraid." Ebenezer smiled apologetically. "But I think you like seafood, don't you? I might have a very tender shark fin in a piquant marinade to offer. Or squid, grilled, not fried in fat, with an outstanding—"

"Wait." Griffin silenced him with a wave of his hand. "I'm sorry I struck at you just now, but—

"You didn't hit me. I stumbled, that's all. One so rarely meets anyone alive down here, you know? That's one of the reasons I hardly ever come out. Entirely aside from this unpleasant smell." He laughed merrily. "You gave me quite a fright before."

Griffin shook his head. Countless drops of water sprayed from his braids in all directions. "I . . . don't understand that. Where are we?"

"In a whale, of course."

"Of course."

"Don't tell me you didn't know that?"

"I was swallowed . . . by something. But a whale?" Said

aloud, it sounded a thousand times more incredible. "I thought I . . . oh, I don't even know. Maybe I'm just imagining all this."

"Most certainly not. And if you'll permit me, my marinade according to a Breton cloister recipe will definitely convince you."

"So we really are inside a whale?"

"Certainly."

"But no ordinary whale has—"

"I didn't say it was an ordinary whale. On the contrary."

"What, then? Something out of the Mare Tenebrosum?"

One of Ebenezer's eyebrows twitched higher. "Certainly not. But I might have guessed you'd know of that. You appear to be an unusual young fellow, or you would not have arrived in this place unhurt."

"You know the Mare Tenebrosum?"

"Not from my own experience. But I know the stories. I know a great deal about the islands and the mainland. I even wrote a book about it."

"About the Mare Tenebrosum?"

Ebenezer waved his hand. "About the coastal regions of the Caribbean. As a young monk I was a member of a small mission station. I was the first to collect data and facts about the animal and plant world. I was almost finished with my work when the provision ship on which I was visiting one of the islands encountered a storm and went down." He expelled a deep sigh. "God knows what became of my manuscript. But that was long ago, thirty years or more."

Griffin's eyes widened in disbelief. "You've been here that long?"

Ebenezer nodded. "He swallowed me at that time. I survived and . . . well, and discovered something."

"Didn't happen to be a way to get out of here, did it?"

"Oh, *that*! Certainly I know a way, but that wasn't what I meant."

"You know how to get out of this thing—I mean, how it spits a person out again?"

The fat man laughed. "Very possibly. But first you'll try my marinade."

Griffin looked at the unappetizing environment. He had a murderous hunger, but he doubted that he'd be able to get anything down here. And nothing at all that smelled of fish. Or even tasted like it.

"Come with me." Ebenezer began moving. He pulled up his cloak, which Griffin now recognized as something like a monk's habit, only more colorful. Carefully he stepped over rubbish and ribs. "I'd like to show you something."

Griffin was about to resist, but then he changed his mind and followed the strange bird. The candle illuminated only a narrow circle, leaving the walls of the stomach cavity—if indeed that's what it was—mostly in the dark.

"What do you do down here?" Griffin asked. "Besides cook, I mean." But before Ebenezer could answer him, Griffin stopped, rooted. Something had occurred to him. "Wait . . . that's *you*, isn't it?"

"Who do you mean?"

THE MAN IN THE WHALE

"The man in the whale!"

"Well, yes, I am a man, and this is definitely a whale."

"You're known all over the Caribbean. I've heard the stories as long as I can remember. Everyone is afraid of you. It's said you have the whale ram ships, and then he eats the seamen, and . . . and . . ." Griffin's voice failed, and now he raised the rod to the level of his torso, ready to strike.

But Ebenezer's voice didn't sound the least bit angry. Quite the contrary. "They say something like that about me?" he asked sadly. "About me?"

"On every ship."

The man had stopped and now turned to Griffin in the candlelight. "That's just terrible."

"Is it true, then?"

"Of course not! I have never yet . . . that is, never really . . ." He fell silent, thought for a moment, then nodded slowly. "There was once this whaler, about—God, that was so long ago—about twenty years ago. He wanted to harpoon our friend here, and . . . oh, well, I couldn't allow that. But he would have rammed the ship anyway, even without me. Whales are very smart, you should know, and this one is smarter than all the others. Even if he probably doesn't look that way from the inside."

"The whaler went down?"

"With every man."

"And that was the only time?"

"But definitely."

"Then there must have been survivors," said Griffin. "One of them saw you."

Again Ebenezer nodded. "I was standing outside, in the mouth, because I thought I could convince those men to leave us in peace."

"Someone must have survived and told others of it. That must be how the stories got started. Everyone has added something to it, and so you've become the bloodthirsty man in the whale."

"Bloodthirsty! Good heavens!" Ebenezer put a hand to his temple in shock. "But I want nothing except—But wait, you will see it right now."

Griffin wasn't completely convinced that he could trust this extraordinary stranger. On the other hand, Ebenezer knew a way to the outside. And Griffin had to have something to eat, too, right away, no matter how bad it smelled.

The monk climbed up a hill of all kinds of debris and rubbish. He'd built makeshift steps of boards so that their feet didn't sink into the sludge.

At the top of the hill was a door.

It was of massive oaken planks, mounted with metal that gleamed in the candlelight. That really should have rusted in the damp, salty air, but Ebenezer appeared to polish it regularly, the hardware shone so. The door was fixed in a frame that was anchored to the top of the hill with slanting supports. Griffin guessed that more stakes led deep into the interior of the rubbish hill, so that the frame would stand even if the whale was at a steep angle while diving or surfacing.

They approached the door from the side, and so Griffin saw that it led nowhere. If you went through it, you'd come out on the other side but still be standing on the hill. He was growing more and more doubtful about the condition of his amazing host's mind with every passing second.

Ebenezer reached the door and waited until Griffin had come up to him. Then he turned the heavy knob and pushed the door open. Flickering firelight greeted them. Suddenly the smell of grilling fish hung in the air.

Behind the door lay a room. Not the other side of the horrible rubble and bone hill, but a real room. With wood-paneled walls, an open fire, and cozily gleaming wooden flooring. And at the opposite wall there was something that might have been a bar.

"Welcome to Ebenezer's floating tavern," the monk announced proudly.

Griffin blinked. Then he stepped outside the door and walked around it. It was open on the other side too, and when he looked through the frame he saw Ebenezer standing there and smiling.

"It only works from one side," said the monk.

Griffin turned back to the starting point of his round and looked again into the room behind the door.

"Walk in," said Ebenezer, walking in.

Griffin scraped the last bits from the plate with knife and fork. He'd just demolished his second portion.

"That was good," he said, licking his lips.

"Nothing like practice."

"I thought you were a monk."

"The good Lord does not fill one's stomach by Himself. Even monks must eat. And someone has to cook for them."

Griffin cast a regretful look at his plate, but it was empty. "So then, were you the cook at the mission station?"

"Cook, scientist, illustrator. One learns such a great deal when one is suddenly stranded in the wilderness."

"And you never wanted to go back there?"

"In the beginning, certainly. But then I said to myself that it was a sign from the Lord to allow me to survive in this place. After all, I'm not the first brother in faith who has met this monster."

"No?"

"The Old Testament also told of it. There was a man by the name of Jonah, to whom God had given a highly unpleasant task. But Jonah decided to run away instead and fled to the sea with a ship. However, God followed him with storms and thunder and lightning. When the sailors realized that Jonah was to blame for the bad weather, they threw him overboard on the spot. But before he could drown, Jonah was swallowed by a gigantic fish, who threw him up three days and three nights later, safe on a shore."

"And you think that was this whale?"

"Very possibly. There are still more stories about him. Have you ever heard of the Irish monks who sailed the sea in ancient times? The best known of them was the monk Brendan, who encountered him during a seven-year search for the land of the saints. His story was written down at that time, under the title *Navigatio Sancti Brendani Abbatis*. In any case, in the sixth century after Christ, this Brendan met a mighty fish, bigger than an island, and he gave him the name of Jasconius. Brendan and the other monks even celebrated a holy Mass on his back, it's said." Ebenezer scratched his head and smiled a little apologetically. "It's a fact that there are others like us. And in some ways I've become accustomed to my situation. This whale is also a land of sheer milk and honey. You cannot imagine what all he swallows. Especially when we're in the vicinity of a trade route. Day after day entire cargoes go overboard, ships sink, and so forth. A quantity of the stuff that goes missing lands here with me sometime. Meanwhile, Jasconius has developed a good feeling for it."

Griffin shook his head. He could comprehend nothing of all this. "And the door? This room?" He waved a hand at the room. "Are we now in the stomach of this whale or . . . or somewhere else?"

Ebenezer's eyes followed Griffin's gesture through the room. The wooden paneling, the fire in the fireplace, even a handful of paintings seemed to be appropriate to the country house of a European nobleman. Anyway, it didn't look like a piece of stomach.

"To be honest, I can't give you any correct answer about that," said Ebenezer, with a shrug.

"Have you tried to look behind the paneling?"

Ebenezer nodded. "Stone."

"A wall?"

"Quite right."

"But that's utterly crazy!"

Pirate Emperor

"One gets used to it." Ebenezer waved a hand. "In the beginning it's certainly a little strange, but after a while . . . And you know: Don't look a gift horse in the mouth. And it has its advantages. I'm not sure if I could have held out for very long in that damp hole outside there. But here inside . . . why not?"

Griffin stood up, walked to one of the walls, and knocked on the paneling, testing. Then he went back to the door, opened it, and looked out: As before, there lay the dark swamp of parts of wrecks and bones from the insides of giant animals. With a shudder he closed the door and turned to the second one, which was located behind the bar.

"May I?" he asked.

"But of course."

He found himself in yet another room, just as big as the first. Here Ebenezer had set up his kitchen. There were several tables and chopping blocks of rough wood, as well as shelves and cupboards with a jumble of various dishes, which apparently came from some wreck. Griffin saw a cast-iron oven with cooking plates and a gigantic fireplace with a smoke catcher in which one could have roasted an ox. Where the smoke was drawn off to, however, wasn't possible to tell.

Shaking his head, Griffin crossed the room toward the only door. He placed each step very timidly, as if careless movement could make the surroundings burst like a soap bubble.

Behind this door lay a third room, just as large, in which stood an iron bed; at the head was mounted a coat of arms that was unfamiliar to Griffin. Perhaps it had once belonged to a captain or been in a nobleman's cabin. An open wardrobe held nothing more than a dozen monk's robes of different materials and of various colors. At least as far as clothing went, Ebenezer had learned nothing new in the past thirty years. On the floor, strewn all over in piles and careless heaps, lay books, some half-disintegrated, others wavy from the time spent in the water. Some had no covers anymore, others consisted only of bundles of loose pages, which Ebenezer had obviously sorted and then tied together with string. There was a wooden globe with a dent, exactly where Europe must have been located; a chessboard that was set out in an unfinished game; on the walls several paintings that were damaged from their meeting with the salt water; a grandfather clock that was still ticking; a candle stand; a fringed carpet with an Oriental pattern; a stuffed crocodile with a glass eye; a drafting desk, and numerous cracked glass cases full of butterflies and insects on pins.

There was no other door in this room, so Griffin made his way back to the first of the three rooms. Ebenezer, still seated at the table, looked at him expectantly.

"Well? What do you think?"

"Quite impressive," said Griffin.

"Isn't it? For an animal's stomach, very comfortable."

"But how . . . I mean, how did you . . ."

"Luck. Trust in God. Act of Providence. One day this door lay amongst all the other plunder. Jasconius had swallowed it with the remains of some ship. I haven't the slightest idea where it came from or who made it for what purpose.

I also doubt that I will ever unravel that secret. But maybe that's all to the good anyway. Secrets are like the fire in the stove: They go out if one pokes around in them for too long." He grinned as if he'd just uttered a deeply philosophical bit of wisdom. "Anyhow, the door opened when I fell on my stomach—I almost fell in headfirst. Then I stood up and—*voilà!*" He made an inclusive gesture with his hand. "Here we are now."

Griffin had been pacing nervously up and down while he was listening to Ebenezer. Now he let himself fall onto a chair, exhausted, rubbed his eyelids, and took a deep breath.

"Here we are now," he repeated with a sigh as he opened his eyes again and looked at the grinning Ebenezer. "I still have one question."

"Just ask it. We have all the time in the world."

"When you found me, out there in the stomach, you said then that you were in the . . . 'hospitality trade.' And then you said something about a floating tavern." He indicated the bar with a nod. "Besides, there's that bar, and I'm wondering . . . oh, well . . ."

"Whether I have possibly lost my mind, is that it?"

Griffin looked embarrassed. "Something like that."

"Not at all, my young friend. Not at all." Ebenezer shoved back his chair. He walked over to the bar on his short, thick legs and almost tenderly stroked his fingertips across it. A dreamy shine appeared in his eyes. "I am completely serious. Tell me, boy, what is your name, actually?"

"Griffin."

"Good, Griffin, then you will be the first to whom I tell my plan." He leaned his back against the bar and supported his elbows on the edge. With lowered voice and conspiratorial expression he went on: "This whole thing will become a legend in the business of hospitality. Something the sailors from the North Sea to the South Pacific will speak of. Oh, what am I saying—the world will speak of it, on land *and* on water!" He smiled archly. "But the unusual thing is: Only the very fewest will have the pleasure of a visit in person. And that's just what will make the business so marvelous!" Ebenezer threw his hands into the air as if he had just revealed to Griffin a plan to subjugate the whole world. "Everyone will talk of it! Everyone will wish to have drunk his rum at this bar once. The first floating tavern! The first and only tavern in the stomach of a giant whale!" His eyes were now round circles and stared at Griffin expectantly. "Well, how does that sound?"

Griffin swallowed. "I . . . am speechless."

"Right you are, my dear fellow, right you are! People will give their eyeteeth to be allowed to come here. They will then pine with longing for a second visit—but Ebenezer's Floating Tavern will have moved on and be anchored in another spot. Sometimes here, sometimes there. It will become a *myth*! Can you imagine a better business idea?"

"You know, I don't have much of an idea about the hospitality trade, but . . ."

"But?"

"Why should anyone give their eyeteeth to eat in the

stomach of a whale? That's . . . oh, well . . . disgusting?"

"Disgusting? Nonsense!" Ebenezer guffawed. "It's quite amazing. People will eat fish inside of a whale. Who else can offer them that? Only—"

"Ebenezer's Floating Tavern."

"Exactly right!"

It must be the loneliness, thought Griffin, full of pity. *The poor fellow hasn't seen another human soul for decades, and now he's fantasizing himself an entire tavern full of them at once.*

"Anyway, I wish you much luck with it. Really." Griffin stood up. "Now, would you please show me how I can get out of here?"

"But I need your help!"

"My help?"

"Certainly! For months I've been waiting for someone to turn up who can take part of the work from me. You must of course begin small, on the lowest step, so to speak—as kitchen boy. But just think of the chances for advancement! If you do well, I promise you a fast promotion. I'll teach you to prepare small dishes. Then bigger ones as well. You'll serve the guests at the tables, pour the rum and the beer." He clapped his hands happily. "It will be so *wonderful!*"

The room suddenly seemed to become smaller. The walls closed in on Griffin as if they intended to press him into a shape, like dough. Behind his back he clenched one hand into a fist. "That may indeed be a marvelous offer. Honestly. But I have two or three other things that I have to get done. Besides, I was always a dud in the galley. What I cook is not edible. And . . . oh, well, and therefore I would like to go now."

"And where? Outside there's nothing but the endless sea. Do you perhaps want to swim to the next island?"

"How far away is the next island?"

"Too far, that much is sure."

The surroundings seemed to peel like a banana before Griffin's eyes. Beneath what had just a minute ago seemed to him fantastic, strange, and a little crazy, the reality now became visible as a rotten fruit. The scenery remained the same, as did Ebenezer's joyful laughter, even the cozy room in the glow of the fire in the fireplace—and yet now it was all different.

Ebenezer was mad. And he obviously intended to include Griffin in his madness, whether Griffin wanted it or not.

"You're going to keep me imprisoned here?" Griffin asked.

"Do you perhaps see bars? Or keys? Nothing of the like, my boy. I ask only for your help. I will even pay you. Believe me, I have gold down here. We will of course earn more of it when our reputation is established. A twentieth of everything for you. Is that a deal?"

Be very calm now, Griffin told himself. *Give him no occasion to mistrust you. Then the chance to get away will occur all by itself.*

"When do you intend to open the tavern, then?" Griffin found it difficult to speak seriously about a matter that was the craziest thing he'd ever heard of. Against a tavern in the stomach of a whale, even the marvels of Aelenium paled to a paltry heap of coral.

"Well, we have a lot of work ahead of us. Are you a good carpenter?"

"I've often helped with repairs onboard."

"Outstanding! You can build the chairs. And tables. There's wood enough outside, and you'll find nails in the piles of debris. What do you think? Fifty places? Will that be enough for a start?"

"I should make *fifty* chairs?"

"Too few?" Ebenezer was dancing around excitedly and reveling in the images of an overfilled barroom. "Better eighty? Or a hundred?"

"Fifty might be enough."

"We don't want to overdo it, do we? Just fifty, then." Ebenezer hurried behind the bar and pulled out a hammer and a pair of rusty pliers and pushed both of them across the bar. "Oh, yes, and you should take off that horrible uniform. Just look around in Jasconius's stomach." He winked exuberantly at Griffin. "I'd guess you'll find everything you need there."

At the Council of the Captains

The pirate fleet was anchored in a wide ring around the island of Saint Celestine. In the darkness, the lamps aboard the ships were hard to differentiate from the constellations and their reflections on the water.

"It'll be just crawling with lookouts here," said Walker gloomily as, crouching, they headed across the beach toward a grove of palms. Their sea horses had withdrawn into the security of the open sea.

"Of course," Soledad retorted. "But they're on the lookout for uniformed Spaniards or English. Not every pirate knows the members of all the other crews. If anyone blocks our way, we simply claim we belong to the crew of another ship. Who's going to check on that?"

Saint Celestine was a tiny island, fifteen sea miles west of the Antilles island of Martinique. French colonists had tried to settle the island many years before. But the changeable weather and the swampy ground had finally brought them to their knees. Nature had recaptured what the settlers had wrested from it in their years of labor.

The remains of old farmhouses were overgrown with bushes and vines. In other places, jagged remnants of walls rose out of the thickets like the bony jaws of a giant. Directly in front of a rock wall, under a mantle of fleshy leaves and vines, was an astonishingly well-preserved church tower. Its tip showed nearly intact above the jungle.

Everywhere there was flitting, chirring, and screaming— the nightly hunters of the jungle were awake and on the prowl. It smelled of damp foliage and a lush array of exotic flowers.

They'd gone only a short distance when Walker, in the lead, soundlessly pointed upward.

Ahead of them rose the incline of a volcanic slope. On the flank of the mountain, exactly at the height of the tip of the church tower, gaped a huge gash, forming a natural platform. Voices could be heard, too far away to be understood. A cluster of torches illuminated the back wall and the overhanging rock roof of the plateau: without doubt the place of the secret meeting.

They carefully followed the path and a little later came to a set of stairs cut into the rock. It must have been cleared of vines and bushes very recently. Chopped-off branches were still strewn around. Someone had stuck a single torch in a rock niche. Its firelight flickered over the wall of stone and vegetation that towered in front of them.

AT THE COUNCIL OF THE CAPTAINS

"There's no point in playing hide-and-seek any longer," said Soledad decisively. "Either way, I have to show myself. Why not right now?"

Walker closed his hand more tightly on the grip of his saber. Soledad saw that he didn't like the situation. However, it wasn't the fear of discovery that was causing him uneasiness but the fact that he wasn't the leader of their troop. Even the Ghost Trader kept still and left the leading to Soledad. This was her terrain.

"Ho there!" she called when they'd climbed halfway up the stairs. "We come with peaceful intentions!"

Out of the darkness above them emerged two figures. One wore a cocked hat and a striped shirt, and in his hands were two pistols, cocked. The other held a saber and wore a weapons belt diagonally across his naked torso. His muscles gleamed in the light of two torches beside the stairs' upper landing.

"Who's there?" called the pirate with the pistols. "Do you belong to Tyrone's people? It's about time."

"No," she replied. "I am Soledad." The princess spoke in a loud, clear voice as she mounted the last steps. "Scarab's daughter. Presenting my unusual request to the captains: According to my birth and name I challenge Kendrick to a duel before the council of the Antilles captains."

Walker and the Ghost Trader exchanged alarmed looks. The captain laid a hand on Soledad's shoulder from behind. "There was never any talk of a duel!" he whispered indignantly. "Will you quit this nonsense!"

Soledad turned around and gave him a brief smile. "I

never concealed anything from you, Walker," she said. "It's about Kendrick's throne. That's why I'm here."

From behind her came a rough voice. "And *I* am here because of you, Soledad," the man called scornfully, now stepping onto the upper landing into the circle of torchlight.

The princess whirled around.

Kendrick, the pirate emperor, had drawn his saber, but the point was directed at the ground. His smile was icy, his eyes squinting with hatred. The golden ring in his left ear glowed in the firelight. The right had been shot off years before in a duel, but vanity made him cover the scar with his abundance of wavy hair.

"Soledad," he said, and he spat on the ground in front of her. "Before the sun rises again, your head will be stuck on my bowsprit."

"Hear me!" cried Soledad, as her eyes moved from one face to the next. At the moment she had the sure attention of the twelve Antilles captains. She asked herself only how long that would remain so.

"The pirates of the Lesser Antilles have preserved their independence for decades, and I know that the quarrel between Kendrick and me is not yours. Kendrick is not your leader, as my father also was not. But before you consider allying with him, you should know that Kendrick's rule over the pirates of Tortuga and New Providence is built on lies, treachery, and fraud. And on cowardly assassination."

Her voice rebounded loudly from the rock walls. The tables at which the twelve Antilles captains had gathered in a circle stood in the center of the natural platform slashed into the volcanic rock by a mood of Nature. From here one looked out over the leafy roof of the primeval forest onto the night-dark sea. The ships lying at anchor out there were clearly visible in the moonlight. Only three or four yards from the edge of the rock rose the partially disintegrated framework of the church tower roof. The rest of the settlement's ruins lay some fifty feet deeper, concealed in the thickness of the jungle.

The old fireplace, where flames now blazed again, must stem from the time of the settlers.

Torches were stuck into rusty holders on the rock walls. The shadows thrown by the light of the flames fell intimidatingly large across the rough stone.

"We're listening to you," said the captain who sat to the right of Kendrick. "Say on." He was a rough seadog with a voice that decades of rum and whiskey had transformed into a hoarse wheeze. He wore a dark red frock coat with a wide collar and a black sash diagonally across his chest. His feathered cocked hat lay before him on the table, right beside a silver wine cup. Soledad knew his name, just as she could name all the men gathered here. Rouquette was the oldest in the circle and did the talking, as tradition required.

Kendrick had sat down beside him after he'd led Soledad to the table. Walker and the Ghost Trader stood outside the circle. They hadn't been disarmed, but Kendrick's men watched them with blades drawn. Indeed, Soledad's throwing knives were still stuck in her belt.

"We thought highly of your father," said another man, before the princess could continue. He was younger than Rouquette and had black hair and an eye patch in whose center a ruby sparkled, large enough to buy a whole island with. His name was Galliano. "If we didn't recognize your father as our leader, still we never quarreled with him and always counted him as our ally."

"You all know that Kendrick murdered my father. After that he had his body dragged through the streets of Port Nassau like a dead dog."

None of those present changed expression.

"You all know it," said Soledad once more, "and it is clear to all of you that I have a right to retribution." She pointed at Kendrick. "And to his place in this circle."

"There has never yet been an empress of the pirates," said Rouquette. "Still, that is of no matter to us. We admire you for your courage, Princess. But do you seriously believe that the pirates of Tortuga and New Providence would accept a female at their head?"

"When this female throws Kendrick's head at their feet, they will have to."

"Your retribution has nothing to do with your claim to the throne, Soledad. And that cannot be a matter for this circle. We are not in Port Nassau here."

A murmur of agreement sounded from the circle of the other captains. One thumped his approval on the table with his pipe. The thumping was thrown back from the rocks and resounded out into the jungle.

"Perhaps you'll change your thinking if I say to you that a danger threatens the whole Caribbean—also the Lesser Antilles—which we can only confront together. All the pirates together, the same whether they sell their takings in Martinique or New Providence."

Kendrick waved that away with a nasty laugh. "What a cheap trick. Something like that should be beneath even your dignity."

"I am here not only to demand my right," Soledad continued, without paying any attention to his interjection. "My warning is serious. A deadly danger threatens us all."

"What are you talking about?" asked a captain with a forked black beard. His right arm ended in a three-pronged claw, whose end he scratched across the surface of the table over and over. "Who threatens us? A Spanish armada from New Providence? Perhaps an alliance of the Spanish with the English?" That was absurd, and he said it in a tone of voice that left no doubt that he considered Soledad's warning a ruse.

She chose her words very carefully. At this moment no one here would take seriously a mile-wide maelstrom, gruesome creatures from another world, and a war host of kobalins.

She must approach the matter differently. "It is a danger that will sweep over us all like a storm and against which none of us has a chance alone."

"Hear, hear," shouted Kendrick, laughing.

Some of the pirates joined in the laughter, but a few of them scrutinized Soledad expectantly.

"I cannot ask that you pay more attention to me than I am

entitled to in this circle," she said. "You shall learn everything—but only after I've proven through a victory over Kendrick that I am worthy to speak before you."

The Ghost Trader leaned toward Walker. "A clever plan," he whispered appreciatively.

"One that's going to deprive her of her life," retorted Walker.

"That's only a silly trick!" shouted Kendrick into the circle of the Antilles captains. "She's fooling you by making your mouths water!"

"No," said Rouquette, without taking his eyes off Soledad as he spoke. "She's right."

Kendrick leaned forward angrily. "But she—"

"She is Scarab's daughter," the oldest councillor interrupted him. "You yourself have confirmed that. On the other hand, you've made us a good offer, Kendrick, which also is entitled to our appreciation. Probably none of us would have thought you capable of such a plan. And if it's true that Tyrone would stand on our side in it, we wouldn't hesitate to join in the business."

"What's he talking about?" Walker whispered, staring at Rouquette as if he could read the answer in his face.

The Ghost Trader remained silent, but in his expression there was alarm that was now no longer directed entirely toward Soledad.

Apparently Tyrone hadn't arrived on Saint Celestine yet. But if Kendrick actually had succeeded in entering into an alliance with him, the pirate emperor was holding the better cards here in the council of the Antilles captains.

"But," Rouquette continued, "even if we join with you in an alliance, that doesn't mean we can close our ears to the princess's just challenge."

Galliano nodded in agreement, and one by one the other captains agreed. It remained uncertain whether it was their sense of honor that Rouquette was appealing to or only their anticipation of a duel.

"This is ridiculous!" Kendrick slammed his fist on the table. "I come here, promise you fabulous wealth and a victory over the Spaniards, and you ask that I undertake a duel with . . . with a half *child*!" He spat across the table in Soledad's direction.

"If you refuse," said Galliano, smiling craftily, "that could mean that there's some truth in her accusations. Consider that, Kendrick."

Soledad used her opportunity and struck the same note. "I tell you, he's a coward! Murder from an ambush, that he can do. But you hear it yourself: He doesn't even have the guts to stand and fight a woman."

Kendrick leaped to his feet. Obviously he was seeing his position endangered now. "This is neither the place nor the time to—"

"It's not for you to judge that," said one of the other captains, a man with fire red hair and jagged scars on both cheeks. "You're a guest here in the council. It's reserved to us to judge the honesty of the princess, not you."

Again the murmur of agreement grew loud.

"That decides it," cried Rouquette to the circle. "Kendrick must accept the princess's challenge. The fight will take place here and now. Are there objections?"

Kendrick looked as if he had a whole lot of them, but he compressed his lips determinedly and shook his head.

Soledad did not allow her triumph to show. She nodded to Rouquette, noticing out of the corner of her eye that Galliano winked at her suggestively, and planted herself confidently in front of Kendrick.

"Here and now," she said grimly.

Rouquette raised a hand and brought the men to silence again. "Since Kendrick was challenged to this fight, the choice of weapons falls to him."

Kendrick supported himself with clenched fists on the tabletop. His eyes bored through Soledad like steel blades. Then he smiled.

"Grappling irons."

The Cannibal King

"That scurvy bastard!" swore Walker, hardly able to keep from rushing at Kendrick. One of the guards still had a pistol trained on him. "He knows very well that she doesn't have a chance against him with a grappling hook."

The Ghost Trader also looked concerned, but he said nothing. He remained a quiet observer of the event, perhaps because that was a role that he had filled elsewhere for an eternity.

The captains' tables were drawn apart into a wide semicircle. They formed one boundary of the fighting area; the other was the rock ledge with the gaping drop-off behind it. There were no railings there, only the deteriorating roof of the church tower, which rose above the edge like a rib cage of wooden beams.

Rouquette had directed his men to fetch two grappling

hooks from one of the ships. Each of the two fighters, who had taken positions on opposite sides of the semicircle, received one of the lance-shaped weapons.

A grappling hook consists of a six-foot-long wooden shaft with a steel point; branching off the steel point is a claw-shaped hook. Originally they served during a sea battle to pull on the railing of an opposing ship to make it easier for the pirates to board the enemy deck. A long time ago, however, the freebooters had begun using the grappling hooks for attack as well—often with devastating effect. The steel point was easily a foot and a half long and rammed through any body without difficulty, while the sharp hook left hideous wounds behind it. Anyone who was strong enough could even whirl the long shaft in a wide circle and mow down several opponents at once.

For a woman, even for one as skillful as Soledad, the grappling hook was a cumbersome and unmanageable weapon. Point and hook towered over her by almost a head, which made it difficult for her to grip the shaft securely and keep it in balance—not to mention make moves of attack and defense. Handline a grappling hook depended on muscular strength alone; it was a coarse and inelegant weapon. Soledad could have taken Kendrick on with saber and dagger without any trouble. But with this weapon the pirate emperor clearly had the advantage.

Soledad grasped the shaft with both hands and was trying to find a good balance when Rouquette gave the signal: He fired his pistol once over the drop-off, out into the night.

Kendrick let out a wild yell and plunged forward. He crossed the semicircle of tables with a few quick steps, intending to bore a hole through his adversary on the very first attack.

Soledad avoided him and ducked under the thrust. Only seconds later she tried to pull him off his legs with the hook. Her attack also went awry, but it showed Kendrick that he wouldn't have an easy game with her.

The Ghost Trader placed a quieting hand on Walker's shoulder as he saw that the captain was ready to intervene then and there. "No!" he said sharply. "They'd kill all of us on the spot."

"I can't look on while he—"

"She wanted it that way."

Walker was silent, staring worriedly at the fighting ring. Sweat beaded his forehead. His hands opened and closed with every attack, every parry.

The boots of both opponents made the dust swirl up. Now and then an "ohh" and "ahh" went through the group of Antilles captains when one of the fighters—usually Soledad—got into difficulty. But most of the time the men were silent. They all lived a life full of fighting and bloodletting, and each of them had witnessed hundreds of such duels. Nevertheless, they couldn't turn away from the spectacle.

Soledad was managing better than the pirate emperor had calculated, evidently. In the beginning Kendrick bellowed and snorted in order to disconcert her, but when he noticed that his threatening behavior had no effect, he fought as silently as she, with a taciturn expression and clenched teeth.

Kendrick might be a coward, but he wasn't a bad fighter. He hadn't gained his position among the pirates by trickery and treachery alone. He moved quickly and decidedly, his attacks often came unpredictably or were targeted at places that were difficult for Soledad to protect.

The princess possessed only one advantage: She was more agile than he, and what she lacked in the strength of her arms, she made up for in speed. That gave her little opportunity to attack, but she could often avoid his savage blows. Several times she let him stumble into emptiness, as his own momentum almost snatched him off his feet. Each time she then tried to run at him with the grappling hook, but he repeatedly succeeded in escaping her strikes and stabs.

Soon both were bleeding from small wounds. Kendrick's velvet breeches were torn at the knees, while Soledad's jerkin hung in shreds on her back: One of his lance thrusts had almost shattered her spine.

It was only a question of time until the strength of one of the two would fail. It was becoming apparent that not skill but exhaustion would determine the outcome of the fight. And none of the onlookers, not even Walker and the Ghost Trader, had any doubt as to who would inevitably be the first to wear out.

The weight of the clumsy weapon was exhausting Soledad. She was slowly losing the feeling in her arms. Her fingers were so tightly clenched around the shaft that she doubted whether her hands would ever open again on their own.

Kendrick was wielding the grappling hook with undiminished strength. Each time she succeeded in parrying one of his blows, she felt the force of the strike throughout her entire body and was in danger of being knocked off her feet.

She had to try something before it was too late; somehow break through the storm of blows and thrusts that he was raining down on her.

She could think of only one possibility.

With a few broad leaps she broke away from the radius of his weapon and ran toward the rock edge. For the first time in many minutes Kendrick let out a triumphant yell, for he now believed that he'd put his opponent to flight. But Soledad planned something else. At full speed, she headed for the drop-off—and for the fallen-in church tower timberwork. Nine feet of emptiness gaped between the rock platform and the beams.

Still running, Soledad hauled back and flung the grappling hook like a lance over to the roof.

A murmur went through the row of captains.

The steel point penetrated the wood and remained sticking in a timber, vibrating violently. The roof creaked dangerously. A swarm of birds, which until then had been invisible in the shadows, fluttered up screeching, hung for a long moment over the abyss, and then shot away in the direction of the forest.

Soledad pushed off from the edge of the platform and cleared the gap in a broad leap. She crashed against the beam with a bloodcurdling oath, quickly grabbed hold with both arms, and swung around. She'd landed right next to the grappling hook, which was sticking horizontally into one of the beams. The roof's groaning grew to a despairing convulsion of rotten wood. But still the framework held. Soledad instinctively looked down: on one side of the overgrown tower wall she saw the crowns of trees, vague in the darkness; on the other, in the interior of the tower, nothing but a pitch-black shaft.

Sliding, Kendrick had come to a stop at the edge of the drop-off. He stared over at her grimly, uncertain for a long moment whether he should dare to follow her. Soledad slung a leg around the beam and silently hoped it would give her enough of a hold. Then, using both hands, she pulled the grappling hook out of the wood. She let it rotate in her right hand, now holding it like a spear, hauled back, and flung it across the chasm straight at Kendrick.

The pirate emperor screamed when the point hit his thigh, smashed the bones, and came out the other side. The force of the blow threw him backward, and the steel point drove against the rock and struck sparks. Bellowing, Kendrick fell on the ground and, holding his leg with both hands, rolled in torment from one side to the other, while the shaft of the grappling hook cut through the air aimlessly above him.

The onlookers held their breath.

Rouquette rose from his chair.

Soledad hung panting on the church tower roof and looked over at the rock platform. Her long hair was stuck to her face, and sweat burned her eyes. Kendrick's pain filled her with deep satisfaction, but also with uncertainty. She couldn't get down from here under her own power. Would the Antilles captains accept Kendrick's wounding as defeat, even though it wasn't fatal? Or was neither of them the victor as long as Soledad was up here as helpless as the pirate emperor?

"The decision," cried Rouquette, in order to be heard over the tormented screams of the wounded man, "is hereby—"

"*Hold!*" A voice as cutting as a saber blade interrupted him.

The heads of the Antilles captains turned. Several men leaped up. Rouquette's eyes narrowed in anger at the interruption. The Ghost Trader also turned toward the man who'd appeared on the upper landing of the rock stairs. Only Walker continued to look desperately for a chance to rescue Soledad. But the man guarding him had his pistols pointed unfailingly at Walker's chest.

"Tend to the man!" ordered the newcomer, and at once two figures appeared from the darkness behind him and hurried to the wounded pirate emperor.

Kendrick was still rolling on the ground. The shadows of the grappling hook shaft fanned across the rock wall like a pendulum. The two men went down on their knees beside him. One pressed Kendrick's shoulders to the ground, the other got busy tying off the thrashing leg above the wound.

"Tyrone?" asked Rouquette, coming out from behind his table. "We expected you earlier."

The man on the stairs walked into the glow of the firelight. He wore wide black breeches, boots with wide cuffs that reached above his knees, and a black frock coat, embroidered in finest silver. His face was a stark contrast to his elegant clothing: Tyrone's features, indeed his entire skull, were covered with a network of drawings. Archaic patterns and wavy lines framed his eyes and lips, ritual paintings that probably stemmed from the culture of the cannibal tribes under his command. A long black ponytail grew from the back of his head, but the rest of his scalp was hairless; even his eyebrows were missing.

When he spoke, Tyrone revealed teeth filed to needle-sharp points. Walker, who was now standing only a few steps away from him, noticed that the cannibal king's tongue was split and the ends were colored black.

"I was held up," he said to the circle. The split tongue gave his words a hissing sound. "As I see, I've just missed the most interesting part." He walked over to Kendrick. The grappling hook had been removed from his leg. The wound was cleanly bound up and was bleeding less. However, the pirate emperor had lost consciousness.

One of the two men who'd cared for the injured man at Tyrone's command looked up. "He will lose the leg. The bone is splintered."

"Take him aboard his ship," commanded Tyrone with a wave of his hand. "His men will look after him."

Soledad was fascinated and at the same time repelled by the nightmare figure of the cannibal king. The arrogance with which he came before the powerful Antilles captains was impressive. One thing his appearance and his tone of voice made clear right off: When he spoke, no one else spoke, neither Rouquette nor Galliano nor one of the others. He sucked all attention toward himself, until everything revolved around him alone.

The princess was still clinging to the church tower. Her arms were slowly becoming numb. Nevertheless, she did not move. It was no longer up to the captains whether she would come down from this tower alive. Tyrone would decide that now.

"A plank!" he called, without deigning to look at her. "It's not fitting for a princess to be crouching up there like a monkey."

No one laughed. No one contradicted. At once two pirates hurried away and returned with a sturdy board, which they slid over from the edge of the rock to the tower. Soledad wasn't sure that her legs would bear her, but she had to take the risk. Swaying, she balanced over on the plank. The chasm pulled at her, the darkness reached toward her feet with shadowy fingers.

When she reached firm ground, she collapsed onto her knees with clenched teeth.

No pistols could hold Walker any longer. He stormed straight across the fighting ring, put his arms around Soledad, and helped her up. "Are you in pain?" he whispered to her. "Did he wound you?"

"Everything's all right," she replied hurriedly, adding softly, "So far."

Tyrone smiled. The two rows of sharply filed teeth gleamed behind his lips like coarse saw blades. But he spared himself any comment on the pair at the rock's edge and instead looked from one Antilles captain to the next. Finally his eyes rested on the Ghost Trader. Silently both men stared at each other. The Trader did not change expression, did not show the slightest trace of uncertainty.

Tyrone's smile grew even broader.

Soledad fought against dizziness. The figures swam before her. Did the two know each other somehow?

The silent moment between the two men passed, and Tyrone turned again to the assembled captains. Behind him the unconscious Kendrick was lifted by two of his men and carried to the steps.

"Too bad," said Tyrone without any pity, "that we must do without his presence."

"Kendrick is no longer the leader of the pirates of Tortuga and New Providence," announced Rouquette. Obviously he was no longer willing to put up with the imperious entry of the cannibal king. "Princess Soledad has defended her claim to the throne. She should lead the negotiations in his place and speak for her people."

Soledad became aware with a slight thrill that by "her people" he did not mean Walker and the Ghost Trader but all the pirates between the Bahamas and the Virgin Islands. She had beaten Kendrick in battle. But unfortunately he was only wounded, and she was not certain whether that would suffice. Would the outcome of the fight be accepted in Port Nassau or on Jamaica?

Tyrone had obviously had the same thought, and he did not shrink from expressing it. "Kendrick called this meeting, not the girl. It's his plan that has brought me here. Since I'm in on everything, with your permission, *I* will speak for Kendrick." There could be no talk of permission, his tone left no doubt about that.

"Princess Soledad wished to warn us of something before you arrived, Tyrone," Galliano interjected.

"Oh? It looked to me as if she just wanted to break her neck." He turned to Soledad and Walker with a sharklike grin. He frowned when he noticed that Soledad was no longer supported by Walker but standing with legs astride and on her own.

"Tyrone," she said coolly. "You're a guest here, just as I am, and I wonder why you would do the talking for Kendrick or one of the other captains. If they put up with that—fine, that's not my affair. But for *me*, you will not speak."

The attack was unconsidered and perhaps unwise, but Soledad was fed up with Tyrone's dominating manner. He might command several thousand cannibals on the mainland, but out here on Saint Celestine he was only a pirate like all the others.

Tyrone made a mocking bow in her direction. However, the sharp response she'd expected did not come. "Then tell us your plan. How does it look for the attack on Caracas? That's what we've all gathered here for."

Caracas? Had Kendrick seriously planned an attack on one of the richest and strongest Spanish coastal strongholds? Had he lured them here with *that*? By all that was holy, he was crazier than she'd supposed.

"I'm not here on account of Caracas," she said, "but to warn you all of a peril that can befall us in a few days or a few weeks."

Tyrone remained silent. He listened.

Soledad exchanged split-second looks with the Ghost Trader and saw him nod almost imperceptibly.

"The kobalins have united themselves into a powerful fighting force." After that there was no going back. "They are gathering to the north of the Lesser Antilles, out in the Atlantic. I've seen them with my own eyes, thousands of them. It's said they're commanded by something that calls itself *Maelstrom.*" She purposely kept it vague so that the captains wouldn't be burdened with too much at once. She was walking on thin ice, and it seemed to her that Tyrone, with his looks alone, was stirring up a fire under her feet.

"Kobalins?" Galliano was staring at her, and to her horror she could see the disappointment in his eyes. Apparently he'd expected something more persuasive. "Everyone knows the deep tribes are enemies of each other. They'd never join together for any purpose."

Some of the other captains nodded. A dark-skinned man snorted disparagingly. "So that's your great peril, Princess? An old wives' tale?"

"It is no fairy tale," she replied firmly. "I've seen with my own eyes how the deep tribes are being moved to the east. The kobalins are gathering. And they will attack. It has been reported to me that they've already left the water once and gone onto land. And they will do it again."

"Kobalins *never* leave the water!" shouted Tyrone. He wasn't contradicting Soledad's words but appealing to the listeners. "Even their captains are afraid of the air. They'll never go on land. That's ridiculous."

"And yet it was so."

"And what do we have as proof? Your word of honor?" Rouquette inspected her suspiciously. She was about to forfeit her last sympathetic listener.

"The word of the rightful empress of the pirates," she said vigorously, and then she thought of something else. "Wasn't it always said that the cannibal tribes feuded with each other? Nevertheless, Tyrone has succeeded in uniting them. Why shouldn't that happen with the kobalins, too?"

Tyrone's facial muscles twitched. "Cannibals are only men," he said icily. "Men are afraid, and that makes them weak and pliable. But kobalins? Who is a kobalin afraid of?"

"And who are cannibals afraid of?" she countered.

A tense silence now reigned among the Antilles captains. Here was a new battle emerging that none of them had reckoned with. A battle without grappling hooks and bloodletting. A battle of words and of the stronger will.

Tyrone's eyes bored into the princess. It was hard to stand fast against those eyes, which promised so much cruelty and horror. And yet she maintained her composure.

The cannibal king whirled around. "Captains!" he cried to the circle. "This girl promises a war with the kobalins. *I* give you the treasuries of Caracas!"

Soledad was about to protest, but this time she was interrupted by Rouquette. "Quiet, Soledad! Now it's Tyrone's turn."

Pirate Emperor

The cannibal king gave her a predator's smile. Then he walked away from her and began to pace back and forth in front of the captains. "In two weeks a great attack on Caracas by the Caribbean pirates will take place. You'll say, 'That has been tried before, and all were undone by it.' Probably true. But the situation is different today. That time it was an attack from the sea side, but with my help we—and *you,* if you choose—will take the city from the sea *and* the land."

The captains' whispering became a murmur, then loud discussion. Soledad threw the Ghost Trader a despairing look, but his face remained unfathomable. Walker was standing somewhere behind her, near the edge of the rock, but he kept his distance so that none of the captains would think she needed the support of a man in this situation.

Tyrone waited until the talk had died down, then he continued his address. "She gives you kobalins," he said once more, relishing every syllable, "but I give you gold! If all the pirates of the Caribbean join together in this attack, dozens of ships will take the harbor of Caracas under fire—a whole armada! At the same time I will attack with my men from the land side. We'll take the city by surprise."

"How many men are you talking about?" Galliano asked.

"Yes," the dark-skinned captain also questioned, "how many men do you command?"

Tyrone's triumphant voice rang out into the stillness. "Five thousand!"

Soledad's heart hammered in her chest. One thing was clear: She could evoke the coming destruction of the world for the captains—but against their lust for gold she wouldn't get very far with it.

"Five thousand," echoed from the crowd.

"Eighteen of the largest native tribes," Tyrone confirmed, "and a few other scattered groups obey my command. And every day more join them." He paused to let his words take effect.

Soledad jumped in. "He says 'native tribes.' But in fact, he means *cannibals!*" She fixed her eyes on Rouquette and Galliano. "Is that what you want? An alliance with *five thousand human-flesh eaters?*"

The two captains exchanged a look but then turned their attention to Tyrone again.

"The best is yet to come," announced the cannibal king.

"Go on!" the captain with the forked beard cried avidly.

"I'm giving you five thousand men—and none of them will cost you a single doubloon!"

Again silence. Open mouths, wide eyes. Then someone broke into laughter, others clapped their hands. The captains' enthusiasm gushed up among them like a tidal wave.

Soledad stood there as if she were turned to stone. Suddenly Walker was beside her, bending toward her ear. "Come on, let's get out of here! Quick!"

"But—"

"No. It's over. They won't listen to you anymore."

She knew he was right. She was powerless against such arguments. The Maelstrom? A war against kobalins? Unimportant in the face of five thousand fighters who would make these captains a great many times richer. Fighters they need not pay for.

Soledad said good-bye to the idea of returning to Aelenium with a large fleet. Even her victory over Kendrick suddenly meant nothing to her anymore. They'd be lucky to get off this island alive. The Antilles captains were going to eat out of Tyrone's hand and fulfill his every wish. Soledad's head on a golden tray? It would only be a question of the sharpest blade.

While the captains leaped from their places, excitedly shouting all at once, Soledad moved over to the steps with Walker. The men who'd been watching them and the Ghost Trader showed no more interest in them now.

"Let's go!" said the Trader when they reached him.

And then they were hurrying down the stairs. Soledad looked back only once and saw that Tyrone had turned around to her.

He opened his mouth and laughed at her. Torchlight fell on his lips.

His gums were as black as a dog's.

Walker and the Ghost Trader were arguing with each other. That is, Walker was arguing—the Ghost Trader remained remarkably under control. The captain was demanding to know why the Trader hadn't simply called up all the ghosts on the island and brought the farce up there to an end. The Trader replied—not for the first time—that everything that had happened during the meeting had to happen that way and no other. Which was of course not an argument likely to persuade a man like Walker. But the Trader remained obdurate, as if he possessed some knowledge about the fate of all of them.

"It was important," he said, "that we meet Tyrone in this way. And it was just as important that Soledad have the chance to humiliate Kendrick in front of everyone. Sooner or later you'll understand that, Walker."

Soledad paid attention only when her name was mentioned. But then she sank into her own dark thoughts again and left the men to themselves.

They had gone almost halfway back when two pirates stepped out of the trees and barred their way.

"What's going on up there?" one of them asked. He carried a long-barreled rifle. The second wore a saber at his waist. Nevertheless, the two didn't seem very intent on involving Soledad and her companions in a fight. Their attention was primarily on the illuminated platform in the rock wall, which from down here glowed like a second half moon in the darkness.

"We're celebrating with Captain Tyrone," said Walker quickly, before Soledad's hesitation could make the sentries mistrustful. "He's brought good news."

"Him? Good news?" The man with the rifle frowned. "He looks like a lunatic to me." Then quickly he added, "But don't tell anyone."

Walker shook his head. "The captains wanted to organize a celebration in his honor. They've just opened a barrel of rum up there."

"Rum?" The pirate with the saber wanted to make sure.

"For everyone."

"For us, too?"

"Not as long as you're standing watch down here."

"You mean . . . ?"

Soledad nodded. "We're on our way to tell the men on our ship. If they're here first, there won't be much left over for you."

The pirates exchanged a look and they hurried off. "Thanks!" called one of them, grinning over his shoulder. "You're true friends!"

Soledad and her two companions crouched and darted into the thicket. Yet they heard one pirate say to the other, "I think I recognized the one fellow. Looked like Walker."

"*The* Walker?" asked the other, but whatever answer he got was lost in the rustling of the leaves as the three comrades hurriedly put distance between them.

They encountered two further groups of sentries, but they were able to avoid them in time. Soon afterward they reached the belt of palms that surrounded the island. Here the trees were at wider intervals, without any protective undergrowth. Their silhouettes showed up like paper cutouts on the snow-white sand. The little group slowed its steps. Walker dropped behind a little when he stepped, cursing, into a hermit crabs' nest, and he busied himself on the way to the water pulling the uncooperative little creatures from his trouser leg.

A sharp wind was blowing across the sea. The waves foamed at their feet, and even in the moonlight they could see that high mountains of waves were boiling up out on the open sea. It seemed almost as if Tyrone had brought the harbingers of a storm with him to Saint Celestine—in several respects.

The Ghost Trader raised the mussel pipe to his lips. Then they waited in silence for the arrival of the sea horses.

The thought that the Antilles captains intended in all seriousness to ally themselves with the cannibal king left Soledad no peace. It was *one* thing to storm a Spanish fortress, even if there'd be a dozen or even a hundred dead; but it was something else to let five thousand flesh eaters loose on the inhabitants of Caracas.

In her mind she saw Tyrone's pointed teeth before her and the black-stained ends of his tongue. She knew what the people of Caracas might expect when that beast made his entry there. And although Soledad herself had taken part in attacks and had seen with her own eyes how pirates fell on the women and girls of Spanish settlements, the idea of a hungry horde of cannibals called up sheer horror in her.

Suddenly everything looked hopeless. Their entire mission was a failure: On land the cannibals raged, on the sea the kobalins. And somewhere in the distance the Maelstrom was turning.

She wondered if he didn't also pull the strings here, in the shape of men like Tyrone and Kendrick. Was there an alliance between them and the Mare Tenebrosum? Was the whole attack on Caracas nothing but a feint to keep the Spanish and the pirates busy while the Maelstrom extended his sphere of influence farther with each day?

She was going to share her thoughts with the others when Walker suddenly pointed to one of the illuminated ships.

"That's Tyrone's ship—the *Quadriga!*"

Against the starry sky and the churning horizon lay a four-master, a former Spanish frigate with a high bow construction. Only isolated lanterns were lighted on the railing and on the bridge. It almost seemed as though someone wanted to keep curious eyes from being able to observe what was taking place on deck.

A shiver ran over Soledad when she thought of the men who were in Tyrone's service. His companions up on the rock plateau hadn't been natives, and she guessed that the remainder of his crew also consisted of men from the Old World. But who would voluntarily follow a monster like Tyrone? What did he use to lure his people? Riches? Battle? Or was it fear that made them obedient?

A good hundred yards away from the *Quadriga* lay the *Mask,* Kendrick's brigantine. While the *Quadriga* was primarily good for sea battles, the small and racy *Mask* was best suited for a fast journey.

"The ship's boat!" Walker pointed to a small silhouette on the dark water. "They're taking Kendrick back on board. He'll never forget this defeat, whether or not the other Caribbean pirates keep on following him or you." He was about to put his arm around Soledad's shoulders when she took a step to one side, as if by chance.

"I'm not afraid of him," she said.

"The man who bandaged him was right," said the Ghost

Trader. "Kendrick will lose the leg. The wound was too severe, and they'll only be able to give it emergency treatment on board. He's finished as a leader."

She shrugged, even if she was shivering inwardly. She'd already killed any number of men—but she'd never yet maimed one and left him alive.

"Whatever happens, I'm with you," said Walker.

She was about to make a caustic reply when she suddenly realized how serious it was with him. She'd never seen him the way he was now. He was a cutthroat and a rogue, some-one who couldn't easily accept another as an equal—until that moment up there on the platform, when he'd put his arms around her. A change was taking place in him that touched her but also alarmed her. She feared for her own courage.

"There they are!" said the Ghost Trader, pointing at the three sea horses, who were gliding through the water to the shore.

Soledad was the first into the surf and waded to the horses. The sea horses stopped a stone's throw from land. Here the sea was just deep enough to offer enough room for their long fish tails under the surface. The animals kept ducking themselves into the water, as if they instinctively felt that danger threatened them from aboard the ships.

A little later Soledad, Walker, and the Ghost Trader were sitting in their saddles. They turned the sea horses and headed toward the open ocean.

The Trader guided his animal closer to the others. "I think it would be a mistake to returne to Aelenium now."

Soledad looked at him in surprise. Secretly she'd thought the same thing, but she hadn't dared say it aloud. She'd defended the throne of her father and was the rightful ruler of the pirates, whether Kendrick accepted it or not. Her place was at the side of the Caribbean freebooters. The attack on Caracas was a bad plan at the wrong time, and it was her duty to prevent it. But at the same time she felt a confusing obligation to Jolly and the others. She was now a part of that group, whether she wanted to be or not.

Walker looked from one to the other in the half light of the moon. "I know what you have in mind. But I wonder why."

"Let's follow Tyrone secretly, when he returns to his base," said the Ghost Trader. "We serve the affairs of Aelenium better if we thwart his plans."

"You felt it too, didn't you?" asked Soledad, alert. "There's more behind Tyrone than can be seen with the naked eye."

The Ghost Trader nodded. "I felt it when he was standing up there and speaking to the captains. Those were his words, but the plan behind them . . . I'm not sure."

"You think Tyrone serves the Maelstrom?" asked Walker.

"That we shall find out."

"Good," said Soledad. "Agreed."

Walker nodded. Maybe he'd have followed her straight into the Mare Tenebrosum. That gave her a guilty feeling, but also an entirely new, unexpected excitement. It was for more than just gratitude that he was sticking by her.

"When the *Quadriga* hoists anchor," the Trader said, "we follow her."

THE CANNIBAL KING

Walker looked grimly from him to Soledad. "You know where that's going to lead us."

She stroked the back of the nervous sea horse's head, as if she could give herself courage that way too. "Yes," she said. "Right into the heart of the cannibal kingdom."

Old Friends

"I don't understand it," said Jolly as she looked out over the Caribbean Sea, which gleamed like tarnished silver in the dawn light. Their follower under the waves had vanished without a trace the day before. "Something happened on Agostini's bridge that I just don't understand either."

The Hexhermetic Shipworm was in his knapsack, which he hardly left at all these days, like a snail. Perhaps even he felt the deep uneasiness that had taken possession of them.

"No one in Aelenium could tell me anything about it. Not Munk, not the Ghost Trader, not even Forefather." She knitted her brows. "Or maybe no one wanted to tell me anything."

Jolly was standing in the bow of the *Carfax* with one hand on the railing, as if the cool wood under her fingers could help her to perceive the world around her as reality and not as another of the Mare Tenebrosum's illusions. She now dreamed of the black ocean every night, just as if she were coming nearer and nearer to the Mare Tenebrosum, and yet she must actually be moving farther away from it with every sea mile.

"The Maelstrom is the gate to the Mare Tenebrosum, so therefore we must shut him in—I understand that. But what about the bridge that Agostini—I mean, the shape-shifter—built? Griffin and I, we were up on it. The bridge was just like a gate too. If it's so simple to open one, why is the Maelstrom so very important?"

"Well," said the worm in his grating voice, "I don't know much about the Mare Tenebrosum."

"But that isn't true! You told me more about it than the Ghost Trader—before we arrived in Aelenium, anyway. You even knew the Crustal Breach!" She threw a glance over her shoulder up to the wheel where Buenaventure was standing. She'd gradually come to doubt that the pit bull man ever needed sleep. He passed the few rests he allowed himself dozing, always on the alert, vigilantly listening to every wind gust, every unusual creaking of the timbers. For days it had seemed as if he and the ship had melted together, body and soul of one creature. Buenaventure was here to protect Jolly—but his concern was also for the *Carfax*, like a dear old friend.

"Come on," said Jolly, challenging the Hexhermetic Shipworm. "Talk to me!"

"So, the bridge," he murmured with a sigh, wagging his head back and forth as if a fakir were luring him out of his knapsack with a flute. "You said the kobalins attacked the bridge. But they withdrew when the soldiers of Aelenium appeared and set Agostini's construction on fire. Right?"

Jolly nodded.

"Doesn't that seem strange to you? The kobalins are under the orders of the Maelstrom. And he in turn is a servant of the Mare Tenebrosum. Why should the Masters of the Mare assault their own construction or let it be destroyed at all?"

Jolly frowned. "No idea."

"We-ell," the worm drawled, "because we may have been mistaken the whole time. Perhaps the Maelstrom has been pursuing other goals entirely. His own goals."

"But the Maelstrom is the gate for the Masters."

"Why doesn't he simply open by himself, then? Until now we've assumed he was probably too weak. But then why does he command thousands of kobalins and also stir up other mischief wherever he can? I have another conjecture: For some reason, the bridge was dangerous for the Maelstrom. And therefore he had it attacked."

"Do you really believe the Maelstrom is stabbing the Masters in the back?"

"Indeed. The Maelstrom must have freed himself from enslavement by the Masters. That's the only explanation for the way the kobalins acted at the bridge. Perhaps he's realizing his own power. Why should he share with the Masters if he's now the most powerful creature in this world? He can set himself up as the ruler over all."

The worm's speculation turned upside down a lot of what Jolly had hitherto assumed. But it was the only way the whole business made any sense. The bridge must have been built because the Maelstrom had closed himself to the Masters and they needed another, new entry into this world. Then the only question remaining was, why didn't they simply walk over it when Agostini had finished?

"You are expected," she muttered softly.

The worm stretched his head out of the knapsack a little farther.

"Beg your pardon?" he asked in irritation.

Jolly brushed a strand of hair out of her face. The wind had freshened, and the *Carfax* was clearly picking up speed.

"The shape-shifter said that to me when he was standing with us on the bridge: You are expected."

Jolly stepped away from the railing and began to pace nervously up and down the deck. Why hadn't she thought of that sooner? It was about the polliwogs. In the final analysis, it was always about the polliwogs.

"The bridge wasn't intended for the Masters of the Mare," she said aloud. "Agostini built it for me. It was supposed to lead me to them in the Mare Tenebrosum."

The worm nodded thoughtfully. "I was thinking something like that myself," he said slowly.

Jolly stopped in front of him. "What kind of interest could the Masters have in me?" she asked. "Why didn't they just direct the shape-shifter to bring me to them? After all, I'm their worst enemy."

The worm pushed the edge of the knapsack down a bit farther with his front pair of legs. "Are you? Their deadly enemy?"

Jolly was about to answer when Buenaventure's voice thundered over the deck.

"Land ho!" he called down from the bridge. "Jolly, the coast lies ahead of us!"

A chain of hills was clearly visible on the horizon. The mainland. Somewhere there in the distance lay the mouth of the Orinoco—and, she hoped, a further clue that would lead to Bannon and the men of the *Skinny Maddy*.

She suppressed all further thoughts about the bridge, the Mare Tenebrosum, and the words of the worm. Now she had to concentrate on what lay ahead of her.

"Everything all right?" called Buenaventure.

"Yes . . . yes," she said uncertainly, straightening, yet she thought that nothing was all right. With more clarity than ever before, she had to face the fact that she'd made a terrible mistake. With her flight from the sea star city she had betrayed everyone, the people of Aelenium, her comrades, and worst of all, Griffin. His face appeared before her inner eye, and this time it overrode everything else with such force that she writhed with pain and longing.

The Hexhermetic Shipworm said something more, but she didn't hear the words and looked right through him.

"Jolly!"

That was Buenaventure.

She pulled herself together and turned her head in his direction. "What?"

"We aren't alone anymore. Over there—behind us on the horizon!"

She ran toward him, through several ghosts who didn't get out of her way fast enough, leaped up the steps to the bridge, and looked tensely over the railing. The two parrots fluttered behind her and sat down on the railing beside her.

A ship had appeared in the distance. Its sails were numerous and very large. "Looks like a Spanish frigate!"

Buenaventure said nothing. But after several minutes, when they could see that their pursuer was much faster than they were and was coming closer and closer, his dog eyes narrowed when he glanced behind them.

"That's the *Quadriga*," he said. "Tyrone's ship."

"Can we make it to the coast before them?" Jolly asked, although she knew the answer.

Buenaventure shook his head, his bent-over ears flapping. "No. If they want to catch up to us, they will."

Jolly shouted commands to the ghosts on board. In a flash the cannons were manned and made ready to fire. Torches flamed, barrels were rammed, iron balls rolled down the barrels and clattered into place.

"There's no point in it," said Buenaventure, and for the first time Jolly noticed the strange undertone in his voice. The pit bull man was afraid—not for himself, but for her. And for his ship. She had never before seen him so rattled, and that caused her even greater fright than the appearance of the *Quadriga*.

"You don't want to fight?" she asked, dumbfounded.

"I didn't say that. But it's pointless. The *Quadriga* is a warship and has three times as many guns as we do. And if they want to board us, the ghosts will be hardly any help."

In her heart she knew he was right. But she wasn't ready to accept it. Not so close to . . . yes, to what? Her goal? But what *was* her goal, anyway?

"Jolly," said Buenaventure, "bring the worm here."

She ran to the bow, picked up the knapsack with the scolding worm in it, and carried him back to the bridge. Buenaventure fastened him firmly to his back.

"Pull in your head, Diamond of Poetic Art!"

"If anyone had so much breeding to declare me——" The worm fell silent when he discovered the ship that was now flying along in their wake, only a few hundred yards from them. "Oh," he said, and he crept into the knapsack without another word.

"Jolly, I'd like you to go below."

She stared at the pit bull man. "Most certainly not!"

"Please, do what I say!"

"I'm the only one who can command the ghosts. They won't obey you. Besides, I wouldn't think of hiding away."

The shipworm showed a tiny fraction of his head shield. "But hiding away isn't a bad idea."

"I'm staying!" she said to Buenaventure.

"And what if it's you they're after?"

She thought about that. Was that possible? What interest could the cannibal king possibly have in her?

"I will not go below," she said finally.

Buenaventure let out a wheeze, which in an ordinary human would probably have been a deep sigh. "Then at least hide yourself behind the chests on the main deck."

The monotonous hissing of the sea behind them was broken by the thunder of cannon.

"Oh, dear," whimpered the shipworm deep in his knapsack. "They're shooting at us!"

"That was only a warning shot," said Buenaventure. "They want us to heave to." His right eyebrow rose in his flat forehead. "Well, *Captain* Jolly?"

"Do what you think is right."

"Then you'd better disappear now."

She leaped down the steps to the deck and took cover behind some chests that stood next to the *Carfax*'s mainmast. "Ready to fire!" she called to the ghosts. When she saw Buenaventure nod to her from the bridge, she gave the order to heave to. The *Carfax* slowed.

A little later the larboard of the *Quadriga* slid into Jolly's field of vision. She had to pull in her head not to be seen.

"Ahoy, *Carfax*!" someone called. Jolly didn't dare raise her head. A ship like the *Quadriga* had a crew of more than a hundred men, and just as many pairs of eyes were at this moment directed to the deck of the *Carfax*. The risk of being discovered was too great.

"Ahoy, *Quadriga*!" replied the pit bull man. There followed a long pause in which Jolly wondered if Buenaventure had seen something over there that stopped his voice. There was a lump in her throat that she couldn't swallow down.

Then finally the pit bull man called, "We have no cargo aboard, if that's what you're after."

"Commander Tyrone wants to know if you have a young girl aboard."

Anyway, it was now clear to Jolly that the voice did not belong to Tyrone himself. In fact, it seemed familiar to her. Where from was hard to say, however, as long as the man was shouting across the gap between the two ships and the wind was distorting the syllables.

Buenaventure let out a barking laugh. "*Commander* Tyrone? Did he name himself that?"

"Answer, dog!"

"The *Carfax* has no children aboard!" the pit bull man said grimly.

"We'd like to convince ourselves of that personally."

"Do you intend to board us?"

Jolly changed her position a little so that she could see up to the bridge. Buenaventure's left hand rested on the wheel, but his right held a cocked pistol. Something wasn't right. He was acting strangely, much more restrained than usual. Was he only doing that in order not to irritate the crew of the *Quadriga*?

"We will indeed board you if we don't receive your permission for a goodwill visit," called the voice.

"An important word that you're using carelessly there, traitor!"

Traitor? What the devil was going on? Damn it, she had to see why Buenaventure was acting so strangely.

Very slowly she rose between the chests and looked over the larboard side.

The railing of the *Quadriga* towered more than six feet over that of the *Carfax*. Dozens of figures were standing up there, staring down at the deck of the smaller ship. They all wore the colorful, ragtag clothing of the Caribbean pirates, even though some of them were islanders. She avoided looking into the faces of any of them. She walked briskly over to the steps and mounted to the bridge.

"Jolly, you ought not to—"

"That's my decision, Buenaventure. Otherwise they'd sink the *Carfax*."

He sighed, and it sounded almost like a whimper. "I'm sorry."

Only when she turned toward the bridge of the opposing ship and saw who was standing up there did she understand what he meant.

She fell back with a scream of surprise. It was as if she'd banged her head on an invisible wall.

"I'm really sorry," said Buenaventure once more.

"Jolly," called the man. "It's great to see you again."

She couldn't answer. Her jaw felt as if it were screwed shut, her tongue was paralyzed.

"Bannon?"

He gave her the beaming smile that she had always liked so much. His straw blond hair fluttered in the stiff breeze, and his white shirt bellied out in the wind like a sail. On his chest hung a silver amulet. His father, who'd been the first cannoneer aboard a freebooter in the pay of the English crown, had presented it to him before he was strung up in the harbor of Maracaibo. Bannon had intended to pass it on to Jolly someday, he'd always said. *Someday it will belong to you.*

"But . . . how come . . . ?" She spoke so softly that the words didn't even reach Buenaventure.

The pit bull man lowered his gaze. Anger and pity in equal amounts gleamed in his eyes.

"Jolly, come aboard to us," Bannon called. "We've missed you. Look around, everyone is here!"

Her gaze wandered over the faces that inspected her from the *Quadriga*, some smiling, others serious. She recognized every third one of the men. There was Trevino, the cook on the *Skinny Maddy*, who'd designed the tattoo on her back; Cristobal, the steersman; Abarquez, who'd taken her up to the crow's nest for the first time; Long Tom, who didn't fit into any hammock on the *Maddy* and had sewn himself a bigger one out of plundered brocade; Redhead Doyle; old Sam Greaney; Guilfoyle, and the black giant Mabutu; the silent German, Kaspar Rosenbecker; Lammond and Lenard, the best cannoneers on the *Maddy*; and also Zargoza, who swore by all that was holy that he wasn't a Spaniard, even though everyone knew better.

Jolly recognized them all again and some others too.

She took a deep breath. She'd reached her goal. What she had longed for most: to find Bannon and her crew again. But it wasn't at all the reunion she'd imagined and for which she'd given up so much—if not everything.

"What . . . what are you doing on that ship?" she called, and her voice didn't sound half as firm as she wanted it to.

"I saw the spiders . . . and . . ." She stopped again. Tears came to her eyes. She hoped no one could see them at a distance.

"We're fine, Jolly!" replied Bannon. "Come aboard the *Quadriga* and I'll tell you everything."

She looked helplessly at Buenaventure, who shook his head almost imperceptibly. Why, devil take it, didn't he say something?

"What are you doing on the *Quadriga*?" She called. She was too churned up to listen very carefully to what he replied. But she needed time. To consider, to weigh, to . . . Suddenly she didn't know anything anymore. She doubted if she could ever make a decision, even if she were to mull it over for hours.

But she didn't have hours. Not even minutes.

Behind Bannon appeared a man in black, towering almost a head over him. His skull was shaved bald up to a long black ponytail, which he vainly wore draped forward over his right shoulder. Paintings decorated his face, and there was something wrong with his mouth that Jolly couldn't properly make out at this distance. With his teeth.

Bannon and Cristobal moved to one side to make room for the man at the railing.

"We're all very touched by this heartfelt reunion," he said in a tone of voice that belied his every word. "But we're frittering away our time here. Either you come over on your own, girl, or I'll send someone over to get you."

At his wave, a plank was shoved over from the main deck of the *Quadriga* to the *Carfax*.

"And hurry up!" he called over to Jolly. "I've heard so

much about you, I'd really like to get to know you myself."

"That's Tyrone," Buenaventure whispered to her. "The cannibal king of Orinoco."

So this was the man who'd cut off the ring fingers of Munk's mother many years ago and shredded her earlobes because she hadn't taken her jewelry off fast enough; the same man who, people said, led more than a thousand cannibals, whose atrocities had plunged even the bloodthirstiest tribes of Orinoco into utter terror.

But even more than all that, she was shocked by Bannon's submissiveness to him. Tyrone's appearance on the bridge had made all the men freeze, and Bannon, who'd never let himself be ordered to do something by anyone, acted like a ship's boy toward him.

This observation finally roused Jolly from her numbness. Her goal of finding Bannon and the others and possibly rescuing them from the fangs of a tormentor dissipated like a cloud of smoke and left her with a huge emptiness. An emptiness that now gradually filled with the knowledge that she ought not to have been there at all. Her place was not with Bannon, who had betrayed her. Her place was with her true friends. With Griffin and Soledad and Walker and . . . yes, even with Munk.

Once again she looked at Buenaventure, and this time he must have realized what was going on inside her. He nodded, almost with his eyes only.

Do we need more time? she wondered.

No, the ghosts were already in their positions. The cannons were ready to fire.

"Give up, little girl!" said Tyrone. He didn't have to bellow in order to be heard as Bannon had done. He spoke quite quietly, as if they were standing directly opposite each other, and yet she understood him without any straining. His voice halved the distance between them without any effort. "We have a full broadside aimed at you," he added.

"Jolly," shouted Bannon again, "be reasonable!"

"Do you remember what you taught me?" she replied in a trembling voice. "Never give up. You've said that to me over and over again, Bannon. Never give up, no matter who your opponent is and how bad your chances are."

"There *are* no chances," said Tyrone, savoring his words. "Not for you."

There were about fifteen feet between the two ships, and the steep plank that connected them was scraping loudly on the railing. Several men aboard the *Quadriga* held grappling hooks on ropes in their hands, which they would hurl over at Tyrone's command; with their help the ships would be firmly roped together so that the pirates could move from one ship to the other without risk.

Once the hooks were firmly seated, it would be too late to fire the cannons. Even now the ships were too close for a firefight; Tyrone and Bannon must know that. If a ball hit the powder magazine of the *Carfax*, the explosion might be big enough to seriously damage the *Quadriga* too.

Did Tyrone think he could take her in with a bluff like that?

"The commander gave us the antidote," said Bannon, and

for the first time he paid no attention to the look that Tyrone sent him. "He saved us. He won't do anything to you, either, Jolly. Don't forget, we're pirates—you too! We're always on the side of the ones who promise us the best take. That's the way it's always been in our business."

"I learned from you that freebooting is more than just a business, Bannon." Jolly shook her head sadly. "And as for the antidote: Maybe he did give it to you. But he was the one who lured the *Maddy* into the trap in the first place! Right, Tyrone? The galleon with the spiders, that was your idea."

"Certainly." The cannibal king grinned coolly. He had the face of a hungry predator.

"Who gave you the job of catching me?"

The cannibal king stretched his arm and pointed his bony forefinger in her direction. "I'm not here to chat with a child! Either you come over or my men will fetch you."

"Was it the Maelstrom, Tyrone?" Her knees were trembling, but no one on the deck of the *Quadriga* could see that. "Spill it to them. Tell them whose service you're in!"

Bannon frowned, but he didn't dare look at Tyrone.

"Go, men!" cried the cannibal king. "Go get her!"

But Jolly was faster. Before the first grappling hook could sail over, she sprang to the *Carfax*'s little bridge gun, reached determinedly right through the ghost at the cannon, and aimed it directly at Tyrone. The arm-long gun barrel was mounted on a swinging joint and glided around, screeching. Jolly snatched the torch from the ghost and held it to the powder opening.

OLD FRIENDS

Several men on the bridge of the *Quadriga* cried out at the same time. They all stormed in different directions, and even Tyrone started back in surprise. He might have reckoned with much, but not that Jolly—the *child*, as he'd called her—would attack.

"Show 'em!" Buenaventure roared grimly and pulled the wheel around.

The jolt of the cannon shot almost tore Jolly's right arm out of her shoulder. She was thrown backward, and the pressure wave hit her in the face like a box on the ear. For a moment smoke veiled her sight, and tears now ran down her face whether she wanted them to or not.

Piercing screams pealed over from the opposing deck. But in all the smoke it was impossible to tell if she'd hit the cannibal king.

She didn't wait but bellowed orders to the ghosts, as she had once learned from Bannon. In a flash, the *Carfax* was moving again.

"They're going to shoot us to pieces," shouted Buenaventure doggedly. "But they certainly won't forget this day for a long time."

At first she didn't know what he meant. But when she looked back at the *Quadriga*, it was instantly clear to her. The bridge railing on the starboard side had almost vanished. Their shot had torn a wide breach in her planking and exposed the cabins that lay behind it. Men had fallen into the hole and now found themselves one deck deeper. She recognized Bannon, who stared back at her, his face grim, perhaps in rage, but perhaps also because he knew that she'd signed her death warrant.

Where was Tyrone?

She discovered him a few seconds later among the men who'd fallen into the open cabins. He scrambled up in the midst of the debris and rubbed the blood off his face, obviously not his own, for soon he roughly pushed the injured aside and stepped into the breach that Jolly's hit had blasted in his bridge.

He called something after her that she didn't understand.

Bannon stood farther up, on the edge of the hole, supporting himself on a split wooden post and shaking his head. He knew what was going to happen now, but before Jolly could tell whether his expression was of sadness or at least sympathy, a cloud of smoke drove between the ships and covered her sight.

She had no time to consider the reactions of her former friends, all those men who'd raised her as if she were their daughter. Instead she wiped the tears from her cheeks, swallowed down her grief, and turned around to Buenaventure.

"They're going to sink us," she said matter-of-factly.

"Yes," he answered, likewise outwardly unexcited. "But that was worth it. Almost."

Now for the first time his jowls drew into a sad smile. He might have the face of a dog, but his smile was more human than that of the cannibal king.

Suddenly she thought of Walker. The *Carfax* had been his mother's ship, the ship of the first woman pirate in the

Caribbean. This sloop was her remembrance, her legacy. There was even an urn with her ashes in it in the captain's cabin.

She'd gambled with all that. And lost.

"I'm—," she began, but the cannon fire drowned out her words. The *Carfax* shook, and Jolly was thrown off her feet. Balls shredded the sails, and barely a second later the air was full of iron. Shredded ropes whipped around like snakes' bodies. Splinters of wood rained down on the bridge and onto the deck. The foremast dropped like a felled tree. The ghosts crowded into a nebulous whirl that seemed to be everywhere at the same time, yet they could no longer stop the sinking of the sloop.

"Jolly!" shouted Buenaventure, who was still holding the wheel. "Over the side! Quick!"

"Not without you."

"Stop arg—" Billows of smoke wafted up to the bridge and separated them. Fire had broken out somewhere, at the guns, probably. Again the cannons sounded, instantly followed by further hits.

The *Carfax* sank.

The ship screeched and moaned and groaned like a dying animal as its boards and masts convulsed one last time. Jolly felt through the smoke for the wheel, but the wheel was gone. Instead a deep hole of devastation gaped there.

"Buenaventure!"

She looked around, panicked, but she could discover no one.

"Buenaventure!"

The bow pointed down. Water rushed and slapped as the stern was raised out of the waves. At any moment the ship might break in two.

"Just say something!"

But she received no answer. Not from the pit bull man, not from the Hexhermetic Shipworm. Both were gone.

She wanted to go down with the *Carfax*. She alone bore the blame for all that had happened. If the two of them were dead, then she wanted to die too.

"Jolly!"

Someone was calling her name. Bannon? Tyrone? The *Quadriga* was no longer visible on the other side of the wall of smoke.

"Jolly! Down here!"

Perhaps she was only imagining the words. The noise around her was deafening. The ship beneath her convulsed, everywhere wood shattered, and she had to avoid the remains of the rigging so as not to get caught in it.

Nevertheless, she heard something again.

"Jolly! Jump!"

In a last burst of reason, she recalled what she had learned in Aelenium. The stern was now up in the air at such a steep angle that she had to fight against the incline to get to the railing. When she reached the spot, there was no railing left, just a row of shattered wooden stumps.

Jolly threw herself into the deep. Head forward, she shot downward, arms outstretched. It was her only chance;

otherwise, as a polliwog, she would shatter on the surface.

She broke through the waves, pulling a trail of air bubbles behind her. Instantly, the noise around her was cut off. How deep she glided down before she remembered her arms and legs and began to kick she did not know. There was blue-green half light around her. Churning water. Debris falling, spinning, to the bottom.

And then a murderous drag.

Right beside her, not twenty feet away, the *Carfax* sank into the sea. When her broken, exploded stern was finally underwater, there was no more holding her. The hollow spaces inside her filled immediately. In a chaos of ropes, rags of sails, and knife-sharp broken timbers, the wreck plunged down and pulled everything in its vicinity with it.

Jolly struggled in vain against the suction. She could of course breathe underwater, and when she wanted to, her hands parted the waters like air. But she couldn't make any headway against the force of the sinking ship. She saw the light pale above her, desperately fast. The deep caught with invisible fingers at her clothes, at her limbs.

Jolly shot downward, half on her back, lying almost horizontally, her face turned upward, her hands outstretched, as if over her there were something to which she might have held fast.

But there was nothing.

Only emptiness and the daylight, which was becoming ever weaker.

The Water Spinners

The suction dragged Jolly through dismal nothingness.

Around her reigned the uniform gray that she owed to her polliwog vision. It made her realize even more clearly the hopelessness of her plunge to the bottom.

If she didn't drown, she might be buried under the debris. Or speared by the tip of a mast.

Odd that she could still think so clearly. She might possibly be the first shipwreck victim who perceived her fall to the bottom consciously, without panic robbing her of understanding. The wreck of the *Carfax* had sunk faster than she was doing; it was somewhere beneath her, wrapped in a mantle of air bubbles. Pieces of debris kept detaching themselves and shooting to the surface, so that she had to take care not to be hit by them.

She could change her position within the vortex and turn

herself belly and face downward—but she could not *escape* from its force, which was pulling her relentlessly toward the bottom. Like a nail pulled by a magnet, she followed the shipwreck down.

How deep might the sea be here? Five hundred feet? Five thousand? No, probably not that deep; they were too close to the coast for that. It wouldn't be much longer, probably, before she reached the bottom.

She saw no fish during her fall. The animals avoided the colossus that had invaded their kingdom from above. Later, when the *Carfax* was lying on the seabed, they would draw near curiously, explore the debris, and gradually incorporate it into their world. Morays would then nest in her splintered stern, algae cover her boards, and crabs go searching for prey in her cracks and splits. Someday the misshapen mountain would be no different from its surroundings, ensnared by plants, half-buried under sand and slime.

These images chased through Jolly's head at top speed, flashed up, and were extinguished again. She thought that the suction was letting up a little now. The stream of air bubbles dwindled, and she could see the destroyed ship beneath her again, cocooned in waving ropes and bulging sails.

And she could hear! More and more quickly her ears were getting used to the new environment. When she and Munk had dived through Aelenium's undercity, they'd been able to converse. But she'd been too excited to perceive the underwater world's own sounds.

As silent as a fish, the saying went. Not at all! In the

distance Jolly could hear a confusion of whistling and peep-
ing and roaring, uttered in the chaotic rhythms of bird
twitter, except it wasn't twittering but the voices of the fish
that must be there somewhere beyond her sight.

The noise of the wreck's breaking up also rose toward her.
The pressure was squashing the wooden interior spaces. It
must long since have pulverized the cabin with Walker's memories of his mother. Again Jolly felt such a powerful stab in her
chest that for a moment she thought her body had been
pierced by a piece of debris. But it was only her bad conscience
that was hurting her, the certainty that she had saddled herself
with terrible guilt.

And still she continued to fall.

Now she wept—there was no one she had to hide it from
anymore. And her tears became one with the water as soon
as they came to her eyes. She didn't need to wipe them
away—even while crying she could see as clearly and sharply
as if she were on the surface.

Any moment she expected the impact that would probably break all her bones, given the speed of the suction. She
wouldn't drown, wouldn't be crushed by the pressure—she
would plainly and simply lie there, unable to move. God,
she would become the first human to die of thirst on the
bottom of the sea.

Suddenly a second drag seized her. It pulled her out of
the grip of the first and drew her to the side, much faster
than before, as if she were sliding through a narrow tunnel. Perhaps she lost consciousness for a moment, perhaps

even for hours. Or did she merely blink her eyes?

When she opened them again, she was in another place.

She'd just been seeing the *Carfax* below her, a tangle of wood and rope and bent iron. But in the next moment the ship was gone, as if it had dissolved into nothing from one heartbeat to the next.

The stream of falling debris was also gone.

Below her, Jolly now saw the sea bottom, a gray wasteland, which reminded her of the descriptions of the Crustal Breach. But this couldn't be the Breach or even a place in its vicinity. They were thousands of sea miles from it, entirely aside from the fact that there was no trace of the Maelstrom anywhere.

Was she dreaming? Was this the first step to the other world? Was she perhaps dying faster than she'd feared?

The suction faded away. At a height of about fifty feet over the bottom of the sea, she got her fall under control, hovered, and looked down.

There was something that puzzled her.

At first look it looked like a dark spot in the gray sand in the shape of an equilateral triangle. Only as she slowly sank deeper did she make out three figures. Three old women were sitting there, facing outward, with long white hair that divided at the backs of their heads into two skeins. They were linked together by these skeins, which stretched taut among their heads and wove over and under one another so that it wasn't possible to tell where the hair of one ended and the other began.

Pirate Emperor

The three women perched on low stools; before each stood a spinning wheel. Jolly rubbed her eyes, so very much did she mistrust her perception. But with a careful look there was no doubt: The women were sitting at spinning wheels at the bottom of the sea.

Now Jolly floated about twenty-five feet over them. She tried to remain on guard, but she was so fascinated by the strange sight of the spinners that she couldn't tear herself away.

Why did the three have their backs turned to one another? Why were they bound together by their hair? And what the devil were they doing down here?

"Hail, young polliwog," said one of them without lifting her head. Jolly couldn't tell which of the women had spoken.

"What . . . is this here?" she asked tentatively, sounding to herself quite simpleminded. This must be a hallucination, which would make dying easier for her.

"You will not die," said one of the women.

"Not yet, anyway," added a second.

Jolly looked from one to the other but couldn't make out which of them had moved her mouth. "Where is the *Carfax*?" she asked, now a bit more composed.

"Far away from here."

"Or not."

"It depends how one takes it."

Had they spoken one after the other? If yes, then they spoke with *one* voice.

Jolly hesitated to let herself sink any farther. When she realized, however, that this conversation would go nowhere as long as she wasn't looking the three in the eye, she overcame her nervousness. She glided a little to the side, so as not to land in the center of the triangle, and then moved down.

Sand puffed up when her feet touched the bottom. One voice cried, "Careful, child! Don't step on the yarn!"

Yarn? She looked down and discovered that the ground was covered with a sort of net. Countless threads were interwoven into a dense web. They came from all directions, in a star shape, and ended at the spinning wheels of the old women.

"What is that?" She crouched down and stretched out her hand to touch one of the finger-thick strands. She half expected that the women would restrain her, but there was no protest.

A tickling went through her hand and shot up her arm, but it withdrew quickly again, as if it streamed out of Jolly's fingers back into the yarn. The material was soft and smooth and as clear as . . . water?

Indeed. The old women were spinning strings of water. Or of something that was already *in* the water, at any rate, and thickened under their hands.

"Magic," said one of the old ones. "But you would have realized that yourself, wouldn't you?"

Amazed, Jolly looked away over at the network, whose end vanished at the edge of her range of vision. "Are these the magic veins?"

"We call it yarn," said the old one sitting nearest Jolly. Her lips scarcely moved as she spoke.

"But that is probably the same thing," said another.

"Who are you?" Jolly asked.

"Spinners."

"I see that. But I mean . . . what are you doing down here?" She knew the answer already, before the women said it. "We spin the yarn."

"What do you want with me?" Jolly knew without a doubt that her presence here was not coincidental.

"We have observed you."

"You and the other polliwog."

"Did *you* create us?" Again Jolly looked down at the magic water strands, which, although they were surrounded by water, never lost their shape. As if they were firmer and thicker. Or even more magical.

"The yarn created you," said one of the women.

"Not we."

"But that is unimportant."

"It is time that you learn certain things."

"We thought others would explain it to you."

"But no one has."

"So we will do it."

All three nodded, and the band of hair between them stretched to the breaking point. They seemed not to feel any pain from it.

Jolly slowly circled around the three women. The sand whirled about her feet, erasing her tracks in seconds. "Tell me first what kind of a place this is."

"It has no name."

"We are spinners."

"Here we spin."

Jolly clenched her lower lip in her teeth. Instead of asking more questions, she inspected the women as she walked past them. All three wore long gowns, which covered their feet even as they sat; like everything else down here, the material of their clothing was a monotonous gray. The long, fleshless fingers of the old women worked the spinning wheels nimbly and with no extra movements. None of the three looked up at Jolly as she walked past them. But they spoke alternately, even though it wasn't clear in what order.

"You were created out of the sea, little polliwog."

"Out of the magic of the yarn and the power of the water."

Jolly stopped. The yarns were the magic veins she'd heard about in Aelenium. This was the place where they originated. She grew dizzy at the thought of how much power was concentrated here. It was said that the Crustal Breach was full of magic power, and only some veins intersected there. But this was the source, the root of the vein network. And the three old women were its creators.

And thus, to be precise, also the creators of Jolly and Munk.

No, she contradicted herself. They haven't created me. Only the polliwog magic in me. But somehow this thought couldn't reassure her either.

Who were these three? Sorceresses? Witches? Goddesses? Or something that lay beyond the origins of the gods?

Moments later she learned how close to the truth her guess had come.

"The sea is the place from which all life stems," said one of the women. Her fingers danced on the spindle and yarn like insect legs. "Every animal, every human, had its beginning in the ocean. Out of the water were born the first living creatures, and the water has made them into what they are today."

Jolly nodded impatiently. She'd already heard something similar. Hadn't the cook Trevino told of it during one of his speeches about God and the world, which he always held forth on when he was drunk?

"The gods also came from out of the sea long ago."

"Not out of *this* sea."

"Not out of *this* water."

Jolly crouched down in front of one of the women to be able to look her in the face. She now had no more fear, felt not even a trace of shyness with them. Like a young animal that still knows its mother by her scent even months after its birth, Jolly was suddenly overwhelmed by a feeling of deep trust. An aura of the wondrous surrounded the three women like something she knew from dreams.

"Not out of this water," she echoed in a whisper, and then her eyes widened. "Out of the Mare Tenebrosum? Is that what you mean?"

"The oldest of all seas," said the woman in front of her, and another agreed: "The mother of all oceans." And the third said, "The father of all waters."

Excitedly Jolly tried to follow the spinners' words. What sort of talk was this about gods? She didn't even believe in one God, never mind several.

"They have all lived."

"And they live still."

"But they are gods no longer."

"Or what humans understand by that."

"They have become like you."

"Almost like you."

"They have lost their power since they created all of this."

"This world has cost them all their strength."

"It has sucked them empty."

"But so that no more powerful one follows them from the sea of seas, they have closed the entry and guard it jealously."

"Many ages long."

"They have hidden away and mourn the old days of their power. In order to be near the water out of which they were born, they established a city on the sea, which serves them as a hiding place and a fortress."

"A city that seals the passageway."

"Aelenium."

Although Jolly could breathe underwater, for a moment she was breathless with excitement. "You mean to say that the people of Aelenium . . . are not humans at all? But gods?"

"Not all."

"Only a few now."

"They were too weak, even for the simplest things. Many have gone, simply disappeared."

"Like a dream in the first rays of the sun."

"No one remembers them anymore."

"They needed help and lured humans through the fog to Aelenium. Men who took over the tasks for them."

"But these men had children. And they again had children. Generation on generation."

"And while the old gods who had withdrawn to Aelenium died off, the number of humans grew. Today there are only a few of the original inhabitants left."

"Forefather?" Jolly asked hesitantly.

"The oldest of all. The Creator."

Jolly held up her hands defensively, as if she could push away the things the spinners were saying. "But Forefather is only an old man with a lot of books!"

"He is that today."

"But he was not that always."

"He had a name then."

"Many names."

"But he was always the same. The Creator. The first who came out of the sea of seas and kindled a light in the darkness."

All at once Jolly felt the weight of the sea over her, a column of water as wide as her shoulders and many thousands of feet high. Powerless she sank to her knees, let herself fall back, and pulled her legs into a cross-legged position.

"Forefather is God?"

"Not *the* God. Only a god."

"The oldest."

"What about the others?" Jolly asked. "Count Aristotle and d'Artois and—"

"They are men. Eager hands with a spark of understanding."

". . . and the Ghost Trader?"

"The One-Eyed One."

"The Raven God."

"Formerly his birds bore other names. Hugin, the one. Munin, the other. They were ravens then."

For a long moment there was silence, as if the three spinners were aware that they were already forgetting things. That their strength too was weakening, just like that of the gods.

"No matter," said one of them finally.

"No matter, no matter," the two others agreed.

"But the Masters of the Mare Tenebrosum," said Jolly, still trying to wring a meaning from all this, something that she could take in and comprehend. "The Masters are . . . bad!"

"What is that?"

"Who said that?"

"Above all, they are young. And powerful. Just as the gods of this world once were, an infinitely long time ago."

"They are curious."

"Greedy, perhaps."

"Or envious."

"But bad? What is bad, Jolly?"

It did not escape her that the women had called her by name for the first time. And she knew what that meant. The women expected an answer from her. Nothing parroted, nothing she had been taught, but *her* answer.

What is that—bad?

The Acherus had murdered Munk's parents. That was bad. Or not? Was it bad if Spaniards killed Englishmen?

All a question of point of view, thought Jolly, and felt sick and guilty about it. But it didn't change the answer. All a question of point of view.

No! she pursued the thought. *Killing is bad, no matter what the reason is.* Perhaps that was the solution. But how could she presume to judge the Masters of the Mare when she herself had taken part in countless forays and privateering expeditions? Certainly there were people who would have described her—Jolly—as bad. So it couldn't be that simple.

"If the Masters of the Mare Tenebrosum are not bad," she said thoughtfully, "then why are we fighting against them?"

That earned her nothing but silence.

"Why?" she asked once more, and she jumped up. She was just about to grab one of the women by the shoulder and shake her.

"These are the facts," said one spinner. "Produce a meaning for yourself."

Laboriously Jolly attempted to put everything she'd learned into a reasonable order. Forefather was born out of the waters of the Mare Tenebrosum. He had "kindled a light," as the spinners had called it, and created this world. Jolly's world. More and more life had arisen from the new oceans, other gods, then animals, then humans. And as the gods had finally used up their power and become weaker, they withdrew to Aelenium, with which they sealed the door to the Mare Tenebrosum. They were no longer strong enough to savor the fruits of their creation to the fullest, but neither would they grant that to anyone else. They were not prepared to share with the powers of the Mare Tenebrosum, not even Forefather, who'd originally come from there himself. They jealously guarded what was theirs; they were not protecting humanity but defending their position. Like a child who withholds a plaything from another even if he no longer plays with it himself.

So that was the secret of Aelenium. A city of gods who had ceased to be gods a long time ago. Some gone and forgotten, others still alive but already on the threshold of oblivion.

What did that mean for Jolly? For her friends? For the battle against the Maelstrom? She was much too confused to find answers, so she asked her question aloud.

"It means nothing," said one of the women.

"Or everything," another added.

Rage mounted in Jolly. Rage at everything that the Ghost Trader had withheld from her the whole time. Rage at herself because she felt so terribly helpless. And rage at these three women (who were certainly anything but ordinary women). Why tell her these things if they couldn't give her a solution?

"Because the solution stands only at the goal of your journey," one spinner said. "Perhaps."

"You thought everything was simple. Go to the Crustal Breach, close the Maelstrom back into his mussel, and everything is over."

"Nothing is over."

"Nothing is ever over."

Jolly stamped her foot angrily in the sand. Dust arose from the bottom of the sea and, before she realized it, surrounded her like a fog. She quickly took several steps to one side, but that just made it worse.

Only when the swirls had settled again did she see what purpose they had served.

The water spinners were gone. The bottom was smooth, the magic strands vanished.

Not fifty paces away lay the wreck of the *Carfax*, and that was also what had stirred up the ground: It was still raining debris, which landed in the sand around the ship, very near Jolly.

A dream? A hallucination from the fall into the deep?

No, she thought. *Most certainly not.*

Her legs were wobbly, but she flexed her knees, summoned her strength, and pushed off. Like an arrow she shot upward into the dim light, toward the crystal roof of the distant surface.

The brightness of the day came nearer, sunlight breaking on the glassy crowns of the waves. Golden-white beams pierced the surface, only to vanish several fathoms into the deep.

From down here it looked as if someone had brushed through the waves with a golden brush; the sparkling bristles combed the waves, now in this direction, now in that.

Jolly slowed her ascent a few feet below the surface of the sea. She wondered if sharks had already been lured by the spectacle of the battle. As long as she ran over the water, she was safe from them. But when she swam, she was a prey for the predator fish like any other shipwrecked person.

Buenaventure! seared through her mind. How could she have forgotten him and the Hexhermetic Shipworm while she was speaking with the spinners in the deep? Had she squandered valuable time? On the other hand, they'd hardly left her any choice. As had so often happened in the weeks past.

She cautiously stuck her head through the surface. The sparkling of the sunshine on the wave crests blinded her for a moment. The unaccustomed low angle of sight, from which she'd seen the sea only a few times, made her uneasy. For the first time she felt restricted by the masses of water, something almost like claustrophobia.

The *Quadriga* was gone.

Jolly's first thought was: *How long was I under there, actually?* And her second: *Where are Buenaventure and the worm?*

Ship debris can stay on the surface for days, or even longer, depending on its composition. The fact that until a few moments ago pieces were still falling to the bottom didn't mean that the *Carfax* had sunk only a short time ago. Anything was possible.

Nonsense! Don't obsess over it. You only spoke to the spinners for a few minutes. Only a few minutes.

And then Jolly caught sight of them: three silhouettes rising from the horizon, narrow and high and remarkably shaped. About two hundred feet away. Not ships, most certainly not. In the first moment she thought the spinners themselves had risen up from the bottom.

An instant later she recognized the truth.

It was sea horse riders!

Humans on three hippocampi.

"Ahoy!" she called as loudly as she could. "I'm here! *Here I am!*"

She placed her hands on the water on each side of her as

if it were a ledge and pulled herself up. From one second to the next, she was standing upright on the waves. And she realized at once that there was no going back: For miles around there was no high point to dive—and without the dive she couldn't go under again. So she was at the mercy of the riders, whoever they were.

"Jolly?" cried a disbelieving voice. And then breaking with joy: "Jolly! There she is! That's Jolly over there!"

"Soledad?" She rushed toward the riders. "Walker? Is that you?"

The sea horses were nearing so fast that Jolly's eyes could hardly follow the movements. Soledad was the first beside her and made her sea horse sink deeper into the water so that her face was on the same level as Jolly's. With a shriek of joy, the princess embraced her. "Blast it, Jolly! We were just thinking we'd lost you!"

Walker and the Ghost Trader guided their animals to Soledad's side, and now she saw who was sitting behind the captain in the hippocampus's saddle.

"Buenaventure!" Jolly loosed herself from Soledad and ran over to the pit bull man, who looked so relieved that he would probably have preferred to leap off the horse and run to meet her on the water.

"Jolly! You're alive! By Poseidon's algae beard!" They embraced each other, as well as they could. The pit bull man was so overjoyed that he wouldn't let go of her again. His barking laugh rang out over the water, and he grinned with relief.

"Good to see you, Jolly," said Walker. He was also relieved, although dark shadows lay on his face, shadows of grief and loss: His ship, his mother's ship, was destroyed. The *Carfax* lay on the bottom of the sea.

"I'm sorry," Jolly stammered. "I—really—I don't know what I can say."

"I'll tan your bottom for it later," said Walker somberly. Numbly he looked over the pieces of flotsam that were still floating on the waves. Then he quickly shook his head. He visibly had to pull himself together. "But now—"

"First of all, we're glad that you're alive," the Ghost Trader finished Walker's sentence. Jolly turned around to him. The water spinners' words rose to her mind when she saw him sitting above her on his sea horse, a dark silhouette in front of the sinking sun. His robe bellied out, fluttering in the sea wind. Above him hovered the two parrots, their wings beating frantically.

She straightened her shoulders and looked from one to the other. "I was dumb. I would like to apologize to all of you and . . . Wait! Where's the shipworm?" Her eyes had fallen on Buenaventure's knapsack, which hung flat and empty on his back. "Oh, no."

The pit bull man shook his head despondently. "He didn't make it, Jolly! I looked for him right after I went overboard. . . . But the knapsack, it was suddenly empty. He must have slid out and . . ." He fell silent and dropped his eyes.

Jolly whirled around to go look among the flotsam, but the Ghost Trader's voice held her back.

"No, Jolly! It's pointless. We've found no trace of him."

Jolly's gaze slid over the sea and the floating remains of the *Carfax*, far out to the horizon and then to the distant stripe of coast.

Again it was Soledad who was the first to come up beside her and gently place a hand on her shoulder. But this time the princess said nothing, only listened with her to the whispering of the wind.

Jolly felt salty tears on her lips, and for the first time in her life it occurred to her that sorrow tasted exactly like the sea.

The Fleet of the Enemy

The fortress of the cannibal king had been erected on a mountain, half of which had long ago tumbled into the sea. This had produced a steep rock wall that fell away some sixty feet to the ocean and ended in a foaming wall of spume. The winds here blew sharply from the northeast and drove the sea relentlessly against the coast. Remains of the sunken mountain stuck out of the water as jagged reefs, surrounded by foaming surf. It was next to impossible to maneuver ships through the rocks from the north and east. The only passage through the reefs was to the south and west, and it led into the shallow waters of the Orinoco delta.

On a side arm of the river, beneath the cliff fortress, there was an extensive settlement of huts and wooden houses, whose outskirts overflowed to a huge tent city. It had long ago spread out over the cultivated area and merged with the dark green thicket of the jungle.

"Where's the harbor?" Walker asked, when they saw the fortress and the settlement lying in the distance. He was still having trouble keeping the sea horse steady under him. In contrast to Soledad, who controlled her mount as surely as if she'd had years of experience with it, Walker obviously didn't find it easy to ride on the hippocampus, even after several days. Having the heavy Buenaventure behind him in the saddle didn't exactly contribute to his well-being either.

The Ghost Trader squinted his one eye as if he could see the coast more clearly that way. "That is strange," he said. "Where do they moor all their ships?"

Walker scratched his head. "Maybe Tyrone was telling the truth. If his cannibal tribes intend to attack Caracas from the land side, they don't need any ships."

"A march from here to Caracas on foot?" Soledad shook her head decidedly. "Very unlikely. That's more than a hundred miles through thick jungle."

"The natives know their way around the area, though," Walker said, but his tone showed that he was anything but convinced himself.

"We're east of the delta here, aren't we?" asked Jolly.

The Ghost Trader nodded. "The outlet there must be the easternmost arm."

"Then I know where the ships are lying."

All heads turned toward her in surprise. Soledad inspected Jolly over her shoulder. "Really?"

"I told you about the book where I discovered the drawing of the spider. There were also maps of the Orinoco delta in it. I tore one out."

"Do you have it with you?" asked the Trader.

"No. It went down with the *Carfax*."

"Like so much," said Walker grimly.

Jolly still couldn't look him in the eye, she was so very ashamed for the loss of the ship. "Anyway, I had enough time to look at the map and compare it with the ones in the cabin," she explained in a low voice. "I think I know exactly now how the arms of the Orinoco run."

"And?" Walker asked.

"The fortress wasn't shown, of course, but the cliff it's on was. Otherwise the coast is flat here. I think that behind the bluff there's a kind of lake, with a connection to the delta. We can't see it from out here because the mountain with the fortress is exactly in front of it."

The Ghost Trader looked toward the coast. "That means the fortress itself is on a kind of spit that's bounded by the sea and the river on two sides and on a third, landward, by the lake."

Jolly nodded vigorously.

Soledad was visibly impressed. She gave Jolly a smile, then turned to the men. "Tyrone is a pirate. He wouldn't build himself a fortress like this if he had no way of providing a protected anchorage for several ships in its vicinity. What Jolly says sounds reasonable."

Walker had to agree. "In any case, we should take a closer look."

"That's why we're here," said the Ghost Trader decidedly and drove his sea horse forward. Immediately all three animals were shooting along in the direction of the coast, in a wide arc, so that no one would see them from the battlements of the fortress.

They came on land about two miles east of the rock. The sea horses withdrew to deep water again, while the five comrades waded through the surf to the shore. Before them lay a narrow sandy beach, which disappeared into the shadows of the ancient jungle after just thirty or forty feet. A few crabs crept over the sand; coconuts lay under the palms along the edge of the jungle. Walker broke some in two with his saber, and they drank the sweet milk inside, ate some of the meat, and shared a ration of meager provisions that the Trader, Walker, and Soledad had brought in their saddlebags.

Not really fortified, but still halfway satisfied, they began moving again. Jolly stayed close to Buenaventure and observed with amazement how familiar Soledad and Walker were with each other. During the ride to the coast, the princess had told her what had happened on Saint Celestine and what Tyrone was planning; but as to what had happened between her and Walker, about that she'd said nothing.

Anyway, Jolly's thoughts were someplace else entirely. She grieved over the Hexhermetic Shipworm, and she could tell from looking at Buenaventure that it was the same with him. The little fellow might have been a pain in the neck, but during their voyage on the *Carfax* he'd become very dear to them.

And then there was Bannon. Every memory of him was

like a blow in the face. The man who'd raised her and whom she'd loved like a father had sided with her enemy. An enemy who—if Soledad's suspicions were right—was not only a human-flesh-eating monster, but an ally of the Maelstrom.

The Ghost Trader believed that Tyrone's plan for taking Caracas was intended to distract the pirates. The truth was plain: The Spanish armada and the pirate fleet were to mutually demolish each other in front of Caracas, while the kobalin armies could attack Aelenium undisturbed. It was now clear why the Maelstrom had waited so long for his attack on the sea star city.

But how important to all that was what Jolly had learned from the water spinners? Now that she was with her friends again, the meeting with the three old ones seemed even more unreal—blurry, like a dream. But could she make it so simple? It was tempting to divide the world into good and bad again, as before—Aelenium on this side, the Mare Tenebrosum and the Maelstrom on the other side—but her reason told her that it hadn't been that simple for a long time.

The mere fact that the Maelstrom might have broken away from the Masters of the Mare disarranged the image that she'd made for herself until then, even if it didn't make that image any less terrifying. She wondered once more what would have happened if the bridge had not caught fire and Griffin had not pulled her back.

One thing was certain: The answers to these questions were only to be found in Aelenium. Whether the gods who had withdrawn there were now acting in their own interest or not, they commanded the knowledge to save humanity. The kobalins must be stopped before they started their campaign of annihilation. And the Maelstrom must be halted.

What is bad? the water spinners had asked. Now Jolly realized that the answer to that question wasn't important. The goals of the inhabitants of Aelenium were unimportant, so long as their battle served to protect the entire Caribbean. Jolly need not care whether jealousy or the old interests of the gods were driving them.

What was Griffin doing now? Was he still safe in Aelenium? When would the great attack of the Maelstrom begin, and how long would the city be able to withstand it?

And what about Munk? She shook her head so hard that Buenaventure, who was tramping along beside the others just as reflectively as she was, turned to her.

"Don't reproach yourself on account of the worm," he said.

She was grateful to be diverted from Griffin and Munk for a moment. Not that the reminder of the shipworm meant any relief. "If I hadn't set out in the *Carfax*, you wouldn't have had to follow me," she said dejectedly. "And the worm would be in Aelenium now."

"Where the good people of the Poets' District would probably have roasted him on a spit, they were so upset."

She gave the pit bull man a halfhearted smile. It was dear of him to want to relieve her of the responsibility for what had happened. Nevertheless, she knew the truth. She alone bore the guilt.

They sank into silence again as they hiked westward among

the outermost trees of the jungle, just far enough inland not to be seen from the sea. In other circumstances, the walk to the bluff wouldn't have taken an hour. But the soft sand delayed them, and they were all moving tensely and cautiously, for the danger of meeting enemies became greater with every step.

For a while they encountered no enemy sentries. Soon the land began to rise and grow rockier. The sand dwindled to soft drifts and then it was entirely behind them. There were no paths here; they had to hack their way through the increasingly dense bush with their sabers, through vines and leafy shoots. Walker and Buenaventure went ahead and cut a path in the thicket. Every stroke seemed to Jolly treacherously loud, and she was afraid the startled birds taking to the air would alarm Tyrone's guards.

Their ascent now grew increasingly difficult. They were moving over a natural ramp of rock that on their right fell steeply to the sea. The fortress must be somewhere in front of them. But what was on the left side? Jungle, certainly. But if the lake lay there in the south somewhere, the land in between must drop away as well.

They found out a little later, when Walker and Buenaventure stopped. The forest thinned in front of them. The red-gold of the setting sun streamed through the tree trunks in small stripes, coloring their faces blood red. They'd already turned away from the cliff a while ago and had been walking farther to the left, always going where a break through the jungle seemed easier and caused less noise. And so they had reached the western edge of the rock ramp.

Pirate Emperor

In front of them opened a chasm, as steep as the cliff at their backs and just as insurmountable. A wider strip of jungle hugged the rock wall a hundred feet below them. On the other side of it, shimmering like a plain of gold in the evening twilight, lay the lake.

"Jolly, you limb of Satan, you were right!" Walker took a deep breath. Here on the rock edge the air was clearer and fresher than under the oppressive leafy roof of the jungle. Jolly, too, felt that breathing was easier.

Tyrone's fleet lay at anchor on the lake.

There were at least two hundred ships.

For a while no one said a word. They were all probably having the same thought. Each one recognized how hopeless a battle against such superior strength would be.

Finally Buenaventure spoke. "Where did he get them all?"

"Built them," said Walker. "Look. Most of them have never been to sea yet." He pointed to a row of piers, ramps, and wooden houses to the south, on the far side of the lake. "That over there must be the workshops."

"But I don't see any half-finished ships," said Jolly. "Do you really think they were all built here?"

The Ghost Trader nodded in the shadow of his hood. "The fleet is ready. Those ships down there are only waiting for the order to run out."

"Even if all the pirates of Tortuga, New Providence, and the Lesser Antilles joined together, there wouldn't be such a large fleet," Soledad said dully. "It must have taken years to build so many ships."

As far as could be seen in the twilight, the jungle to the south had been extensively cleared. It was hard to make out where the forest began again. The humidity rose steaming from the ground, obscuring the horizon.

"That can't have been done without help." Walker said what they all were thinking. "The natives are no shipbuilders. He must have had architects, carpenters, sailmakers."

"Spaniards," said Soledad.

"Spaniards?" Walker repeated. And then he understood. "Of course! He isn't just committing *one* treachery, but two at once. I'll be damned!"

"Two?" Jolly asked.

Walker ran his hand excitedly through his long hair. "That damned whoreson! He guarantees the Spaniards he'll lure the pirates into a trap. And he promises the pirates an easy victory over the Spaniards. As thanks for his double-cross, the Spaniards provide him with men and material to build his own fleet. Maybe they later intend to leave part of the Caribbean to him or to support him in his raids against the English."

Jolly stared at him. "Don't forget the third move in his game," she said softly. "He betrays the Spaniards, because in truth he intends to use the fleet for an entirely different purpose."

"The destruction of Aelenium," murmured the Ghost Trader. "Tyrone is also a servant of the Maelstrom. He'll send his ships to Aelenium to support the kobalins."

"And I'd like to bet"—Soledad took the thought further—"that though the Spaniards are certainly figuring on an attack by the pirates of Tortuga and New Providence, they aren't in on the fact that they've joined up with the Antilles captains. So the Spanish armada will face a much larger pirate fleet than they expected. Tyrone has also provided for that. This way he plays our people against the Spaniards, and vice versa. And in thanks for it, he receives a powerful fleet."

"That is rotten," growled Buenaventure.

"That is clever," said Walker appreciatively.

"Indeed," agreed the Ghost Trader. "Tyrone and the Maelstrom will take Aelenium in a pincer movement. The fleet on the water, the kobalins underneath. And who knows what other surprises he's prepared for us."

Jolly was silent. While the others still spoke of Tyrone's plans, she was looking into the future. Forefather and the others had been right from the beginning. There was only one way to stop ruin: She and Munk must go down to the Crustal Breach and face the Maelstrom.

She stepped closer to the edge of the cliff and looked past the others to the west. A few dozen yards away rose the outer wall of the fortress. Still farther to the west a snaking path led down through the rocks to the city of huts and tents on the shores of the lake. Only now did she see that a broader, deeper water channel cut the settlement in two—the outflow of the lake to the Orinoco delta and to the open sea.

"Are we going farther?" Walker asked. "Or shall we turn around and warn Aelenium?"

"Farther," said the Ghost Trader. "Maybe we can learn even more down there."

"In that rats' nest?" Soledad frowned. "Is that really a good idea?"

"Have you a better one, Princess?"

But before Soledad could answer, there was a sudden racket down below. At first they heard only individual cries, but then came the sounds of shattering wood.

"There!" cried Jolly excitedly and pointed down below. "There, in front of the *Quadriga*!"

Just then they all saw it.

One of the ships had listed and sunk. It must have been a huge leak, for it went down with such speed that the water was sloshing over the railing within an extremely short time. Two other ships were also listing steeply, followed by a fourth. And a fifth.

"What's going on down there?" Walker asked.

"Sabotage," growled Buenaventure with satisfaction. "Someone's making sure the tubs fill up with water."

"Someone?" Jolly gasped breathlessly. Then suddenly she exulted. "Damn it all! I know who it is!"

How had they passed the fortress wall without being discovered by the guards? How had they succeeded in descending the path unseen, in spite of the troops of workers and tribal warriors who met them? How did they manage, against all reason, to pass the outlying houses of the settlement and get straight into the confusion of little streets without someone pointing a finger at them and identifying them as spies?

Afterward, Jolly didn't have an entirely satisfactory answer to any of these questions. In her thoughts, the path through the rocks melted to a confusion of crouching and sneaking, stolen looks into the darkness, wide detours around sentries, toneless whispers, fingers clenched on saber grips, and rivulets of sweat running down her forehead and into her eyes.

But none of that really counted. Her relief outweighed any other feeling, even her fear of falling into the hands of Tyrone's cannibals.

The Hexhermetic Shipworm was alive! No one had any more doubt of that now. *He* was responsible for the leaks in the ships around the *Quadriga*. After the *Carfax*'s sinking he must have eaten through the hull of Tyrone's flagship, so close to the surface that hardly any water got in during the short trip to the harbor. Jolly found the whole thing astonishing: She wouldn't have credited him with so much foresight. He could just as well have sunk the *Quadriga* out there on the sea. But instead he'd let himself be carried into Tyrone's harbor in order to create even greater destruction there.

She imagined him snaking through the water from ship to ship. With his stumpy legs he wasn't a good swimmer—in fact, at their first meeting Jolly had saved him from drowning—and yet it seemed that somehow he'd managed to go from one hull to another.

Good, dear, wise worm!

Jolly and Buenaventure exchanged looks, and both felt the same relief. The others still might not know how to cherish the worm properly, maybe didn't even believe he was really responsible for the damage to the fleet. But Jolly and the pit bull man were agreed. Nothing was going to keep them from rescuing the little fellow now—at the very most they'd wait until he'd assisted a few more ships to the bottom of the sea.

And while Jolly was still indulging in her high spirits, the Ghost Trader suddenly said, "It won't be enough."

Jolly looked up at him. "What?"

He shook his hooded head. "There are at least two hundred ships lying out there. How many hulls can he eat a hole in before they catch him? Seven, eight? Possibly a dozen. And they may even be able to save some of the ships, if they stop the leaks fast enough. The fleet itself will scarcely be weakened; Tyrone won't have to change his plans."

The paths between the huts and wooden houses were full of men. Many were natives with teeth filed to a point like Tyrone's, but most were in European clothing and had obviously been trained by Tyrone's subordinates to become sailors. So he wasn't manning his ships with only Spaniards and the scum of the Old World, but also with cannibals. Jolly shuddered at the thought of how long Tyrone must have planned this conspiracy. Many years, that was certain. And no pirate had known of it.

None except Kendrick, the pirate emperor himself. Or had he also fallen into a trap? Did he really think that the attack on Caracas had any chance of succeeding? It looked frighteningly likely. Kendrick was a perfect idiot if he trusted a beast like Tyrone.

The comrades reached the shore of the lake and hurried around it in a southerly direction. When they looked up at the rock over their shoulders, they saw the fortress of the cannibal king enthroned over the landscape. It was an unadorned building, similar to the defense installations the Spaniards had built on many Caribbean islands: high, sandstone-colored walls, along whose long defense galleries were places for numerous guns; no towers, but low buildings, which were protected from cannon shots by the parapets; and few entrances, probably only a main gate, which was secured by a moat and a drawbridge.

Tyrone had received more from his Spanish allies than just help in building his ships—they had erected for him on this rock at the end of the world a fortress that could match a governor's palace in strength and defensive might.

It was gradually dawning on Jolly that Tyrone was far more than a mad despot who had forced the native tribes of the jungle to accept his command. He also knew how to influence the governors of the Old World.

The friends had almost reached the place where the sinking ships were anchored. Workers and sailors were running around excitedly. Apparently they were vainly trying to bring order to the chaos. Everywhere, orders were shouted and instructions given. Men with knives between their teeth leaped into the water to search out the culprit. They'd quickly realized that it must be someone who was diving from one hull to the next and hiding in the labyrinth of narrow waterways between ships.

Oaths rang out from dozens of throats, some in English, Spanish, or French, others in languages that none of them understood. The noise was deafening. One of the ships leaned to the larboard and rammed its masts into the rigging of a neighboring frigate. Yards splintered, ropes tore. Men who found themselves on the deck of the sinking ship leaped overboard, screaming, and landed across the paths of those who were already in the water looking for the saboteur. Soon it was so crowded down there that every attempt to catch the malefactor was inevitably doomed to fail.

Jolly gained new hope for the Hexhermetic Shipworm. If he didn't drown, it had become highly improbable that anything would happen to him. No one was figuring that such an inconspicuous creature as he was responsible for the destruction. Maybe he could, small as he was, vanish unnoticed among the excited men.

"Well, I'll be goddamned!" escaped from Walker. "Look at that!"

They were standing in the shadow of some boxes and piled lumber not far from the quay where the damaged *Quadriga* lay at anchor. There was frantic activity in front of them, and yet now they clearly heard shouting ring out over the wharf from Tyrone's ship. The cannibal king and Bannon seemed not to be aboard any longer, but among the men who now streamed hastily onto land, Jolly recognized a whole line of members of her former crew. The sight of the familiar faces pained her. She hurriedly stepped back into the Ghost Trader's shadow.

"Serves them right," murmured Soledad, as the *Quadriga*, too, listed and slowly sank.

"There's Bannon over there," said Buenaventure, laying one of his huge hands on Jolly's shoulder as if he wanted to keep her from running over to him.

Bannon and some of his men were making their way

through the mass of men who were running around in confusion on the quay. Obviously no one had any idea how to stop the sinking of the ships, and so they followed all the different orders or stood around uselessly and in the way.

Bannon was yelling orders, gesticulating frantically, and trying to shoo some of the sailors who'd just left the *Quadriga* back on board to fix the leaks. The stench of hot tar wafted over from somewhere, but it was obvious that neither this nor any other measures would save the *Quadriga*. Bannon and his crew had to look on helplessly from the quay as the ship sank into the waters of the lake. It didn't tip but sank down with majestic calm until water was washing over the deck. When it finally landed on the bottom, only the masts were still sticking out of the boiling surface. The rest had vanished into the lake.

Jolly counted thirteen ships that had already been sunk or could no longer be saved. Ever more new ones were added to them, but cannily, the worm wasn't running along one row but apparently randomly flitting back and forth in the crowd of close-lying ships.

"It's getting too dangerous," said Walker. "We have to get out of here."

Now men were streaming past them from all over; several hundred were already on the quay. More crowded onto the decks of every ship that had not yet been affected. And still it appeared that no one knew who or what was responsible for the catastrophe. Countless ships had let rowboats down onto the water. Other crews simply jumped overboard to get away from the suction of the sinking ships. And the ships damaged each other, too, if they poked one another or the broken masts shredded a neighbor's rigging.

"Walker's right," said Soledad. "Someone in this hurly-burly is going to recognize us sooner or later."

Jolly's heart raced as she replied, "I'm not going without the worm!"

"You don't even know that he's responsible for all this," said Walker, but a growl from Buenaventure made him throw up his hands in defeat. "All right, all right! Maybe he really is. But how are we going to get him out of the water?"

Jolly walked out in front of the Ghost Trader. "I'm getting him!"

"No, Jolly! Wait!" But Soledad's cry came too late. Jolly got free of Buenaventure's hand, ducked under the Trader's arm, and rushed away.

Walker was beside himself. "That—that *child*!" she heard him raging behind her, but she'd already disappeared into the crush on the quay, snaking between sailors, natives, and harbor workers and approaching the water yard by yard. Was someone calling her name? As she ran she looked in the direction from which the voice had come. But she saw no face that seemed familiar. Nothing would be worse than having Bannon cross her path now.

She'd scarcely finished thinking of him when he was standing in front of her.

"Jolly?" he asked incredulously, and for a tiny moment she actually weighed the idea of stopping. But then she simply ran on, rammed her shoulder into his belly, and saw him collapse like a marionette with snapped strings. She leaped away from his clutching hands, escaped the grasp of another man, and two steps later reached the harbor wall. Without hesitation she pushed off and jumped.

She landed with both feet on the waves without sinking. She stumbled and almost fell, catching herself at the last moment. What was this? Polliwogs could only run on saltwater. But this was a lake! She'd intended to dive under the water like all the others, so in the middle of the confusion she could look for the worm unnoticed. But obviously enough saltwater flowed in from the passage to the sea to bear a polliwog.

Then make the best of it! Get moving!

She sprinted forward as fast as she could. The surface seemed to boil with all the turmoil, the suction of the sinking ships, and the quantities of air bubbles that were foaming up from the wrecks. There were men in the water everywhere, some paddling in panic like children. Others grabbed at her when they guessed that the polliwog running past them had something to do with this catastrophe.

Behind her a whistle sounded. Was that an alarm signal? Or was the Ghost Trader trying to call the sea horses to him?

Jolly didn't look around. She didn't want to see if Bannon had given the order to shoot at her with pistols and rifles. And if he didn't, if he remembered in spite of everything how important she'd been to him only a few weeks ago— well, so much the better.

Smoke bit into her nose and her throat. At least two of the sinking ships had burst into flames. Before the water could close over the fire and extinguish the flames, it had already spread to the masts and sails. Flying sparks and rags of torn cloth bore the fire in all directions. Soon two or three neighboring ships that had until then been lying safely in their anchorages were burning as well.

Shots whipped past. Whether on Bannon's instructions or from another direction, Jolly didn't know. She only hoped that her friends hadn't been discovered. In front of her, the water flowed over the deck of a sinking ship, and she had to cut a sharp turn to avoid being caught in the vortex of the wreck. A powerful current arose beneath her, and for a moment she was fighting in vain against the roaring surge. But then she reached a broad lane between two undamaged ships that offered her protection from the shots on the shore. Her goal was a sloop some fifty yards away from the quay, which was one of the last ships to begin to sink. She hoped to find the worm somewhere nearby. Her advantage over the pirates and natives was that she could move faster on the surface of the water.

A dull thump sounded beside her, and suddenly a feathered spear rose from the wall of planks. Several cannibals appeared on the ship to her left, not in the outfits of the sailors but in leather aprons and strange bands they had wound around their arms, legs, and bellies.

A second spear missed her. A third clattered into the water beside her, brushing her leg, but only with the shaft. Then she was out from between the two hulls and, on a zigzagging course, approached the ship where she guessed the shipworm might be.

"Worm!" she hollered across the water. She could see no

more than ten yards in front of her, because the smoke was now befogging the entire harbor. At least it protected her from the men on the shore.

"Worm!" she cried again, looking around her.

Beside her a ship leaned to the larboard. She just managed to jump out of the range of the tipping mast. Again and again she called for the Hexhermetic Shipworm, at the same time having to avoid a hail of spears, which whistled down from one of the other ships. Now someone with a pistol opened fire at her from somewhere, but he gave up after two shots. Occasionally she still saw men in the water, but the farther she went from shore, the fewer they became.

"Worm! Damn it, where are you?"

She was slowly becoming aware of how crazy her plan was. How was she supposed to find the tiny fellow out here, somewhere in the water between the ships, in the waves, in the smoke, and under the attacks of her enemies? But she didn't give up hope.

The Hexhermetic Shipworm had inflicted more damage on Tyrone's fleet than Jolly and the others would have thought possible. The Ghost Trader didn't have to grumble so loudly: Just the fact that Tyrone had suffered such a defeat in his own harbor damaged the reputation he'd enjoyed among his men. Tyrone, the mad ruler of the Orinoco, suddenly didn't seem to be half so mighty.

"Jolly!" came a wail somewhere to her right.

There was something in the water that looked like a piece of wood and was being rocked up and down by the waves. It was moving itself forward with wiggling, serpentine winding, but was obviously too weak to resist the play of the waves much longer.

"Worm!" Beside herself with relief, she bounded over to him, pulled him out of the water, and pressed him to her. She cradled him in her arms like a newborn, and even pressed a smacking kiss on his shell head. His breath was rattling, and his short legs dangled lifelessly from his body.

"So . . . exhausted . . . ," he panted, "from much . . . eating." He belched so loudly that it echoed from the walls of the nearby hull.

"Don't worry," said Jolly, starting to run again. "I'll take you to safety."

"I think . . . I couldn't have . . . much more." He fell silent. He seemed a little heavier in her arms. He'd fallen asleep. He was snoring.

At first she was quite drunk with joy, but reality caught up with her all too quickly. They couldn't go back to the quay and to their friends. It was now thronged with their enemies. Perhaps Tyrone had even come down to the harbor by now.

She considered briefly, then decided against a return to shore and ran out into the lake, away from the burning and sinking ships. She hoped with all her might that the others had been able to get away in time. If she managed somehow to get out into the delta, away from the tent city and the huts at the foot of the fortress, then, yes, perhaps . . .

She stumbled and forced herself to concentrate. Every step counted, every minute she distanced herself farther from the eyes and the bullets of her enemies.

Having eaten his fill, the Hexhermetic Shipworm slumbered peacefully in her arms as she bounded over the water. Everywhere lay ships at anchor, no longer so close together out here as nearer shore. It was only occasionally that she saw men on board, but they posed no danger to her in the approaching dusk.

Jolly was gasping with exhaustion when at last she reached the inlet. To her right and left, torches were burning on the beaches of the tent city. Still, she had enough strength to run on. Men were observing her from both sides of the shore. Some waded right into the water toward her, but after a few steps the channel was too deep. Now and then a few bullets whistled past her ears, but most of them went so wide that they didn't even make her jump.

She reached the eastern arm of the delta river and followed it out to the Atlantic Ocean. The worm stirred in her arms, purred and rumbled something, and fell asleep again. Breathing hard, she carried him farther, along beneath the fortress, towering dark and threatening above her. She followed the coastline toward the southeast at about a stone's throw from land.

The sun had finally gone down and now the night spread quickly over the jungle and the sea. Tyrone's fortress melted into the sky; soon it was distinguishable only as a lighted point in the distance. The noise from the lake on the other side of the spit carried out over the ocean. Along the way Jolly had seen several dark outlines rushing past her under the surface of the water in the opposite direction. She clung to the hope that it was the sea horses, following the Ghost Trader's signals.

The fortress was falling farther and farther behind her. The black wall of the jungle moved closer and gave way to the sandy beach on which Jolly and her companions had come ashore. In the dark she could make it out only as a ghostly line, a vague shimmer where the sand reflected the moon.

With her last ounce of strength she turned in the direction of the shore, fell to her knees in exhaustion, and let herself be carried the last hundred feet to the beach by the surf. With the shipworm in her arms, she rolled away from the foaming froth onto the land and remained lying there. She no longer felt her legs, and she was too weak to drag herself into the protection of the palms.

She drew up her knees, wrapped her body protectively around the worm, and fell asleep on the spot.

Sometime, perhaps soon, perhaps much later, she awoke to the sound of several voices. The night was pitch-dark. Clouds must have come up, for neither the moon nor the stars were visible. She had sand between her teeth. The worm also awoke and wordlessly pushed closer to her warm body.

Jolly sat up in the sand. She was dizzy, and her legs hurt. She felt a cramp coming in her left foot and quickly moved it back and forth a little to limber it.

The voices were coming from the sea, carried in on the salty wind.

She jumped up, moved slowly to the palms, and sought protection behind a trunk.

She heard crashing and splashing. Something was moving out there. A dark knot of shadows drifted apart, hardly more than a black spot in front of the darkness of the night ocean.

"That isn't them," the shipworm whispered peevishly.

Jolly placed a finger on her lips. Her heart was thumping so hard that she was afraid the entire palm would shake with the vibrations.

"Jolly?" Hardly more than a whisper and nevertheless unmistakable. Soledad's voice!

Jolly leaped out from behind the palm and stumbled over the soft sand. "Here we are!" she replied, and she had trouble lowering her voice. She would much rather have screamed with relief. The worm also relaxed. Before he'd rolled himself almost into a ball, but now he stretched out and nearly slipped out of her hands.

She could hardly make out the princess's face in the dark, but her slender body and her voice were unmistakable.

"Hurry, Jolly!"

"I'm so glad you made it!" Jolly looked over at Soledad. "Are they all there?"

"Yes, don't worry." Soledad embraced her briefly, which made the shipworm grumble angrily because he was squeezed between them. "And the little one is all right, it appears," said the princess, with a glance at the cursing bundle. "Anyway, well done, little man."

"Man?" snarled the worm. "Men are humans. And I'd rather be a stone than a human."

"We're not sure if they're following us," said Soledad to Jolly.

"Tyrone?"

"Not he himself. His people have enough to do to douse the ships. Besides, it's too dark to run out." She pulled Jolly to the water with her and waded out into the surf, while the girl ran along on the waves beside her.

"Who, then?"

"Kobalins."

Ice-cold fear rose inside Jolly. Uneasily she remembered the night that the *Carfax* was followed. Her eyes slid over the sea's surface, but it was too dark to see anything.

"We aren't sure," said Soledad, as she fought against the waves with difficulty and they approached the spot where the others were waiting on their sea horses.

"Don't ever do that again, Jolly," was the first thing Walker said when they'd come close enough.

"Don't listen to him," Buenaventure contradicted from the saddle of his sea horse. "He's glad to see you. He just doesn't want to admit it."

Jolly grinned, even though she could hardly see the two of them. She quickly ran over to them. "Guess who I brought with me."

Out of the darkness Buenaventure stretched out his hands, tousled her hair approvingly, and fished the shipworm out of her embrace.

"Looks as if we have something like a real hero here," he said to the worm.

The remarkable creature proudly stretched out to his full length. Parts of his shell scraped against each other.

"Quite true. I think someone should forge this great deed into verses. A mighty epic about the heroic battle of the Hexhermetic—"

"With a tragic outcome," Walker interrupted, "if I hear a single rhyme."

"Fishbrain! Philistine!"

Jolly helped Buenaventure stow the scolding worm into his knapsack. The hero slid in, fell silent immediately, and breathed a contented sigh. She noticed that something was left sticking to her fingers, something fine, soft, like spider-webs, but she didn't think anything of it and wiped it off on her trousers.

"Hurry!" The Ghost Trader steered his sea horse next to Soledad's. The princess pulled herself into the saddle. Jolly leaped up behind her and shoved her hands and feet into the holding loops.

With rallying cries they urged the sea horses to start moving. Soon they were whistling over the black sea.

"We really spit into Tyrone's soup in a big way," Soledad called joyously over her shoulder when they were out of hearing distance of the coast. The sea wind whirled her hair into Jolly's face.

"I thought a few destroyed ships wouldn't be enough to weaken him," said Jolly.

"Not that. But he knows that we'll warn the people of Aelenium. So he has no other choice now than to run out tomorrow morning and begin the attack as soon as possible."

"And that's good?"

"Well, he has to go through the Antilles captains' territory.

THE FLEET OF THE ENEMY

A fleet like that won't be overlooked, and they'll ask themselves what's become of the great land campaign against Caracas he promised them. The captains will realize that Tyrone has taken them in."

"So no more attack on Caracas?"

"Hardly. Without the Antilles pirates, our people on Tortuga and New Providence will think three times about whether they have a chance. And the Antilles captains won't tolerate the passage of Tyrone's fleet. They're proud men, and Tyrone's treachery will injure their honor deeply."

"Does that mean they'll attack him?"

"Quite possibly. They have no chance against such superior force, but I guess they'll attack his flanks and rear. With a little luck they'll weaken Tyrone considerably. And that again will be to Aelenium's advantage."

Jolly leaned forward in order to look into Soledad's face. "How do you know all that?"

The princess laughed, and for the first time in a long time there was no sound of bitterness in it. "They're pirates, Jolly. And men. If I learned one thing from my father, it's the ability to think like one of those fellows. Believe me, it's much easier than it looks." Soledad had said something similar to Jolly once before, about Griffin and Munk, and she'd been right that time, too.

"Kendrick was wrong," said Jolly.

"What do you mean?"

"When he said no pirate would follow a woman. I think you'll be quite a good pirate empress someday."

The princess shrugged, but Jolly sensed her proud smile in the dark.

They saw no kobalins that night, and not on the following day, either. The friends spoke little and allowed the sea horses no rest. The shipworm remained hidden away in Buenaventure's knapsack; Jolly guessed that he was writing his heroic epic. Vaguely uneasy, she remembered the substance that had stuck to her hands.

The comrades breathed a deep sigh when, early on the morning of the third day, the fog wall appeared on the horizon. High over them fluttered the parrots, and for the first time the mysterious birds acted almost frolicsome.

Although Jolly could hardly wait to see Griffin again, she was the only one who felt no relief. She was unhappily anticipating her meeting with Munk.

But even that dismay paled in the face of the task that lay ahead of her. She looked past the fog to the northeast, over the breadth of the endless ocean. Suddenly she felt panic rising.

Somewhere out there lay the Crustal Breach, many thousands of feet under the sea, in icy cold and everlasting night. She had recognized her opponent and made her decision. Aelenium was only a station on the way, not the destination.

The rising sun filled the heavens with gold, and the comrades rode straight into the light. But Jolly's descent into the shadows had begun long before.

Catch a sneak peek at
The Wave Walkers, Book Three:

Pirate Wars

On the morning of her last day in Aelenium, Jolly visited the Hexhermetic Shipworm.

His house in the Poets' Quarter of the sea star city was narrow, just wide enough for a low door with a window beside it. As everywhere in Aelenium, there were no right angles here and hardly a straight wall. The city's buildings were formed from the ivorylike material of the coral, some having grown in a natural way, others created by stonecutters and artists.

"It's me," she called as she walked past the guard and opened the door. "Jolly."

She didn't expect an answer, and she received none. She knew how things stood with the worm. If his condition had changed, she'd have been told about it.

Jolly closed the door behind her. What she had to say to the Hexhermetic Shipworm was none of the sentry's business. Furthermore, she was afraid Munk might have followed her and stolen into the house behind her, unseen. The last thing she wanted was for him to overhear what she said to the shipworm.

This was her farewell. Hers alone.

She mounted the uneven stairs to the upper floor. There, in the largest room in the house, the worm hung in his cocoon and dreamed.

The room under the peaked roof was largely filled with the fine web being secreted by the worm's motionless body—the only sign that he was still alive.

A few days before, when the first signs of his transformation became visible, Jolly had begged for him to be housed in the palace, even in her own room. But Forefather and the Ghost Trader had refused. They'd given no reason for their decision.

Jolly wasn't really surprised. She and Munk were the two most important people in Aelenium, they were told over and over again. No unauthorized person was allowed to come too close to them. Certainly not some unknown thing that might hatch from a cocoon when the worm had finished his pupation. *If* something should hatch.

"Hello, Worm."

Jolly stopped at the wall of silken threads. The windows of the roof chamber were covered with translucent material to impede the view from the houses opposite, but also because it was feared that hungry gulls might discover the helpless worm. Windows were glass only in the palaces of Aelenium's rulers, not in the dwellings of the simple folk; here they used wooden shutters to protect themselves from wind and weather, but those also blocked out the light. Instead, the fabric that had been stretched across the attic's windows turned the light streaming in milky, dissolving the edges of the shadows. There was no longer any sharp delineation between light and dark in the entire space; everything blended together, mingled.

"Hello," said Jolly once again, because the sight of the eerie thicket of silk affected her more than she'd expected. Buenaventure, the pit bull man, came here twice a day to make sure everything was all right. He'd told her of his visits, but this was the first time that she'd seen the extent of the cocoon with her own eyes.

The silken threads were woven into a mighty net stretching from the floor to the peaked ceiling—not unlike a spiderweb, only with much finer mesh and without an obvious pattern. The uncanny thicket of threads was several feet deep. In its center hung an oval thickening—the worm's cocoon. He seemed to float. The threads that held him over the floor at shoulder height were almost invisible.

The Hexhermetic Shipworm was no longer recognizable in the center of the cocoon, his form buried underneath a layer of silk a handsbreadth thick. Only a weak pulsing showed that he was still alive.

"This is quite . . . impressive," said Jolly tentatively. The sight seemed to glue her mouth shut, as if it were filled with the webs too. "I hope you're feeling all right inside there."

The worm didn't answer. Buenaventure had warned her that conversation with him at this time was a one-sided affair. Nevertheless, the pit bull man was convinced that the worm could hear them. Jolly wasn't so sure of that.

"You gave all of us quite a fright," she said. "You could at least have warned us that something like this was going to happen. I mean, none of us knows a whole lot about Hexhermetic Shipworms." She sighed and stretched out her hand cautiously to touch the foremost threads of the web. The surface billowed like a curtain. It was as if a slight breeze had stroked her fingertips.

"I've come to say good-bye." She pulled her hand back and hooked her thumbs awkwardly into her belt. "Munk and I, we're going to start out. To the Crustal Breach. Everyone here in Aelenium—the nobles, Captain d'Artois, the Ghost Trader, Forefather—is hoping that we manage to seal the source of the Maelstrom. We do too, of course. And I don't know . . . Munk is really good at mussel magic. Perhaps he actually will manage it." She stopped for a moment, then went on. "Myself, I'm not ready yet, even if no one wants to admit it. Anyway, no one says it to my face. I'm not half as skilled with the mussels as Munk. He . . . well, you know him. He's so ambitious. As if he's possessed. And he's still mad at me—because I turned the mussel magic against him on the *Carfax*. But did he give me any choice?"

She began to walk back and forth in front of the web. She'd rather have had this conversation with someone who could give her advice. But even if the companions here in Aelenium were on her side—the pirate princess Soledad, Captain Walker, and his best friend, Buenaventure, the giant with the face of a dog— none of them could really put themselves in her place.

Except perhaps Griffin. But Griffin had vanished. His sea horse had returned to Aelenium alone. At the thought of him, Jolly felt her knees grow weak. Before they could give way, she dropped down onto the floor, rather clumsily, and sat cross-legged. It was too late to hold back the tears that were running down her cheeks.

"No one can tell me what's become of Griffin. Everyone thinks he's dead. But that can't be. Griffin's not allowed to be dead. That's just an expression, right? I mean, *not allowed to* . . . pretty silly, huh? As if there were some sort of rules and regulations." She shook her head. "I firmly believe he's still alive."

The cocoon in the heart of the web pulsed on undisturbed. With every faint expansion, every contraction, a wave ran through the silk like a deep breath.

"What will you have turned into when you come out of this stuff?" she asked. "Do you yourself have any idea? What about the wisdom of the worm *now*?"

She noticed that as she spoke her fingers were clutching her knees so hard that it hurt. Frightened, she let go.

"Forefather and the Ghost Trader whisper together from morning till night. They say the attack on Aelenium is about to happen. And this morning they decided."

She brushed a strand of hair out of her face. "We're leaving," she said wearily. "The practices are finished. I don't think Munk and I can do half of what we're *supposed* to be able to. But there's no more time. Tyrone's fleet will be here in two or three days, at the latest, and the deep tribes will probably attack at the same time, or even sooner. No one knows how long the soldiers of Aelenium can hold out. Maybe a few days. Maybe only a few hours."

Again some time passed in which she said nothing, staring thoughtfully at the attic floor in front of her. She imagined what would happen when the servants of the Maelstrom reached the city. The monstrous whirlpool thundering on the open sea out on the horizon had brought the kobalins under his rule. Thousands of them were moving in on Aelenium in mighty swarms. And the dreaded cannibal king, Tyrone, would fight on the side of the Maelstrom with his fleet.

Sooner or later Aelenium would have to acknowledge defeat. Sooner than ever if she and Munk weren't successful in conquering the Maelstrom. But the fight for the sea star city was supposed to create the necessary time for them to do just that. Dozens, perhaps hundreds, would lose their lives to gain precious hours and minutes for the two polliwogs to try to close the Maelstrom back into his mussel deep on the floor of the sea.

And besides everything else—Griffin's disappearance, Munk's ambition, and fear of the gigantic whirlpool that was bringing all the evil to Aelenium and across the Caribbean— that was what concerned Jolly the most: the fact that men would die in order to support her and Munk. Because they placed all their hopes in two polliwogs.

"I don't deserve so much trust!" she whispered sadly. "They must know that, mustn't they? That I'm going to let them down for sure."

She was just not ready yet. Maybe she never would be. But it no longer mattered. Her departure was decided.

She'd resisted, rebelled against it—all in vain.

The Crustal Breach awaited her.

Her fate.

Jolly stood up, blew a kiss to the cocoon in the center of the web, and wiped the tears from her eyes.

"The rays are ready to leave," she said. "Captain d'Artois is going to lead us to the Maelstrom. The Ghost Trader is going with us." She smiled wearily. "And Soledad. You know her—she insisted on coming with us as far as possible. No one dares to contradict her."

She pulled herself together. "Farewell," she said sadly. "Whatever you are when you hatch out of that thing— farewell!"

Then she turned, left the cupola chamber, and walked

slowly down the narrow stairs. The eyes of the sentry at the door widened when he saw that she had been crying. But he said nothing to her, and for that she was grateful.

"The whale is being attacked!"

Griffin started up. He lowered the hammer with which he'd just struck the first blow and turned his eyes from the coarse wooden chair that lay in front of him on the floor. The twenty-eighth. He'd counted as he went. Twenty-eight chairs for Ebenezer's Floating Tavern——the first tavern in the interior of a giant whale.

"Harpoons, Griffin! They're attacking Jasconius with harpoons!"

"Who is?"

"Who, who . . . kobalins, of course!" The former monk had appeared in the doorway, arms flailing.

Griffin had believed himself to be looking certain death in the eye when he was swallowed days before by the gigantic animal. But in some amazing way he'd landed in the stomach of the whale very much alive and had been rescued by Ebenezer.

The monk must have gone crazy in the long years of solitude down here, of that Griffin was convinced. His plan to open a restaurant in the stomach of the monster was the best evidence of it. This mad plan was the reason that Griffin was spending his time making chairs and tables. Until he was finished with the job, Ebenezer had threatened, Griffin would never walk on land.

"Harpoons, Griffin!" the monk repeated excitedly. "The kobalins have harpoons."

Indignant, he was running back and forth in the wood-paneled room. Outside, in front of the opened door, stretched the dark stomach cavity of the giant animal. But here inside, on the other side of the magic doorway, the atmosphere of a solid country house prevailed: very cozy, very comfortable, very well appointed.

"How many kobalins are there?" Griffin asked.

"How should I know? Have you ever heard of a whale that could count?"

Griffin opened his mouth to reply, but at that moment there was an ear-splitting noise in the dark grotto of the whale's stomach. Something shot toward the open door like a wall of shadows, accompanied by a roaring and raging as if someone had torn a hole in the body of the whale.

"Flood!" Griffin bellowed, and then they both plunged forward, threw themselves against the door, and together pushed against it with all their strength.

The house-high wave crashed against the outside and brushed aside the man and boy along with the door. Water shot into the room, swirled over the parquet, flung tools and finished chairs together, and smashed some of them against the walls. Griffin and Ebenezer both howled with pain as their heads and backs were shoved against corners and wooden edges.

The water withdrew just as quickly as it had come. A second flood wave never came. In no time the water began to seep away through the cracks in the floor. When Griffin staggered to his feet with a groan, there was only a damp film still lying over everything—but it was enough to make it slippery. With a wild pirate oath he sailed backward onto his behind, landing on his tailbone, and wanting in his pain and rage to throw around all the dumb chairs he'd just made so laboriously.

Ebenezer's breathing was wheezy. He was sitting on the

floor, his back against the wall, listening to the voice of the whale. He claimed that he and the whale understood each other through the power of their minds alone, and Griffin had become convinced that there was something to that.

Suddenly Ebenezer gasped. "He's swallowed them," he said. "Griffin, he's swallowed the kobalins!" His eyes swept worriedly to the open door and searched the splashing, gurgling darkness out there.

"How many?" Griffin was on his feet in one leap.

Ebenezer groaned. "Not many. But they're hardly likely to have drowned. It might be that he's squashed a few of them."

Griffin hurried to a chest where Ebenezer stored some of the weapons that had collected in the whale's stomach over the years. Whole shiploads of sabers, daggers, flintlock pistols, and rifles had been swallowed by Jasconius. Unfortunately, the guns were of little use in the whale's stomach—the dampened powder made it impossible to fire them. And besides, the danger of missing the target and wounding the stomach wall was too great.

Griffin pulled a saber out of the chest, tried its weight in his hand, and also stuck a long knife into his belt. Ebenezer looked from the door back to Griffin. "Are you really going out there?"

"Got any better suggestions?"

The monk was torn. "Jasconius has never swallowed a kobalin. Until now they've always given him a wide berth."

Griffin picked up a lantern and pushed through the door past Ebenezer. "Stay here and bar the door. I'll see what I can do."

"We could both hide."

"And what would become of your tavern? Besides, we'll have to go out anyway to look for food soon. The supplies in the kitchen won't last forever."

Ebenezer nodded, but he didn't seem convinced. Contrary to expectation, Griffin was touched by the older man's concern. Until now he'd rather felt himself the prisoner of the whale and his occupant, just good enough to cobble together the chairs and tables for Ebenezer's cockeyed dream. But now he realized that the monk liked him. And he couldn't really deny that it was the same on his part. Ebenezer was certainly a little crazy, quite definitely odd, but he was a lovable fellow.

"I'll be back soon." Griffin said it more to himself than to Ebenezer. The words made him sound braver than he really felt. His voice wavered, which Ebenezer must have noticed.

Kobalins with harpoons. Even if they'd lost their weapons when they fell into the throat, that didn't make them any less dangerous. Their long claws and sharp teeth were as lethal as knife blades.

Griffin walked out of the light of the room and climbed slowly down the hill with his lantern. He looked watchfully about him, taking pains to appear determined as he did so. No victim is more preferable to kobalins than one in deadly fear; it makes it easier for them to strike at their prey from ambush.

Ebenezer closed the door behind him. Griffin heard the bolt snap. The rays of brightness around him were cut off and only meagerly replaced by the weak shimmer of the lantern. The edges of the circle of light were just three or four yards apart. Beyond it, all was darkness.

Everywhere there was bubbling and splashing as the water dripped off parts of wrecks and seeped into the mire. The sounds were hardly distinguishable from the whispering speech of the kobalins.

Griffin nervously shoved some of his braids out of his face with the crook of his arm. His blond hair was plaited into dozens of them. That was really a hairstyle of the slaves brought over to the New World from Africa. It was only rarely seen on one of the white inhabitants of the Caribbean, so Griffin was especially proud of it.

He'd just reached the foot of the hill when he heard a snarl. From the right. Out of the darkness.

He raised the saber high, and then something shot at him as if it had been slung in his direction with a catapult—a spindly, thin body with scaly skin on which the lamplight broke in oily rainbow colors. The kobalin's hands, with their long claws, were wide open, and its mouth gaped like the jaws of a shark.

Griffin let himself drop, and as he did, he thrust the blade upward. Steel cut through skin and muscle, a scream sounded, then the body disappeared somewhere in the shadows and moved no more. A long-drawn-out smacking indicated that it had sunk into the mud of the stomach.

That was easy, Griffin thought as he struggled to his feet. An oily shine gleamed on his blade. The kobalin must have taken him for a confused, starving castaway. But now the others were warned.

If he only knew how many he had to deal with!

He held the lamp on an arm stretched over his head. A rustling was audible somewhere in front of him, followed by the lightning-fast *splish-splash* of rushing feet.

At least one, thought Griffin. *Probably two or three*. He hoped not more.

Something hit him in the back and made him stumble forward. He cried out, stumbled into a depression between the wrecks, and plunged forward. A moment later it was clear to him that the fall had saved his life: A claw swished through the air over his head. The blow would probably have broken his neck.

But then he rolled onto his back and hit his spine on something hard. The lantern slid out of his hands and sank into the morass a yard beyond him.

In its last light Griffin made out his opponents. There were two of them. Their furrowed grimaces were like unfinished accessories arranged around their wide-open mouths—as if the creator of the kobalins had concentrated all his powers on the gigantic throats and sharp rows of teeth, like a child who loses interest in a piece of clay and apathetically squashes the rest of his work together.

Griffin struck blindly over him with his saber in the darkness and at the same time tried to prop up his body with his left hand. But his fingers sank into the dark muck with a sound like a smacking kiss. Again he slashed, but his blow went wild. Instead he felt something grab his right ankle in the dark and pull on it, just outside the range of his reach. A second hand gripped his other leg, and now the creatures began to pull in opposite directions.

They're going to tear me apart! The thought flashed through Griffin's mind in the fraction of a second. Without stopping to think, he sat up and slashed a desperate stroke across his spread legs toward his feet. The pain that seared through his back with the abrupt movement was murderous.

Then—resistance! A cutting sound, followed by a mad kobalin screech.

His left ankle came free. But the strength of the creature to his right forcefully pulled him farther, away from the wounded one.

Kobalins are sly, mean creatures, but they are stupid and a little childish. If they can kill an opponent slowly and painfully, they prefer to, rather than slaughtering him the quickest way—because killing is like a game for them and the longer it lasts, the greater their pleasure.

This characteristic came to Griffin's aid now. They could easily have killed him in the darkness. But the feared attack did not come.

Griffin tried to kick away the claws that held his leg. In vain. The creature's long fingers sat as firmly as C-clamps. Now the kobalin was pulling him along through the bog, through puddles and mud holes, over hard wooden edges, fish skeletons, and bones, which broke beneath him and tore his clothing and his skin. Once it seemed to him that his face was being brushed by grass—until he realized he was lying with his head on the matted fur of a lion cadaver.

The cries of the wounded kobalin behind him became softer, turned to gurgling and sobbing. Then they broke off.

Suddenly Griffin's leg was free.

Stuffy darkness surrounded him on all sides.

Smacking steps to his right.

Before he could spring up, claws seized his braids and pulled his head back into the mud. But still the kobalin did not kill Griffin. It snatched the saber from his victim with one grab. In a twinkling, Griffin was unarmed. Steel clattered in the distance. The kobalin had thrown the blade away.

Dumb, thought Griffin. *Kobalins are really terribly dumb.*

Not that this insight was of any help to him now.

He tensed his neck muscles, supported himself on his arms, and sat up swiftly. There was a fearful jerk, and with a yell he realized that he had sacrificed patches of his scalp and at least one or two braids—they remained behind in his opponent's claws. But he was free.

Somehow he got onto his feet, while behind him the muscular kobalin arms snapped into emptiness like scissors.

This time Griffin didn't stop to fight. He'd learned his lesson. He ran, almost blind in the darkness. Suddenly in the blackness he saw a narrow strip of light, floating behind the parts of a wreck, which looked like huge ribs: Ebenezer had opened the magic door, a torch of light by which Griffin could orient himself in the darkness. The monk must have noted that the lantern was out. He knew that Griffin needed a signal that would point the direction to him.

"One's still alive!" Griffin called, panting, toward the doorway. "At least."

If he received an answer, it was lost in the smacking and splashing of his steps. The kobalin was storming behind him, but it also was now entangled in pieces of wrecks and trails of algae. A shrill gabbling sounded at Griffin's back. Was the kobalin laughing? Or was it summoning other survivors of its brood?

About the Author

Kai Meyer is the author of many highly acclaimed and popular books for adults and young adults in his native Germany. The first book in his Dark Reflections Trilogy, *The Water Mirror*, was a *School Library Journal* Best Book, a Book Sense Pick, and a *Locus* magazine Recommended Read. It also received starred reviews in *School Library Journal* and *Publishers Weekly*, and has been translated into sixteen languages. Kai Meyer lives in Germany.

About the Translator

Elizabeth D. Crawford is the distinguished translator of the Batchelder Award–winning novels *The Robber and Me* by Josef Holub and *Crutches* by Peter Hartling. She lives in Orange, Connecticut.